FINDING DUNCAN

A Novel

Gretchen Eick

BLUE
CEDAR
PRESS

Wichita

FINDING DUNCAN *f*

Blue Cedar Press
PO Box 48715
Wichita, KS 67201

First edition
10 9 8 7 6 5 4 3 2 1

ISBN: 978-0-9960970-3-1

"A Happiness" from The Collected Poems of Norman MacCaig, courtesy of Birlinn Ltd.
Cover design: Gretchen Eick
Composition: Caron Andregg/SeaCliff Media Marketing

Printed in the United States of America
at BookMobile, in Minneapolis, MN.

For all who seek to be found and all who learn to be finders.

Wichita, Kansas: Spring 1994

The training for office associates at the Chicago headquarters ended early. He decided to beg off the closing dinner and come home to surprise Amy. He snagged the last seat on the last flight of the day to Wichita, climbed over the hefty man in 24B to squeeze his body into the window seat in the last row of the small, regional jet. His seatmate, thick pink fingers folded over his swelling belly to hide the inadequacy of his seatbelt, looked like a contender for the hot dog eating championship of the world. The man was already snoring. Duncan leaned back against the lavatory wall that jiggled whenever someone opened the door to the toilet. Long day. He closed his eyes and tried to imagine Amy's face when he walked in the door.

It was nearly ten when he parked in the driveway, unable to locate the remote he usually used to access the house through the garage. He turned his key in the lock and quietly pushed open the front door, wanting to surprise her. He heard voices and followed them to the kitchen where his brother, his only surviving relative, sat at the table intensely talking to his wife.

He hadn't known John was coming for the weekend. After their last visit, he was surprised John was ever coming back. Amy was wearing a red sweater that, with her dark hair and eyes, made her look especially lovely. John was John, tall, handsome, well dressed. In the warm light of the kitchen, their profiles facing each other, they made a pretty picture.

Hearing him, they looked up, regret rather than welcome defining their faces as they saw him standing in the doorway. John discretely moved his hand out of Amy's and mumbled a greeting, not meeting Duncan's eyes.

Amy's eyes bore into John as though sending him a message. Her voice greeted her husband with an artificial cheeriness. "You're home early! There's chicken in the crockpot. Want some?" She stood and moved to the counter, taking a bowl from the cupboard and spooning a generous serving into it before he answered. "John decided to come for the weekend. Isn't that great?" She placed the bowl on the table and pulled back the chair for him. Then she poured him a glass of milk.

John stood and carried his dishes to the sink. He excused himself, saying he was tired and would turn in early so his brother and Amy could have time together.

"We thought we'd go to the zoo tomorrow," Amy told Duncan glancing at John and smiling. "Want to join us, honey?"

He felt confused. He had wanted to surprise Amy, to see her broad smile as she welcomed him home twelve hours ahead of schedule, but she had surprised him instead, and he didn't understand what was going on. "I'm beat. I planned to watch March Madness basketball tomorrow at Old Chicago. It's Wichita State's first game of the tournament. I'll beg off the zoo."

Amy was smiling at John. "I told you that's what he'd say," she told him.

Then a memory that he had locked away for most of his thirty years overpowered him.

He was seven and had run from the bus stop and into the house to tell Mom what had happened at school. He wanted to tell her about the large gold star with his name printed on it and his photo pasted in the center that Mrs. Keys had pinned to the bulletin board under BEST STUDENT OF THE WEEK. He knew Mommy would be so proud of him. His big brother's awards cluttered the door of the refrigerator, held in place by an eclectic assortment of magnets. This was his first award and he could hardly contain his excitement.

"Mommy, guess what!" She was wearing jeans and a red wool sweater, beautiful with her dark hair and eyes and her trim figure. He felt so happy to see her. She was sitting at the kitchen table with John, her eyes focused on his brother.

It confused him that her face, like Amy's now, registered regret at seeing him enter the room. She hadn't opened her arms to hug him, which was part of their daily homecoming ritual. Why not?

"Can it wait just a little while, Duncan? John needs to talk with me right now. I'm sorry, honey, but you've interrupted an important conversation that we need to finish. Go on in your room and I'll come shortly." She had smiled at him briefly, then turned her full attention back to John.

Disappointed, he'd gone to his room, changed out of his school clothes, and played with his battery operated toy car, darting it here and there and smiling when it scooted from under his bed bearing two dirty mismatched socks. Mommy would laugh at that. He waited, bored and deflated, but she didn't come. He needed to talk with her. It was hard to wait.

Her preoccupation with his brother John wasn't a major incident. He knew that these things happen in families, one child's needs taking priority for a time. She'd told him this on other occasions. Only, this time she hadn't come.

He'd heard the phone ring and her voice, two rooms away, muffled as though she was speaking from inside the closet surrounded by quilts and winter clothes. Then she'd called something to someone—maybe John? He heard the kitchen door slam shut and the garage door grinding its way up, the metallic screech of her car door opening and the steady put-put thrumming of the tired engine growing faint as she backed it out of the drive and took off down the street. John was always on her to get a new car. Her ten year old Corolla embarrassed him, "Geez, Mom, your car's older than Duncan!" But Duncan liked Mommy's car, found its noises comforting, liked the excitement that he felt in his tummy hearing the familiar Corolla sounds as she drove up the drive, sounds that told him she was home.

He remained in his room a while longer waiting for those sounds to return. Finally he opened his door, hungry and out of sorts and wanting to know why she'd forgotten him. The house was dark, except for the family room where John was playing video games.

"Where's Mommy?"

John didn't look at him. He focused on the screen where action characters fought dramatically to avoid each other's kicks and the explosions of assault weapons. John mumbled, "She went to get Dad. Something wrong with his car, and Grandma needed him to help her with something. I'll make you a grilled cheese sandwich in a minute."

"It's dark." He felt dumb saying something so obvious, but he was still afraid of the dark, a secret only he and Mommy knew. He wanted to see Mommy, to feel her arms around him and see that alert, interested look in her eyes as she listened to him tell about his day. He wanted her to make him something to eat, not his older brother. And he didn't want grilled cheese.

5

He turned on the lights in the hall and the living room and the kitchen. He got an apple from the refrigerator and some cookies from the Kermit the Frog cookie jar that he and Daddy had given Mommy for her birthday. He poured himself a glass of milk and curled up on the sofa, waiting to hear her car turn into the drive.

He must have fallen asleep.

He awakened to the sound of the doorbell and voices on the front stoop. John was shaking his shoulder. He looked scared.

"There're police outside. I think we've got to let them in. Come with me." They'd been trained never to open the door to strangers, but these were police officers. He and John stood together at the door and John undid the locks and pulled it open. He could not remember what happened next, only that everything changed and his childhood ended.

Now, almost twenty three years later, he couldn't shake the coldness in his gut that told him something dreadful was about to happen.

His head was throbbing. He had to get out of there. He stood, awkwardly shook hands with his elder brother, and left the room, his roller bag rattling lonely down the hall to their bedroom, the bowl of chicken and biscuits in gravy congealing on the table, gray and untasted.

Why was John here? In their last conversation John had told him off. "Why is it so hard for you to be affectionate? Your wife deserves more. That woman has loved you for half of her life! Actually, she's probably the *only* person who loves you."

That hurt, and he'd replied defensively, "Amy knows she's the center of my life."

"Duncan, wake up! You float along consumed by your work and emotionally remote at home, oblivious to what your wife needs. The woman wants a baby, a family." His words were a slap in the face. How dare his brother presume he knew what Amy wanted.

John and he were so different, always had been. John was the charismatic one, a star in the classroom and on the stage. But it was Duncan who Amy had chosen when they met in junior high school.

The brothers hadn't spoken since that fraught conversation two months ago.

His sleep that night was troubled. His seven year old self inhabited his mind, leaving no space for rationality. Saturday morning he slept in, emerging for a late breakfast. Amy kissed him good-by as she and John headed for the zoo.

March Madness was beginning to take Kansas by storm as it did each year. John wasn't interested. Basketball—sports in general—did not interest him. Amy usually watched the games with Duncan, but not today. Duncan left about one o'clock for the sports bar.

There he ordered a beer and tried to concentrate on the big screen where Wichita State was playing Bradley and making them work for their win, as far as he could tell in his distracted state. His next door neighbor approached and greeted him, then suggested they move to an area of the bar away from the televisions and the clusters of men talking loudly as they threw back another one. Puzzled, Duncan followed him to a quieter corner back near the kitchen. He didn't know the man well, their contact had been limited to small talk about the weather and sports when they mowed their lawns at the same time. Now the neighbor looked at him with a seriousness that seemed overly dramatic until his words connected with Duncan's fear.

"There's something I think you should know, Duncan. I was walking my dog past your house yesterday. The drapes were open and I saw your wife standing in your living room…with a man." He cleared his throat and looked nervously at the screen, the floor, and back at Duncan. "They were embracing. At first I thought it was you. But the guy was considerably taller than you. Well, I'm not gonna lie to you; it worried me. 'Course, what you want to make of is your business. I thought someone should tell you."

Duncan thanked him and tried to look confident as he assured the man that it was probably his brother, John, come for the weekend. He felt his stomach contract and the sudden onset of a massive headache. Then he excused himself, moving to the other side of the room and ordering another beer to calm himself before heading home. He wasn't much of a drinker, but the beer seemed to calm him so he had another.

Amy had always been closer to John than he was. He and John were very different, John elegant, socially skilled, and intellectual, Duncan quieter, more private.

He tried to put together what he and the neighbor had seen. John must have caught an early plane from New York City. Why hadn't Amy told him that John was coming?

He returned home at seven-thirty. W.S.U. had lost, but played better than in most of this season's games. Amy would be interested in hearing how many three-point shots Darrin Miller had made. The thick wall to wall carpet cushioned his feet as he walked from room to room looking for her. He found her in the guest room. John was lying on the bed and Amy sat beside him, holding his hand in hers and stroking his hair. They hadn't heard him come in. They were talking softly, still unaware that he stood in the hallway observing them. Seeing them together like that, so intimate, knotted his stomach. It was a moment he could recall with photographic precision for the rest of his life. He backed away without interrupting them and hid out in the bedroom he shared with Amy waiting for her to come to bed. When she finally slipped in beside him, he pretended he was asleep.

On Sunday he robotically went through the motions of his weekend life, making minor household repairs, running errands, and leaving the two of them alone, terrified by the fear worming its way into his brain. Amy tried to get him to join them in a game of Scrabble, but he begged off and sat on the sofa watching CBS News with Charles Osgood while she and John played. He had no idea what he had learned from the news, more tuned in to the animated chatter from the game table than to the television.

By afternoon he was drowning in loss, grief flooding and incapacitating him. He could not control the panic that dominated his feelings. Was he losing the woman on whom he relied for care and affirmation?

When Amy asked if he would ride with them to the airport, he declined. He heard her apologize to John, saying he must be coming down with something, it was unlike him to be so withdrawn. As John left, the brothers shook hands, Duncan unable to look directly at John. Amy drove John to the airport, while Duncan sat outside on the patio in the fragile March sunshine drinking beer and seething.

When she got home, he barely spoke, and they ate in silence. She asked what was wrong several times during the evening, her face so warm with concern and caring that he could not look at her. When he didn't respond, she moved to the living room and settled in front of the television to watch a mystery, hands working soft yellow yarn into a small blanket, row by row as the evening dragged on. So like her. Always making something positive out of the worst of situations. He felt desperate. He loved her so. He could not bear losing her.

It was only nine p.m., but he stood quickly and headed for the bedroom, unable to speak, unable to say goodnight, and vaguely aware of her eyes following him, worry drawing lines on her forehead.

He slept intermittently, disturbed by images of his confident older brother with his charming wife. Once he felt her arms encircle him and nearly turned to her, nearly reciprocated, before John's face, laughing heartily, came between them. He remained frozen and unresponsive, facing the wall while the digital clock counted off the minutes and his imagination held him captive.

In the morning he was up early and off to work, making it through an unproductive day preoccupied by pain that kept growing like an aggressive tumor, reaching out to every organ, destroying the barriers he marshaled to keep it from devouring him whole. He had no idea what he was doing; he just knew that he had to confront her. First, he needed a drink. He left at five and found a bar, threw back two beers chased with too much scotch, and got completely knackered, wobbly and red eyed.

He had loved this woman since they were fifteen. The death of both of his parents that icy spring night when he was seven had left a gaping hole in his capacity to trust. But Amy loved him back with such dependable solidity that gradually, tentatively, he came to believe that he could count on her love for him, that she would not leave him. Throughout high school, college, and the launching of his career as a financial advisor, there had only been Amy. A private man with few friends, she was "the love of my life." Her quirky humor and the way she lit up when she saw him flooded him with waves of gratitude for "saving" him from the loveless, lonely young man he had been before her. His pain overwhelmed him.

It had begun to rain, one of those intense, driving rains that shook the windows and combined with the notorious Kansas wind to produce tornado warnings and power outages. He had to get home. He paid his tab and drove slowly, the windshield wipers clicking like a speeded up metronome, keeping time with his pulse. He parked in the garage of the upscale house that had been their home for six years. The lights in this part of the house were out and he couldn't find the breaker box in the dark, which added another layer to his confusion and fury. He was breathing heavily as he threw open the back door and strode into the house, moving to the kitchen with its bright overhead light.

"Where are you?" he shouted, his voice full of grit. "In the kitchen. Half the power just went out, but I've made soup." Her voice was artificially cheery. She stood by the stove in her pale blue robe, stirring a pot of soup, the homey smells of potato, cheese and onion registering in his brain and distracting him for a moment from the rage that suddenly coursed through him.

She turned to face him wearing a pasted on smile that clashed with the fear gathering in her dark eyes. Then she turned back to the stove to resume stirring the soup.

He grabbed her left arm and twisted it to make her face him, her right arm involuntarily coming forward to protect herself, hot soup slopping from the wooden spoon she gripped and spattering his hand, burning and further enraging him.

"How could you???" He pulled her out of the kitchen, through the small dining room to their bedroom, inadvertently knocking over a chair. The part of him that was outside himself, the Observer, noted, collateral damage.

Now, in their bedroom, his hand with a vice grip on her arm, a bellow began in his gut, growing in ferocity as it forced its way up through his chest and erupted from his distorted mouth filling the room. He could not find words. His sounds came from some subterranean place, howls and groans, terrifying and preverbal, sounds that would surely awake the dead and cause them to gather their shrouds and move on in untimely resurrection.

She was talking to him in a quiet, intense voice, but he could not make out what she was saying, only that she was trying to calm him, speaking as though guiding a frightened child down from a too high tree. Now he hated her for diminishing him, for assuming that she could treat him this way, for her betrayal.

The inarticulate part of him groaned again. He released her arm and moved closer to her, hands squeezed tightly into fists. His brain lost any connection to his hands. His right fist struck her once with the dull, flat thump of knuckles against soft flesh. His mind fled his body and observed her pathetic confusion.

"Don't! I'm pregnant!" Her face, eyes huge and terrified, showed her shock, her words her only defense. They'd been trying to get pregnant and what she said further disoriented him. Why wouldn't she have told him? Unless it wasn't his child. She looked at him like she had never seen him before. Then she crumpled into a heap on the floor like a pile of dirty laundry.

He stood over her, his beautiful wife, sprawled face down on the thick white bedroom carpet she loved, long brown hair half out of the tortoiseshell clasp at the back of her neck, shiny in the lamplight, arms out at her sides, hands at shoulder height to protect her fall. One slipper, wrenched from her foot as she fell, sat upright two feet away. He couldn't see her face, which was turned away from him, right cheek on the carpet, couldn't hear anything except the loud mechanical humming in his head. In shock at seeing her lying there so still and vulnerable, he panicked. He'd never hit anyone, ever. His mind reentered his body, and he turned and left the room.

Now he functioned like an automaton. He stopped at the dining room buffet where he took out the checkbook and a black leather zipper bag they had always kept on hand for cash emergencies. He picked up his car keys and walked out of the house, slamming the door behind him. He started his car and backed it down the drive, entered the main road, then the interstate.

He kept driving until the gas tank indicator's blinking red light got his attention. He did not know where he was, only that he'd been driving a long time. He exited Route 29 at the Sisseton exit and got gas, then walked into the McDonalds for a cup of coffee.

"How do you pronounce the name of this place?" he asked the girl behind the counter.

She looked at him as though he was deranged. "What did you say?" she asked.

"How do you pronounce this place?" he repeated.

The girl must have been sixteen and, by the looks of her, nervous taking the night shift. All sorts of weirdos passing through. She paused, and then said in an outside voice, "M-C-D-O-N-A-L-D-S." He stared at her, paid, and left, leaving the coffee on the counter. He could feel her eyes watching him as he walked back to his car under the lights of the parking lot.

In the miles ahead he must have exited Route 29 and turned west on Route 94. He had no idea where he was. He barely knew who he was. He found a Super 8 where he alternated throwing up and sobbing for most of the night, interrupted by the people in the room next to his pounding on the wall and yelling with increasing fervor, "Shut the fuck up! We're trying to sleep!" He had no idea when he finally crashed into oblivion.

Jamestown, North Dakota: Spring 1994

The next morning he awoke disoriented, his head hurting unbearably. An old fashioned cafe squatted adjacent to the Super 8, rundown and seedy, its windows blurred from the residue of cooking fat that lingered in the air. A few sad shrubs half dead from lack of watering lined the sidewalk that led to the entrance. The inside was lit with long fluorescent bulbs attached to the ceiling that gave off a dull greenish-white light. But it was a few steps from his room. He chose a booth at the back and shrank into the side that faced the kitchen. He ordered coffee, black, and a bowl of oatmeal. He asked the waitress what town this was and grunted a jagged laugh when she told him Jamestown, North Dakota. Where the hell was he headed, he asked himself and then grunted audibly again, as he realized that the question had a double meaning.

The waitress, surprised by his question, asked where he was coming from.

"Wichita, Kansas," he mumbled.

"I got no idea where that is!" she said with a smile.

He went back to his room after paying for another night. Then he slept all day. Awaking in the dark ravenously hungry, he pushed aside the rubber lined drapes covering his window and saw that the red neon OPEN sign was still blinking in the window of the cafe. He dragged himself back there, hunger alternating with nausea.

The waitress was middle aged, overweight, and motherly. Her weathered face wore comforting creases and smile lines that, along with her "Hello. I'm Maggie" badge, said she was there to serve, to provide some sunshine for her down and out customers. "Honey," she said, "you look like you fought a bear and he won! We got the perfect thing to ready you to fight and win tomorrow—meat loaf with green beans, spuds and gravy and some of our homemade yeast rolls. Real comfort food. How about it?"

He nodded, gratitude for her niceness to him filming his eyes. He sat at the booth long after he finished eating, trying not to feel, his mind unable to hold onto anything. He was lost. He tried to slide his lead-filled legs and his sodden torso out from the table and with supreme effort stood unsteadily. One step at a time he maneuvered his way across the diner to the exit and across the parking lot to his room and another long night of despair.

Fragments floated across his brain faster than he could extinguish them: his parents' funeral after their violent disappearance. At seven he understood their deaths as "violent disappearances," and never knew who to blame for taking them from his life. Two mahogany caskets, John and he standing forlorn between them, their contents so mangled by the accident that they could not be viewed. He had tried to hold John's hand but John, thirteen, had shaken him off, embarrassed to be holding hands with a boy, even if the boy was his brother. He heard Grandmother's voice telling them that she would provide for them, but, "Don't expect to be coddled. I don't like displays of affection or sniveling."

Those memories tangled with his neighbor's account of seeing John holding Amy and his own observation of their intimacy. How long had this been going on between them? He searched his memory for clues and found nothing.

It was raining the next time he awakened. Water poured from the sky leaving wide puddles like mirrors across the parking lot. Shades of gray clouds littered the puddles incongruous and adding to his confusion. He zigzagged across the lot, avoiding the puddles, and opened the door to the diner, his jacket freckled with dark spots. Water dripped from his hair and clung to his eyelashes and eyebrows. He ordered oatmeal again, and coffee. Sometime during that meal he started tentatively working on what he would do.

He considered driving his car into a guard rail or even a semi, but he feared being trapped in a paralyzed body more than death. On his paper napkin he inventoried his assets.

Strong

Healthy

Only 30

Financial consultant experience [He drew a line through that one. He was done with that.]

Experience driving a forklift and custom combining at harvest

Carpentry/odd jobs

Fast learner

Hard worker used to working 60 hours a week

In another column he wrote WHERE followed by:

Get apartment back in Wichita

Stay here in Jamestown

and

_____???

Maggie the waitress refilled his coffee and asked if he was staying around these parts for long. His reply, "I don't know. I need to find a job," seemed to please her. She was a person who liked to be helpful. It gave her life meaning.

"We need a dishwasher here, not great pay but it can give you some time to figure out other options." When he didn't respond she carried the coffee pot back to its nest.

He needed to operate the way he had when, fresh out of college in his Big Break job with the firm, the market had decisively plunged, affected by a series of international crises causing a panic. He had pushed down his fear and his feelings and plunged ahead, reassuring his clients with a paper thin confidence that they would indeed be all right, it was only a momentary slump. Amy called it his autopilot mode, joking that he could cope with anything as long as he maintained that default response.

Now he summoned that pseudo confidence, but it was nowhere to be found. The voice inside his head that observed and evaluated, that analytical part of his brain, said he needed time to sort out what to do. So what if he was a financial consultant used to being paid a six-figure salary. Now he needed time and a place where no one knew him, where he could figure out the After of his life now that his Before had collapsed around him.

By the time Maggie returned with a refill, he had made one decision.

"Thank you, I would be glad to wash dishes at least for a couple of weeks. When do you want me?"

The next week was a blur. He called his office and told them he was taking leave for a family emergency that he didn't want to talk about. "I will be back in touch."

Amy floated through his dreams like a dazzling phantom, sometimes the Wicked Witch of the West, sometimes the kind and gracious Glenda, the Good Witch of the East. He was certain John would take good care of her, but he missed her terribly. *Amy! How can this be happening?* He banished the memory of her lying on the floor of their bedroom so still. Having to maneuver this unfamiliar land alone, without her reassurance and care, felt like walking a tightrope with no safety net. Regardless of her betrayal, she had provided him stability and love, nourishment for his soul, and relief from loneliness. He owed her for that. He called his bank and arranged for half of his bank account to be withdrawn and wired to him at the café, the rest to be designated solely for her, no POD, no way for him to touch it.

Each day he washed dishes till ten at night and crashed into dream disturbed sleep for the next seven hours, arising to get back to work at the café where he was so busy he could not think. He stumbled along, focused on getting by. He was tired at the end of each day and the bottle of scotch beside the bed that he sipped eased him into a state of oblivion from which sleep was but one gradual descent downward.

He had left his cell phone at the house that night so he had no one's number and no one knew where he was or how to reach him. He lost track of time. How long ago had he left? Sometimes he took out the folded napkin and idly read over his notes to himself. He was getting nowhere with a long term plan, just treading water, head submerged more often than not.

One lunch time he carried a rack of clean glasses from the kitchen to its place beneath the soda machines. As he turned back toward the kitchen, he glimpsed a woman enter the café smiling at Maggie. She was about Amy's build and height with long, dark brown hair. His heart accelerated at the absurd thought that Amy had found him. His feet stuck fast to the linoleum as he watched her remove her jacket, yearning to see his wife's familiar curves and willing her to turn toward him with her inviting smile. But this woman wore a tight, low cut sweater and skimpy skirt, and he heard her say to the skinny older guy with greasy, shoulder length hair who followed behind her, "Fuck it, I'll be damned if I'll be talked to like that." Her unnaturally high pitched voice carried across the room and grated on the ear. Her dress, words, and their pitch hit him like a punch. This woman was *not* Amy. A wave of longing passed over him, and he stumbled back into the kitchen to his station for hosing down the dirty dishes. As the water sluiced rapidly off the plates, carrying with it remnants of meals, his eyes clouded with sadness as the lost opportunities for nourishment circled the drain.

Could he have misread the situation? Could she be innocent? And faithful? Why hadn't he let her make her defense? *Why had he hit her?* Now he was overcome with remorse. Whatever success he had achieved he owed to Amy for building his confidence, loving him through his bouts with depression, charming his boss and work colleagues. Maybe he should get in his car and drive back to Wichita. Maybe she'd receive him with open arms. Maybe she'd forgive him.

He decided he had to phone her. He had to apologize for striking her. But would she forgive him? And could he forgive her if she and John were lovers, if she was carrying John's child? Regardless, he had to hear her out. He decided he couldn't see her--it would break his heart to see her again knowing her betrayal. But he could call.

On his next break he dialed their land line. When no one picked up, he hung up without leaving a message. He tried again the following day. No answer. After that he called obsessively at every break and after ten when he got off work, calling from the phone booth in the parking lot between the motel and the cafe, a remnant of an earlier time.

No one answered. Where could she be? The only possibility he could come up with was that she must have moved in with John, her lover. He choked on the words. He tried John and left an angry, inarticulate message on his answering machine. Standing in the parking lot beside the ancient pay phone, his back against the cafe wall, he slid downward till he was sitting on the sidewalk amidst the trash receptacles and discarded condoms in the shadowed, dismal rear of the cafe, head in hands.

When his shift was up and he returned to his room at the Super 8, he called his office and left a brief message. "This is Duncan Allan. I am resigning my position with the firm effective now. I'm sorry I can't give more notice but that's how it is. Thank you all. My commissions can be deposited into my wife's account at Intrust--that's Amy M. Allan."

That was it. It felt scary but it was making a decision, better than the Purgatory he was stuck in.

The six paychecks in his wallet--payday was Friday--measured the passing weeks. He lurched from dishwashing to scotch-induced sleep in the Super 8. The robins returned outside his motel window, but he did not see them. The lilacs and forsythia bloomed and faded, and he did not notice. He felt he was suffocating, floating in an airtight bubble, separated by an invisible membrane from the people around him who smiled and joked, even laughed, as they came into the cafe and shared their lives over coffee or the daily special. He barely spoke. Not even Maggie the helpful waitress could get much out of him.

Four months into his new dead life he decided he had to do something, go somewhere. At the rate he was going, some cop would scrape him off the sidewalk and consign him to wherever they take drunk derelicts in Jamestown, North Dakota. He didn't much care to live, but he didn't want to die like that. He must find somewhere else to live, some other place where no one would know his name.

On his day off he went to the town library and asked for help locating the most remote areas of the English speaking world. Hudson's Bay, Canada? Robbin Island, South Africa? Fairbanks, Alaska? The outback in Australia? A fishing village on the northeast shoulder of Scotland?

Over the next month he looked up each place to extract whatever information he could find about its ability to meet his need to reinvent his life where no one from his past would know him. Then he priced air fares. He decided to sleep on it and go with whatever locale floated to the top when he awoke. Something about fishing villages facing the Arctic Ocean appealed to him. He did some more research to narrow down which village he might live in, located some "self-catering" cottages for rent, and decided there was no looking back. Never having left the country before, he had to apply for a passport, which took another month. Then he booked a flight, one way. By late October he was saying good-by to Maggie the waitress, who helped him find a buyer for his car and drove him to the airport. Scotland it was.

Wichita, Kansas, USA: Spring 1994

Amy lay unconscious on the bedroom floor for some time. She had cut her head when she fell and bled onto the white carpet. The sticky feel of blood spreading under her right cheek was the first thing she remembered as she emerged into consciousness and hesitantly felt herself to see where the blood was coming from. Shaky, she staggered to her feet, her nose assaulted by the odor of something burning. She hobbled to the bedroom door, hands out on either side to feel her way. She could see smoke pouring out of the kitchen, through the living room and dining room and down the hall toward her, thick, black and acrid. She tried to keep upright and reached for the phone, dialing 911 to report the smoke and probable fire, assured by the voice at the other end that an emergency fire crew was on their way to Eastborough that very minute. The 911 lady instructed her to close the door between the bedroom and the source of the fire and put wet towels under the door to keep out the smoke. "Is there any way to get outside from where you are now without going closer to the fire? If so, take it NOW!"

Amy pulled the quilt from her bed around her and opened the door to the deck just off their bedroom. Stumbling and unsteady on her feet, she managed despite the dark to navigate her way down the step from the bedroom to the deck and two more steps from the deck to the back yard. She was coughing and dizzy and her head hurt. In her state of shock she was only vaguely aware of the danger behind her consuming their dream house. Her mind was stuck on how she could remove her blood from the carpet.

The deck overlooked the back garden where last spring she had put in wildflowers and woodsy plants, stone walkways, and a fishpond. For a moment she stood looking out at the shadowy garden that had been their pride and joy, imagining where the hydrangeas, larkspur, dahlias and crepe myrtle would soon gloriously color the space. Duncan had added bird feeders and birdbaths. They had loved to take their morning coffee out there where they could watch the birds that flocked to this natural playground that she and Duncan had created for them. Duncan...

Suddenly what had happened before she fell came back to her. Duncan. So angry. Drunk, too, smelling of beer. *Hitting her.* NO! Why was he so angry? What had he said before he pulled her into the bedroom? Duncan never behaved like that. Down and depressed sometimes, but never violent. What had happened to him????? She tripped on a tree root and went down hard.

From inside the house the firemen were calling her. "Mrs. Allan? Mrs. Allan? Are you all right? Where are you, Mrs. Allan?"

They found her lying on the grass beside the deck, blood oozing from a cut over her left eye. The ambulance took her to Via Christi hospital where they kept her overnight. When they could not locate Mr. Allan, the hospital contacted Amy's mother, who came right away.

The fire had started in the kitchen with something cooking on the stove that had ignited a hot pad and dishtowels and then the wooden cabinets and the hundred year old Georgia pine floorboards they'd salvaged from an abandoned old Victorian house in Midtown. Substantial fire damage. As it spread into other parts of the house, the carpet and upholstery had released lethal smoke that killed the dog and cat. It was a miracle Mrs. Allan wasn't killed, the fire chief wrote in his report. Fortunately the Allans had the best insurance money could buy for a situation like this. They would come out just fine. He would have to wait to question Mrs. Allan about what had happened. She was definitely too out of it now to respond.

Sedated, Amy did not awake until the next morning. She opened her eyes to find herself in the hospital with her mother hovering over her, stroking her hair and talking gently to her. "You are going to be fine, Amy. We are so lucky the firemen got to you in time."

Mom did not mention Duncan's absence or the fact that her cat and dog had both perished in the fire. She wisely didn't ask about the puzzling abrasions on Amy's arm or the shocking bluish purple bruise distorting her face.

Typically, Mom also ignored the cut on Amy's forehead, focusing instead on the good news: in addition to Amy being fine, it turned out that Amy was pregnant! "Did you know, honey? The doctor said it's only three months but the baby seems to be fine. Praise the Lord! Oh, God is good, Amy. You are going to rise above this little set back, honey. I just know it."

Amy forced a smile at her mom, then closed her eyes and retreated into sleep.

In the weeks that followed Amy tried to locate Duncan, although she refused to go to the police. If they learned he had hit her, perhaps even caused the fire, and if she pressed charges, he could go to jail. She could not do this to him and she could not lie. She wouldn't press charges. Better to look on her own for him. She tried his office, but they had only two cryptic voice mails from him, one saying he had a family emergency and the other resigning his high paying job with Ameriprise Financial. She phoned the bank to learn that he had taken his name off their joint account after withdrawing half of their savings, which he put into a new separate account. "I am sorry, Mrs. Allan, but I cannot tell you any more than that. Mr. Allan was quite clear that no one was to be given his contact information," the bank executive told her.

She called in the insurance agent from American Family, who located an apartment Amy could use while they rebuilt the damaged part of the house. She didn't like staying away from her home. What if Duncan should call? She was deeply worried about his state of mind. She had a sinking feeling he was running away from her, from Wichita, and from his life. She paced the small apartment and kept calling his cell phone, but when she called the phone company, they told her it had not been used since the night he left.

She phoned John in New York City and they talked for a long while. John was six years older than Duncan and his only family, other than Amy. She'd always found the brothers' differences amusing. Duncan was 5'11", of a stocky build, and when he wasn't at work rarely wore anything other than T-shirts too big at the neck and jeans that had holes in the knees. Of course, when he was working he wore Brooks Brother's suits with pastel dress shirts and discreetly-patterned ties, the company's standard uniform. She loved the Duncan who grubbed in the back yard alongside her, coming into the house grimy with sweat and dirt and smelling, well, manly.

She'd never known John to smell manly. He was tall and thin, dark curly hair always well groomed, open, friendly good looks, firm handshake, immaculately attired in shirts with matching ties and pocket handkerchiefs, and cufflinks. When John was off work, he dressed in designer khakis and polo shirts, nary a hair out of place, always clean shaven and smelling slightly of Obsession. The brothers got along for the most part, although recently things were strained and tense between them, though she had no idea why. John's visit last week was actually to see her, not Duncan. She hadn't found the right time to tell Duncan about their conversation.

Now standing in the sterile apartment feeling abandoned and scared, she dialed John's number and hoped against hope that he and not Phillip, his partner, would pick up. He did.

She related what had happened that night a week ago, the last time she had seen her husband, and she broke down. It was the first time she had cried in front of anyone, and John was the only person to whom she told the full story. She'd been piecing together what had happened, trying to remember just what Duncan had said before grabbing her arm, dragging her into their bedroom and hitting her.

John's cultured voice oozed sympathy. "You poor girl! What a terrible mess you are in!" He was a logical person and approached her like a lawyer. In fact, he was a professor of music theory. They talked about Duncan's disturbing behavior, and John told her of his call from Duncan.

"He called tonight and left a message, a rather hostile message. Said he never wanted to see me again. He didn't say where he was, no number or address. You know we haven't exactly been close. I think Mom and Dad's deaths left us each feeling alone in the world, and living with Grandmother Allan didn't help."

Amy was picturing the feisty old lady Duncan and John lived with when she first knew them. She remembered Duncan telling her how she punished them for the slightest infractions of her rules—making them sit on a chair in a locked room for hours if they talked back, beating them with her hairbrush if they broke any of her treasures. Now she heard from John something Duncan had not confided. She listened closely.

"You can't blame her, I guess. If her only child hadn't slid his car into that old oak in front of her stately home, killing himself and his wife instantly, well, she'd have had a lovely rich-lady retirement, traveling the world in style instead of coping with two unique and not very warm and fuzzy boys. She was the one who found them, heard the crash and went to see what had happened. That must have been awful."

"Duncan never told me that she found them." She was remembering how he had told her of his parents' deaths. No details. Only that he'd been waiting for his mother to come home when the police arrived instead.

"My darling Amy, you married into a strange family of traumatized survivors, as I believe I warned you before you decided to marry my brother, who, as is borne out by his recent behavior, may win the prize for the strangest and most damaged of us all. Did he think you were having an affair?"

"I don't know. And I wasn't having an affair! I love Duncan. I've been so happy with him, at least until lately when he started drinking more than a glass of wine over dinner. My dad was an alcoholic and I won't have that in my life or my children's lives." She was silent for several minutes. Then she spoke almost absent mindedly.

"Did I tell you I'm pregnant?"

John's voice modulated and he commiserated with Amy. Then he remembered that she wanted to be pregnant, and he message-switched gracefully to congratulate her. He said something about her not needing to raise this baby as a single mom, that he and Phillip would come and help, at least during school recesses. She understood this was unrealistic and showed John's futile denial of what Phillip's diagnosis would mean for their life together. Hadn't he made the trip to Wichita just ten days ago for the express purpose of telling her that Phillip had been diagnosed with HIV that had already developed into full blown AIDs? She knew both men were terrified. They had seen many of their friends ride out this horrible end game, victim to any and every infection, unable to breathe, in unbearable pain, unable to keep food down, rejected by family, avoided by frightened friends, having to hide their secret or lose their jobs and therefore their health insurance. She knew that she could not count on John to be more than a long distance support, not now.

"This country hates us fags," he had told her as they had talked then, "and your husband, does too. I've heard his comments. What am I to do, Amy? I don't know how I can live without Phillip. I know I must nurse him through this, stay with him and care for him to the end. But I admit I'm devastated and terrified."

Amy had put her arms around her brother-in-law and held him, patting his back. She had made up a bed for him in their guest room and sat beside him holding his hand listening to his anguish until he fell asleep.

She'd seen Duncan standing in the hallway watching them, his face dark and angry. She hadn't known what to tell him. John insisted that only she know, so she couldn't tell Duncan what his brother was going through or even that John's ten-year friendship with Phillip was not just friendship but a loving marriage, as they understood it, a marriage that was destined to soon end in pain and fear, anguish and isolation.

Now, what felt like a lifetime later, she stood in her temporary apartment living room holding the phone and trying to focus on John's situation. She must find some way to help John with Phillip's care, though she feared what exposure to a person with AIDS might mean for the child she carried. It was such a secret disease, never talked about or acknowledged. To admit you had a family member with AIDS was to make yourself a pariah. John suggesting that he and Phillip come help her raise her baby showed her that he was in denial. Was she in denial, too?

She had known that her husband faced demons that she could not imagine. He'd been abandoned at seven by his parents' sudden deaths and ignored by his domineering grandmother. Could he now for some reason believe that she--the woman he had loved since high school, the woman who had loved him back fully and without restraint--had betrayed him in some way?

She tried to see things from his perspective, but, damn it, she had no idea what his perspective was. Why did he run away, rather than talk with her? Didn't their six years of relatively happy married life merit at least a conversation before he jumped to conclusions and fled? She wanted to break things, any things, but this sterile apartment offered only melmac dishes and stainless steel utensils.

Her anger with him--fury, even--came and went. He had betrayed her and their marriage. She had not. There had certainly been no affair, not even the idea of an affair. Yet he never checked out with her whatever it was that so disturbed him. The crazy state he was in and his recent drinking—. Abruptly, as her unfamiliar rage was carrying her rapidly headlong down a precipitous incline, she changed course, blunted her anger, and forced it to skid to a stop. In its place anxiety about her husband poured over her. Her legs went weak and she slid down onto the apartment's sofa, shaking and frantic with worry. That had been her pattern whenever her husband frustrated her, Amy unable to hold onto anger at him, flooded with pity for his past and a sense of responsibility to be his salvation in a present that she, unlike he, unfailingly understood as promising so much more than despair.

He could be lying in a ditch somewhere or in a hospital or even a morgue. And she, who loved him more than anyone else in her world, was unable to do a thing to help him. All she knew for certain was that he had fled, made changes at the bank to provide for her, changes that sounded permanent, and called his office and John, all of which pointed to his being devastatingly undone by....By *what?* It all pointed to his intention not to come back. She knew NOTHING, and that was so unfair, so *wrong.* He simply disappeared.

She stood absentmindedly holding the phone in the temporary apartment. Temporary. Everything in her world was now described by that word. She felt cold, frozen in this moment when she realized that she could do nothing to bring him back, that their baby was likely to know only one parent--her.

"Amy, are you still there?" It was John.

"Yes."

"He hasn't tried to phone you?"

"Not that I know of. I haven't been able to stay at our house since that night. He may not know about the fire."

"Have you put a trace on his credit cards to locate him?"

"No. At least, not yet. I keep hoping he'll come home."

"We will get through this, somehow, kiddo. When Phillip is...gone..." She heard him take a jagged breath. "...I can find a job in Kansas..." She heard him exhale as though it was his last breath. "...and help you raise the baby. You have me, Amy, whatever pieces of me are left. I swear I won't let you down. Got to go." His voice trembled and he hung up the phone abruptly.

Amy was a wheat-and-beef-fed Kansas woman. Her grandparents still owned the 160 acre homestead they had inherited from her mother's grandparents. Now she consciously leaned on the stories she had been raised on, stories of true grit women who moved their lives to the West and shared with snakes and rodents sod houses built half underground, women who raised their children alone while their husbands left this dry, barely habitable land to fight in America's wars. As the weeks without Duncan unwound, she drew on that heritage, those stories of sturdy pioneer women who made do with what Life dished out.

Within a couple of months she was back in their home. Once she moved back into the house, several of her neighbors dropped by bringing in a meal and commiserating about the fire. When they asked about Duncan, she didn't say much, just that he had to go away. Let people talk. It was none of their business.

It was more difficult once she began to show, not that a woman alone in a blossoming body was all that uncommon in Wichita, but a woman alone in a blossoming body in the elite incorporated community of Eastborough, home to many of the city's millionaires? That was uncommon. She was embarrassed and avoided going out in public, preferring to ask her mother to pick up things she needed, not wanting to see what she anticipated would be disapproving looks from her wealthy neighbors, most of whom were her mother's age. Sometimes she sat outside in their secluded woodsy garden and talked to the birds, so desperate she was for companionship. Eventually she got a replacement cat from the Humane Society. She could talk to him all she wanted, even with her angry voice, and he would continue purring, his body curled and warm on her lap, unperturbed and accepting.

She'd quit her teaching job a year earlier, hoping the reduced stress would help her get pregnant. Consequently, there were no colleagues from work to provide emotional support. Because she and Duncan had been each other's best friends for so long, she hadn't really developed a set of women friends. Only her mother, long ago divorced from Amy's now deceased father, prone to bitchiness and oppressively religious. She could take her mother only in small doses. She schemed to give her mother some limited time on a regular basis and usually suggested they meet at Mother's apartment. There Mother's critical, whiny side had nothing to complain about, Mother's taste being impeccable, at least according to Mother. Amy confined her time with her mother to Saturday outings and Monday evening suppers. The rest of each week passed with Amy and her swelling body alone, sitting before the television watching old movies, or reading anything that could distract her from her grief. Most days she could not recall anything she had done other than clean house and watch TV.

Obsessively she tried to untangle why her husband had hit her and why he had left.

Her pregnancy seemed interminably long, though she was healthy throughout and her doctor called her, "My Star Patient." Finally, in January, when her water broke, Mother drove her to Wesley Hospital where she gave birth six hours later to a healthy baby boy who she named for his father and his uncle, Duncan John Allan.

She surprised herself by how well she began coping once the baby and she came home. She found it helpful having this little person to care for. She simply closed the door when anger and grief came knocking. It seemed the right thing to do. She had a child to raise and she was, after all, a strong woman.

Scotland: Winter 1994-95

When he arrived in Scotland, Duncan Allan took Bus 35 from Aberdeen east, the route that called at the villages hunkered down along the northeast coast. He exited the bus at Portsoy, midway along the route, and walked downhill to Seafield Street, stopping in the Coop grocery store to ask directions to the place he had rented online. He had rented what in the States was called a furnished efficiency apartment. Here it was a "wee cottage" on a tiny back alley of this former fishing village. It was neither efficient nor furnished, simply one long room with thick stone walls, a sink, a table and chair, a toilet and a bed. But it was isolated. And remote.

He'd arrived on November first, a blustery, dark afternoon when everything looked black and sullen. He could hear the swollen sea a stone's throw away at the bottom of the hill, angrily eating the stone walls of the old harbor. Those walls that dated back to the 1700s were the only thing holding back the pounding waves. A cottage in this God forsaken place had seemed from four thousand miles away the perfect place for him. Seeing it in person convinced him he'd made a wise decision.

Wee Cottage was shadowed and sun deprived, invisible behind the rectangular stone homes that lined up close to the street and snaked down the hill to the North Sea, seeming to lean on each other's shared walls. There was one way out of the cottage, on the northern side, a narrow path that led down a steep hill less than a minute's walk to the old harbor. There a substantial stone pub, The Shore's Inn, was planted, solidly facing the sea as though daring it to breach the harbor walls four car lengths from its front door. If you looked closely at the front wall of the pub you could make out 1723 etched into the rough stone. Virtually everything else ringing the harbor was boarded up, closed for the winter, except for a one storey building, derelict and forgotten, where they used to process fish in more prosperous times. Now a handful of women hung on there to scale and package the sparse daily catch and sell it to the locals. Apart from their few salt worn cars parked in front of the small building, the only part of the fishing industry evident in the village on this frigid fall day was the smell that still hung in the air. A person could disappear in such a place and no one would notice.

For five months Duncan lived in hibernation in his Wee Cottage, venturing out only to purchase basic necessities like bread and peanut butter--and scotch--from the Coop, or, infrequently, to visit the ATM in the town center when he ran out of pounds. Most days he lay in bed, floating semiconscious, huddled in his duvet, wearing layers and his L. L. Bean down jacket to keep from freezing. Most days he'd not mind freezing to death, though his basic survival instinct prevented him from taking more assertive steps to hasten his end.

The cottage had only an erratic space heater whose short cord kept it tethered to the south end of his room, and the bone chilling cold seeped through cracks and holes of the cottage's thick stone walls. There was a fireplace at the north end of the room but no wood, and he had no will to scrounge for some. Besides, the place had been vacant so long, he doubted the chimney was functioning properly. The stone walls seemed to absorb the icy air and breathe it out into the room, like some bad joke about arctic air conditioning.

He got out of bed to fix porridge or to relieve himself, rarely to look out the one frosted window, never to walk the town. He wanted to disappear. Living under a shapeless mound of covers was the next best thing. Somehow, he survived the winter.

On the first sunny day in April light danced in the window across from the bed where he lay cocooned. Cautiously he opened his eyes to squint at it, at first not recognizing the phenomenon of spring sunlight. He lay there some time, taking in the intricate patterns of shadow and light moving and shifting on the floor and across the walls, allowing his brain to free associate.

The Rorschach shapes moved and morphed hypnotically and motes of dust lit by the overachieving sun jumped and bounced around his room like elated small children.

After some time he slowly emerged from his cocoon. He was emaciated, grimy from an absence of bathing for these months, and rank as roadkill. He ran some water into a large pot and heated it on the cooker till it boiled, adding dollops of cold tap water till he got the temperature right. Then he gave himself a sponge bath, hopping from foot to foot. Nippy to be naked in the freezing cottage, but the warm water felt good shedding his body, carrying away months of old, dead skin. He went to his large duffle bag, the only thing he had brought when he'd wrenched himself from his life and moved continents to hole up here in northeast Scotland. Inside under some papers, untouched for the past five months, were two pairs of jeans and two sweaters that he had overlooked, still clean.

The thought crossed his mind that Amy would have washed the sweaters by hand in the kitchen sink of their dream house. He could picture her bending over to take the slightly damp jeans from the dryer, shaking them out before the wrinkles set in. He had loved the way her slacks clung to her generous bottom and the embarrassment on her face when she realized he was watching. He had loved observing her domestic rituals--washing, cooking, shaking out the clothes, tidying the house. It was comforting and reassuring, though he didn't know why. Sometimes watching her he had felt he was stepping into a seventeenth century Dutch painting, observing one of Vermeer's women in the timeless repetition of small acts of caring for the world, holding it together.

Was she still there? Who was she holding together now? The cold air on his naked body pulled him back to his present. He forcefully dismissed that thought before it undid him, and pulled on the clean clothes.

Then, in an act of supreme courage, he opened the door of the cottage and stepped outside.

During the next several weeks he, like the wildflowers on the cliffs overlooking the harbor, came back to life. He began walking the coastal path, steadily increasing the distance he covered—west to Sandsend and Cullen or back east from Portsoy toward Banff and MacDuff. It gave him something to do, which felt freeing. He made it a game discovering these towns, noticing what made each unique. Feeling the wind off the sea tossing his now shoulder length hair, he felt alive. He'd return to his cottage, legs aching but feeling more whole, stronger. It helped to be in so foreign a place without visual reminders of Amy and their life together.

Gradually he added to his walks stops in local shops and brief conversations with the owners. Well, not conversations. More like sentences exchanged acknowledging each other. That was about all he had managed for a year now.

He knew he had to find employment as he was running low on funds. He asked the owner of the hardware-and-everything-else store if he knew anyone looking to hire help and learned that the Cruickshanks, who were major business people across the northeast, owned Furniture and Fine Housewares shops and were hiring. "You might try them. Or try Old Mr. Cruickshank --he's from a different branch of the family, but, of course, they're all related. He operates antique shops in Cullen, Buckie, Portsoy, and Banff. Nice old man. Stays to himself mostly. But for sartin he can talk the legs off a donkey if ye get 'im started on antiques. Knows more than anyone aboot. He's getting up in years. May be ready to take on an assistant. You might try 'im."

Duncan stopped at Cruickshanks' Antiques in Cullen one beautiful spring day. The bell tinkled as he pulled the heavy door open. He felt uneasy, reluctant to ask for work, even scared, but he made himself walk into the store.

Old Man Cruickshank read furniture and clocks like some folks read books, paying close attention to details—tiny markings stamped or scratched here or there could reveal who the craftsman was and when he, usually but not always "he," had created this piece of functional art. He'd read dozens of books on antiques and retained what he'd learned with an accuracy that other *aficionados* of this business found truly remarkable.

He also could read people, though he kept what he learned of them to himself. Take the young American who had come into his shop looking like he had emerged from a crypt, rail thin and unhappy, mouth sagging at the corners, unusual in one so young. He guessed that the young man felt uncomfortable asking for work. As he was about to leave the store, Mr. Cruickshank said that he was finding it increasingly difficult driving his truck village to village to deliver people's purchases and hauling "new" merchandise he'd located into his stores. The American turned and without forethought asked outright if he would be interested in hiring *him* to help out. Then he flushed noticeably but ploughed on, awkwardly making a case for how he might be helpful to Mr. Cruickshank. It was not an obvious match of experience, qualifications or skills. Mr. Cruickshank asked why he wanted this kind of job, and the American said he'd like learning about antiques because he'd spent half his childhood in a house full of valuable antiques that he was forbidden to touch.

His simple and straightforward answer intrigued Mr. Cruickshank. He processed the young man's response for several minutes while he concentrated on separating a small glass dome from its brass base without jarring the delicate clock with exposed gears suspended inside the dome. The young man was watching him carefully, barely breathing. At seventy-five with his knees bothering him and his once tight arm muscles gone to mush, Mr. Cruickshank worried how he would continue doing this work he so loved. He calculated how much he could pay the American to lift and haul his finds. Meanwhile he could observe how the man worked. If he was truly interested in learning about antiques, Mr. Cruickshank was confident he couldn't find a better teacher across the Northeast coast. When the dome came free of its base, he turned to the young man and smiled. "You're hired," he said.

Amsterdam, Holland: September 1994

They'd vacationed in Scotland for a week, camping and hiking the coastal trail in Fife, then taking the train north to Aberdeen for their flight home to Amsterdam. Ineke dragged her roller bag up the steps and into the lobby of their apartment building. Her three year old, imitating Mommy, pulled her own miniature bag behind her, Disney's Aladdin bouncing merrily up the steps. The child turned to her mother, bestowing a happy smile as she announced, "We're home!" Ineke's husband pushed the call button before the child's small forefinger reached it, and the elevator door opened on cue, admitting them to its mirrored interior. She was surprised to see her reflection looking unlike how she thought of herself. The face of the young woman gazing back at her wore a look of chronic disappointment. Did she really look like that? Her eyes slipped to Jens' reflection. He was unaware that she was watching him. Irritation was obvious in the set of his jaw and the wrinkles gathering between his eyebrows. Why did he look like that so often? It had been a good holiday, hadn't it?

A soft ping announced they'd reached their floor and the door slid silently open. Their daughter, Elleke, bounded from the elevator and ran down the hall, looking back at them hopefully. Ineke had never noticed before how hard Elleke worked at making the adults in her life happy. Jens turned the key in each lock, opened the door, and the three of them flowed into the apartment and down the hall to their separate spaces with—could her intuition be right?—relief. Did they each feel *relief* at being freed from the forced togetherness of their holiday? Certainly it wasn't because this apartment where they'd lived for five years felt particularly homey. Jens had selected the neighborhood and the apartment and had picked the color scheme, if white walls and beige everything else could be called a color scheme. That she was a trained artist whose tools were colors and shapes didn't seem to matter; he needed to be in charge.

She emptied their suitcases, putting things away, and gathered the dirty clothes to start a load of wash. She inventoried the refrigerator, making a shopping list, and pulled a pizza from the freezer for supper. Elleke was in her room chatting to her toys.

Jens came into the kitchen and told her they needed to talk, so while the pizza baked, they moved to the living room. She perched on the beige sofa in the boring beige room. Jens did not sit but paced, towering over her. What had she done now? There was no segue, no niceties to transition them from vacation. In his inimitable way he merely announced that he wanted a divorce. There was no questioning his decision. He'd been bored for some time, he said. It seemed there was a woman in his office he had begun seeing outside of work. Their attraction was stronger than his attraction to Ineke, and he could not help himself. As an obligatory afterthought he mumbled something about regretting the pain and suffering caused by this crossroads where their life paths must diverge.

Clearly he'd thought this all out long before their holiday. He said he wanted to be fair financially and asked only that he see his daughter during her extended recesses from school, once she was old enough to attend school. Ineke could have the apartment; he'd be moving closer to the Old City where his woman friend lived. It was all very straightforward and civil. Unemotional. Simply...over. It struck her later that their living room should have been a clue—monochromatic with barely a photograph to mark times of connection, impersonal, sterile and dull, like their life together.

She felt a slow burn coming on. She muttered something about telling their families, to which he replied that he'd told his family several weeks ago. He was such an asshole. Was their Scotland holiday supposed to be a reward, a last lavishing of attention before discarding them?

Jens walked to their entertainment center and picked up his keys. "I'll be off now," he said. "Tell Elleke good-by for me." He moved to the outside door. That was it. *Finis.* She smelled the pizza and heard Elleke's door open, hoping the child would reach her father before he made it out the door. No,

Jens the Elusive had made another great escape from intimacy.

"Where's Vader?" Elleke's face was quizzical and suspicious. How much of his recitation had she heard?

Ineke sat on the sofa and opened her arms to Elleke, who climbed into her lap. The child watched her mother's face closely and gently stroked her cheeks. Sitting on the sofa in that colorless room Ineke told her three year old that Daddy would not be living with them any longer. Elleke already knew. "It's okay, Mommy. We don't need Vader. We make each other happy." The child seemed unflustered and not surprised.

Why hadn't Ineke seen it before her three-year-old?

Over the next few weeks Ineke scrutinized the past months, looking for missed cues, finding nothing unfamiliar, just the same routines, the same coolness, the same emotional absence.

She found her own lack of emotion confusing. Shouldn't she be undone? A marriage of five years over so suddenly without drama or tears or even regrets? Her husband cheating on her? Well, that did enrage her, mostly because she had been faithful--out of duty, not out of passionate connection to him. Passion had never been part of their equation. She hadn't even considered leaving him. Marriage was compromise, subduing individual needs for the greater good of the family unit. She'd tolerated his bossiness, his criticism, his coldness, and his neglect of their child. Now she had to admit that she felt relief. She surmised that her own lack of emotion was probably because 1) Elleke would remain with her and 2) she and Jens had never been emotional about anything other than Elleke's birth.

Several times over the next months Elleke asked if they could move to Scotland where they had spent their holiday. Preoccupied, Ineke dismissed the idea at first. When Elleke persisted, Ineke spoke with her parents and women friends about the idea, and, with their encouragement to make a fresh start, decided her daughter's idea made sense. Her English was excellent and they'd be only a short plane or ferry ride from home. As an artist she could work anywhere. But they wouldn't return to Fife. They needed some place new without memories. Her parents had brought her to the Northeast coast when she was a child, and she'd loved the villages with their fields of barley and oats and their old stone harbors massaged by the sea. The landscape would be inspirational. Since she already had her own line of jewelry marketed across Europe, she could make jewelry anywhere along the North Sea and simply send it to her distributors.

Buckie, Scotland: Spring 1995

By April she had sold the apartment in the Amsterdam suburbs and located a house in Buckie, Scotland, where the schools were known to be good and where a local shop wanted to sell her jewelry. The house was an old stone two storey with an extra bedroom that she would use as her studio. It was set high on the hills that rolled up from the sea. It had front and back gardens and was only a short walk from the shops. Because Buckie was one of the larger towns along the coast, the center of herring fishing, she expected there would be plenty to do socially and she could easily get home to see her parents in Holland by taking the ferry from Aberdeen.

Uprooting and relocating was easier than Ineke expected it would be. Her parents were excited about her decision, pledging to come visit for the festival of old sailing ships that brought 26,000 people to the 17th century harbor village of Portsoy each June, only a half hour from Buckie.

In Scotland, Ineke and Elleke established new routines. Several times a week for exercise and to expand Ineke's knowledge of the area, they drove to one of the nearby villages and walked along the narrow lanes down to the old harbors. Sometimes they sat together watching the sea from the cliffs, lying back on the grass and making up stories about the Cloud People. Elleke insisted the Cloud People were real and friendly. She reassured her mom that the Cloud People were looking after them and, on their walks, entertained Ineke with accounts of their adventures. Ineke hoped her daughter would never outgrow her imagination.

Ineke enrolled Elleke in a primary preschool on the edge of Buckie for the fall, a half day program that would build her social and English skills through interacting with other children, while providing Ineke time for designing her jewelry. Elleke was soon speaking English with a distinctively Scots accent.

On this particular day they chose to explore the village of Portsoy, walking from the harbor east through the verdant cemetery and climbing up a long flight of steps to High Street and the town center shops. One of their regular rituals was a trip to the bakery chain along the coast, G & H Bakers, for scones with butter and jam and tea with milk for both mother and daughter. They found a branch of G & H Bakers on Seafield Street in Portsoy and entered the shop.

Elleke loved the bakery and, in her best imitation grown up behavior, she sipped tea and chatted with the other customers. The bakery was in the center of town, in a building that had hosted an assortment of businesses over the past hundred years. Round wrought iron tables and chairs with curved iron backs sat by the windows, enticing walkers from the street to come in for a meat pie or a sweet. Once you entered the shop, you relinquished all restraint. How could anyone resist having a coffee or a "cuppa" tea and a yummy bun or pie or shortbread from the ancient display case? The bakers plied their trade in the next room, mixing and kneading and filling the shop with delectable smells of yeast and cinnamon.

The girls behind the display case were young and chatty, and Ineke noticed that they seemed to like talking with foreigners. Did the presence of foreigners in their village give them hope that they might one day see more of the world beyond this quaint town on the edge of the Sea?

Across several Saturdays they ended up taking tea at the Portsoy bakery. On their second visit they noticed a scruffy looking man sitting at a nearby table drinking coffee and eating shortbread. The following Saturday, too, he was there. Like them, he appeared to be a creature of habit, which Elleke commented on. "That man does the same thing we do, Mama." The man looked up and then away. He appeared to be uncomfortable under the child's gaze.

"Is it the same?" Ineke had replied in Dutch. She wanted to hone her daughter's powers of observation. Sure enough, the child caught the differences. Tilting her head to the right she scrutinized him, then speaking in a voice the whole shop could hear, she said, "He drinks coffee but we drink tea. He eats shortbread but we eat scones." Ineke praised her for being so observant. It pleased her to hear the women behind the counter comment on "that darlin' wee one...so wise she is! And all those ruddy curls!"

After that Saturday, Elleke made a point of looking for the scruffy man whenever they went to G & H Bakery. For several weeks he was not there. Then, one Saturday, he showed up and Elleke clapped her hands excitedly when she saw him, embarrassing both the man and her mother. Ineke's eyes took in the man, who was staring at her daughter with an expression she could not read. Odd fellow, but not bad looking. He seemed less skinny than when they first noticed him, and at least his hair looked clean. She tried to distract her daughter, guiding her to the doorway into the kitchen where she could watch the bakers kneading dough. When they returned to their table, the man was gone.

In late June, Ineke's parents arrived for the festival and to see their new home and enjoy the seaside. They drove together to Portsoy to see the sailing ships and nearly got lost amidst the enormous crowd of people from around the world come to see the high masted beauties enter the harbor like elegant ladies decked out in their finest apparel. Among the crush of tourists Elleke, riding on her grandpa's shoulders, called out to her mother that she saw the man from the bakery, "The Scruffy Man." He was standing two people behind Ineke, who, embarrassed by her daughter's enthusiasm at seeing the stranger, turned and introduced herself, explaining that Elleke liked to look for him at the bakery, "It's a silly game we play, like a real life Where's Waldo, and you just happen to be our Waldo. I am sorry if it embarrasses you."

He mumbled in American English something about being honored that the child found him interesting, nice to meet you, see you later and disappeared into the crowd.

For several months after her parents returned to Holland, Ineke was too busy filling orders for high-end designs in preparation for the Christmas promotions at Harrods to give the scruffy man another thought. The first Saturday in October, her deadlines met, she and Elleke walked to the Portsoy bakery, both glad to resume their weekly ritual.

Elleke virtually sailed into the store, pulling her mum behind her. Then she stopped suddenly and stared. The man sat at the table nearest the door *and he was smiling.*

It was a moment all three of them would recall fondly years later. Ineke called times like this kaleidoscope moments, the moment when the tiny pieces of colored glass reflected in the triangles of mirrors fall into a perfectly beautiful design, and you know that you must hold exquisitely still and exercise extreme care or the design will collapse. You know that a new design will form, but if you move, the particular beauty of this design, the one you witness, will be lost forever. The two of them stood just inside the door of the bakery facing The Scruffy Man who was seated at the nearest table, coffee cup half way to his lips, smiling at them. All three of them were frozen in time, even the child, who was always in motion. Intuitively Ineke did not move or speak. She merely smiled.

One of the shop girls, uncomfortable with their silence even as it intrigued her, broke the spell. "Is that the brown bread you be wantin', Mr. Allan?"

"Is that your name? Can I talk with you now that I know your name?" Elleke looked for his nods which were slight but enough for her. She sat on the chair across from him and began her talking-with-grown-ups conversation. Where did he live? In Portsoy. Did he have a dog? No. Did he have a little girl or a little boy "like me"? No. Didn't he like scones? This was in response to her memory that he always ordered shortbread instead. He said he didn't know how to eat them, which delighted Elleke who immediately offered to teach him.

While Elleke animatedly interviewed The Scruffy Man, Ineke pulled up a third chair, looking a question at him first. When he motioned her to join them, she sat down. She had yet to meet people her age in the Northeast and felt excited at this opportunity and anxious to not make any mistakes. She felt glad that her daughter the charmer had taken charge.

Judging by the thawing of his face, the man seemed to be enjoying talking with Elleke. Ineke wondered if the pure act of smiling had tired his face muscles since it seemed he was so out of practice using them for anything other than scowling. As she watched, his shoulders relaxed and he leaned toward the table on which lay the scones that Elleke was showing him how to eat. He mimicked Elleke's actions. When a piece of scone fell off her fork, he dropped a piece from his and was rewarded by her giggles. Ineke liked his looks when he let go of that semi-permanent frown. In response to her question, he said that he helped Old Man Cruickshank run an antiques shop in Cullen, working sometimes in the other branches of the shop in the villages along the coast.

Elleke asked if he had any jewelry. "My mum makes pretty jewelry."

Once they established the basics, Ineke began feeling nervous, unclear what to do or say next. From the expression on his face, he seemed to share her discomfort. The shop girl came to their rescue.

"'Av you 'eard the seals are out on the rocks at Cullen this afternoon? Aye. We no see thim of'n as September turns October so ye might wanna have ye a look."

"Let's do, Mama, pleeease?" Elleke turned to Mr. Allan and extended her left hand which he instinctively took and asked, "Why don't you come with us?"

Leave it to the child! Duncan Allan said there was not much that he had to do as he was off work this afternoon. Looking at Elleke, he said that nothing was more urgent than seeing seals. Of course, he would come. Ineke offered to drive since she had the child's seat in her car and he agreed. In the car they introduced themselves.

Ineke drove east along the A96 and pulled onto the shoulder where several other cars were parked, their occupants looking toward the sea through their binoculars. All the while she was asking herself what she was doing. Just because this strange man smiles a couple of times doesn't mean he's not very odd. Watch out for bad risks, her mother often said. Still, there was something about his smile and the hint of humor in the way he related to Elleke that she liked.

They got out carefully--traffic came fast down that two lane highway. They walked from the car to the cliffs along the worn path. In front of them sprawled the sea, behind them, the high plains of farm fields golden with grain. From the edge of the cliff they could see below them a dozen gray and white seals resting on the sand, swinging their heads awkwardly to look at each other, as though deeply engaged in conversation. Occasionally one shifted position, lumbering up onto the wizened rocks, all the while keeping up a nasal honking sound, loud and imperious. There were so many of them!

Ineke loved this time of day on the North Sea. Nothing but foaming water separated you from the end of the earth. North there was only Sea all the way to the Arctic. If she was observing correctly, Duncan seemed to love it, too.

The Scotland Trails Association had placed wooden benches along the clifftop path that followed coastline. They provided magnificent vantage points for viewing the cliffs and the sea. The Scots called the rolling fields that topped the cliffs "braes." All along the coast these benches on the braes welcomed meditators and the melancholy. Duncan and Ineke with Elleke between them sat on one of the benches, watching the seals converse and the light shift shapes. The tide was coming in. The afternoon light shimmered and slanted along the shore, silvering portions of the giant boulders that time had covered with sea. The lowering sun charged horizontally from the west, lighting the golden fields atop the cliffs and obscuring the crevasses and caves that fractured the cliff faces. As they watched the light shifted. Shadow played with light and, in a breathtaking, prolonged display, Day made way for Night, as dark shadows expanded east across the cliffs. Elleke said it was like a giant Cloud Person was walking toward them. The ridges of black, gray and brown rocks that reached into the sea in parallel rows gradually disappeared under the dark blanket of the incoming tide.

The lingering sun highlighted a patch of rock below where three black cormorants sat chatting.

They could no longer see the caves carved by time and tide that reached under the braes. Colors streaked across the sky—orange and pink and yellow and blue--a magical light show quite wonderful to behold.

Dark arrived suddenly and with it a cold breeze carrying raindrops so soft and fine that they did not know it was raining until they reached Ineke's car and saw its wet, spattered windscreen.

"This was so lovely!" Ineke spoke to no one in particular, needing simply to acknowledge the beauty of the day's end and the Sea, the way you say "Thank You" to the air, or to God, spontaneously, without anything blocking you from vocalizing your gratitude. No need for a consistent theology standing in such beauty, she thought. Duncan seemed to agree.

Ineke dropped him at his Wee Cottage in Portsoy and drove on to Buckie to get some supper into her four year old before the child crashed in one of her meltdowns from the combination of empty tummy and weary body.

She did not run into Duncan Allan again for several months, though she watched for him.

Cullen, Scotland: Late 1995

"Old Man Cruickshank" unlocked the door to his antique shop and stood listening to its cacophony of ticking that sounded like a hundred synchronized metronomes, his own surround sound, he thought. He greeted his clocks with an appreciative smile and commended them for making it through another night. He pulled on the window shades covering his display windows, releasing them to roll up so that the sun and any potential customers would know it was time to come in. He surveyed his shop and blessed it. It was more Home than the house where he slept, and he treasured its eccentricities that mirrored his own. He seated himself at his large mahogany desk and began studying an ivory carving he thought was probably from India, a decade after the Brits colonized that country, maybe from 1867? He delighted in reading antiques, studying each detail closely, checking the massive reference books stacked at the back of his work table when his photographic memory failed him, and opening his clocks and cabinets to the inside as carefully as if he held a newborn. He was looking for patterns and markings that identified their creator and the era in which this piece of art was created.

The people who entered his shops might think Old Man Cruickshank unobservant. In fact, his eyes behind their heavy eyelid drapery took in details that signified a person's emotional state, his physical health, his intelligence, and stored what was revealed where he could easily retrieve it. Almost never would he voice these observations. Like his acute observation of his clocks, he noted the patterns and signs of distress in the people he encountered and analyzed them, drawing on the particulars he had observed in them. Increasingly as he saw his life foreshortening, he pondered his observations and mixed them with his reflections on Life, Love, Good and Evil, attaining along the way what he privately labeled as Understanding, or even Wisdom.

He had not always kept his observations to himself. Those forty-five years that he shared with Molly McDonald Cruickshank, there had been many occasions when he would tell her what he had observed about this or that person, often setting her to laughing in those low extended notes of the musical scale that were characteristic of this woman, who thoroughly enjoyed life in all its peculiarities and let you know it by her frequent, boisterous laughter. She wouldn't always laugh, nay, sometimes she choked up at the dreadful pain he recounted reading on a face. Lord, how he missed her these five years gone!

He'd like to tell her about the young man who came into his Cullen shop many months ago, name of Allan. Came from the middle of America, alone! Thin he was, wearing a face edged in sorrow lines that made him prematurely old, though Cruickshank guessed he wasn't much past thirty. "You never know what burdens a person is carrying so don't add to 'em by judgin' 'em." Molly's words sang in his ear. He was so grateful he could still hear her voice.

Duncan Allan had been staying at the Wee Cottage in Portsoy for a year. Dreadful place now, all run down with holes as big as your fist between some of the rocks. Probably the young man had company for the winter, field mice and shrews and the like, but from the looks of him, he wouldn't have noticed. Cruickshank smiled and chuckled audibly remembering his own times at that Cottage. In better days it had been a servant's home attached to the large house that shadowed it with the unhappy consequence of keeping out the sun. Later owners turned it into a storage building, but they didn't remove the basic furniture—a bed with a straw mattress and an unsteady table, as he recalled. When he and Molly were courting, they'd found Wee Cottage unoccupied, and they'd taken advantage of that bed and the thick walls that kept their sounds from those outside. They'd played a game that it was their cottage and would sneak off to "play" there many an afternoon. He chuckled again. Had anyone been in the store they'd have thought him daft, laughing out loud and talking to his clocks, he thought.

He set the magnifying glass on his work table, leaned back in his chair, and opened himself to the memory of it. A blessing of old age, recalling and savoring those memories that lay on your tongue like thick clabbered cream, melting slowly.

Some minutes later the young man intruded on his thoughts again. Duncan Allan was a hard worker, ready to learn and to take direction, to absorb the trade. He seemed grateful that Cruickshank needed him and would take him on to fetch antiques from country farms back a distance from the coast and haul pieces across the Northeast to those who purchased them. Cruickshank read him as a man with a great tragedy in his young life, maybe more than one, who was desperate for distraction, for something to do that steadied his mind.

Allan is a Scots name. Must have ancestors who crossed the pond in one of the great migrations to America during Scotland's lean times.

He turned to analyzing his most recent acquisition, a clock he calculated had been made in 1804 in Glasgow, probably an early one by this particular clockmaker, possibly a gift to his lady love. He could make out an inscription, quite small letters but readable through his glass: "For Molly." He smiled at the coincidence.

Since the day after he'd hired him the young man was in his shop by ten each morning. He had cleaned himself up a bit, though his eyes still roamed anxiously. Cruickshank had called him to pull up a chair and get started learning how to read these beauties.

That had been the start of their relationship. With almost daily contact and lots of time together pouring over reference books--Cruickshank providing a commentary that the young man seemed so soak up like a sponge--Allan was becoming a fit replacement for Cruickshank. He didn't remember exactly when his perception of the young man's skills crossed the boundary from "competent assistant" to "ready to run the business," but crossing that boundary was significant. He'd not found anyone before who had crossed it, no one who he believed shared his passion for the craftsmanship of these mostly unknown and long dead artists. Cruickshank had discovered that passion when he was yet a lad, and it sustained him all of his life.

All these people with their ability to construct functional art had been here before him and left these tangible constructions that said, at least to Cruickshank, "I was here!" What was he himself leaving behind to make that testimony? That question had long troubled him. He was no craftsman, no artist, just someone who understood and appreciated the creations of others. Molly would have scoffed at this description of him. He could almost hear her say, "Your creations are the people you transform, love. And here is another opportunity workin' right beside you every day."

He guessed there was truth in that.

The arrangement Cruickshank worked out with Duncan Allan solved a problem for each of them. Duncan handled the heavy work and was keen to learn from the expert. Cruickshank did not ask Duncan much about himself; he just treated him fairly and with care. We each carry our burdens our own way, he was fond of saying, and he could tell the first morning that Duncan's burden had been wearing him down.

By late summer Duncan occasionally smiled, though, warily.

Wichita, Kansas: Late Spring 1996

The money Duncan had left for Amy enabled her to stay at home until Little Duncan was nearly two. She used those years to figure out what she would do to support them. She took correspondence courses to earn a certification in accounting and secured a license to buy and sell real estate. She surprised herself by how focused she was. She had to be.

She also faced down what she considered her mother's obsolete religious convictions. On one of their Monday evenings together, they stood in Amy's kitchen, for a change, chopping veggies for a stir fry supper. The house was warm and the air moist. It was too early for air conditioning, but the air in the kitchen swelled with humidity and the pollen of early spring. It filled all the space like an overweight man whose body sprawls over into your seat at the movies. Amy found these moisture laden days disquieting. Summer would soon settle in with an oppressive Kansas vengeance.

Then Mother began complaining. "What is this country coming to with all of these perverts in our government and even in our churches? Did you hear the Episcopal Church is ordaining one of them as Bishop? And Massachusetts is considering allowing them to marry! And all of these single women choosing women over men! It makes no sense! How can any woman choose to love another woman? Not to mention their sexual behavior. No wonder this country is going to the dogs!"

Mother knew about John and Phillip. She knew how offensive this talk was to Amy. That did not stop her.

Little Duncan in his swollen diaper played on the floor, vigorously spinning the lids of pots and pans that clanged and resounded in a cacophony of jagged noise that nearly drowned out their words. Appropriate background music, Amy thought. Then her irritation with her mother seized her, and she turned from her cutting board, eyes blazing.

"Mother, I will not allow you to talk like that around me and my child. Women choose women and men choose men because they fall in love and want to build their lives together. They have that right and should have the right to marry. Homosexuality is neither a sin nor a perversion. I'm sick to death of you spouting your bigoted views as though they are Truth. They are NOT my truth. You will stop attacking people I love."

Now Mother shifted to attack Duncan, railing about how irresponsible he was to abandon his wife and child. But Amy had had enough. Sometimes she privately shared her mother's criticism of Duncan, but anyone else voicing it infuriated her, especially given how generously Duncan had provided for her and her child.

"If you can't control your mouth, Mother, I will have to deny you any further contact with your grandson."

The clanging sounds of lid hitting lid that accompanied their angry words had rattled and reverberated in the somnolent air until that moment when she declared herself. At that moment Little Duncan looked up at them, poised and watchful, aware even at his young age that something important was transpiring.

Mother picked up her purse and jacket and walked out of the house. Amy's stomach churned and her face flushed, but she returned to the business of making supper, dumping the veggies into the hot oil and smiling to herself as they sizzled.

The following day she resisted the voice in her head that said she should call Mother. She simply went on about her life. On Wednesday Mother phoned to ask about their Sunday plans. No mention of their fraught conversation. Amy responded to her cue, and they picked their relationship up as before, except that Mother self-monitored and stayed within the boundaries Amy had set.

It was a turning point for them both. Amy felt proud of herself and even proud of her mother. Mother was pleasant to be around when she kept that language in lockup. And she helped a lot with the child while Amy balanced taking classes, sitting for her exams, and caring for her son.

Northeast Scotland: Spring 1996

By May 1996, Duncan Allan had worked with Mr. Cruickshank for over a year. One day he asked if he could have time off on a Wednesday afternoon to go up to the elementary school in Buckie to speak with a class about antiques. Cruickshank was surprised that Duncan would get such an invitation; the lad was making more progress emerging into life than his boss had realized. Duncan asked if Mr. Cruickshank would like to come along and could they bring two objects to show the children?

Cruickshank lived too far from his sons and their families to get to attend children's functions at his grandchildren's schools--a deficit in their lives that Molly had vocally regretted. So he accepted the invitation with some excitement. He wasn't as mobile as he needed to be. He'd lived here on the northeast shoulder of Scotland all his life, climbed the braes, walked down the cobbled streets to many a harbor and town center more times than could be counted, but now he needed his cane as an extra leg to support his stiff knees and chronically aching hips. His walks to the sea and along the braes were slower, less frequent, and required taking a dose of aspirin beforehand and a pint of ale afterward to motivate him. Going to the school sounded fun.

Duncan picked him up in the old truck he'd purchased from a local farmer, and Cruickshank climbed with some effort into the cab on the left, the passenger side. They had selected a chiming mantle clock with decoratively carved hands and a stationery box covered in cleverly tooled leather that was intricately embossed. Both they carefully wrapped in bubble wrap, boxed, and placed in the bed of the truck on top of several layers of folded wool blankets to protect them from bouncing along the narrow, winding roads. Duncan was a careful driver, Mr. Cruickshank observed.

The school sprawled on a hill like some important monument to the past, three stories of glistening white stone, windows symmetrically placed on either side of the broad front entryway. As they pulled up, a tall, statuesque blond woman probably in her early thirties waved them to a place to park and greeted them both. She greeted Duncan with some warmth, Cruickshank noted with approval. She introduced herself as Ineke and thanked them both several times for coming.

The woman led them into the school and down a corridor off to the left. The old hardwood floors announced their coming. Large bulletin boards had been installed on the old walls and in their colorful drawings you could trace how children's perceptions change over time—circle bodies with stick arms and legs morphed into two circle bodies. Cruickshank marveled at the holistic way of seeing of the very young. They entered a classroom where twenty kindergartners sat in a circle on a rag rug. Cruickshank recognized their teacher, who sat at one side of the circle. He had known her when she herself was in kindergarten and had watched her grow up. She set out two chairs for her guests, introduced Mr. Cruickshank and Mr. Allan, and waited while Mr. Allan placed their two boxes on the floor. Cruickshank's eyes were drawn to a sunny faced girl with short, irrepressibly curly red hair and an excited smile. The father of sons, he had always found little girls delightful, and this one was especially so. He overheard her telling the child beside her, "That's my friend Duncan!"

Duncan showed the children the mantle clock, which conveniently chimed the ten o'clock hour. He explained how it worked and the importance of not winding it too tightly. Then he showed them the stationery box and asked them to move closer so they could see the intricate designs someone had tooled into the leather. They ooo'd and ahhhhh'd as they identified the stylized fish and birds, trees and flowers that its creator had tooled into each square of the surface. Then Duncan asked Mr. Cruickshank to tell them the story of this stationery box. Cruickshank's enjoyment in sharing what he knew was obvious, and his blue eyes were lit with energy. He concluded, "People who lived a long, long time ago made beautiful things as gifts to others, or just because it made them happy to make them. These things that they made are special treasures that tell us about what they did and what they loved. You, too, can make things that you find beautiful for others."

It was the perfect time for the teacher to pass out paper and crayons and direct the children to tables where they could draw the images from the stationery box or create from clay objects they liked to look at or feel.

The girl with carrot color hair who Cruickshank had noticed before had her hand up. "Miss Jones, my mommy makes beautiful jewelry every day!"

"That is wonderful, Elleke. Do you look at what she's made when you come home from school?"

"Yes, I do and it's very, very beautiful."

Cruickshank told the child, "Your mommy's jewelry will live for a long, long time and tell people who see it that she was here."

On the drive back to Cullen, Cruickshank told Duncan that he had handled that very well. "I think those children will remember today. Thank you for including me. That red haired child with the wild curling hair who talked about her mother making jewelry, do you know who her mother is?"

"She's Ineke, the woman you met in the parking lot. She's the person who invited us to talk with the children today."

"Lovely child *and* lovely mother."

Duncan did not reply but Cruickshank could see from the curling of his mouth, in profile, that he agreed. Good! Duncan's recovery was farther along than he had thought. Cruickshank tried to suppress his elation. He wouldn't press his young friend for details.

A week later Cruickshank and Duncan received invitations to Ineke's home for a meal to thank them for speaking to her daughter's class. Cruickshank wondered to himself which of them was the most excited to go.

They sat around Ineke's dining table after the meal listening to Cruickshank's stories of growing up on the Northeast coast seventy years ago. Cruickshank had not enjoyed himself so thoroughly in years. After consuming several Devon ales the old man was mellow and his stories had them all laughing, even Duncan. When Duncan left the room for the toilet, Cruickshank told Ineke, "Ye be havin' a good effect on this melancholy man, lassie." She smiled back at him. "I think it's more your effect than mine," she said.

Cullen, Scotland: Autumn 1996

Duncan Allan came to the shop one Monday morning to find it still locked and the shades drawn. He was concerned. He walked the two blocks to Cruickshank's home, knocked, and, when he heard no response, tried the door, which was unlocked, as was common in this fishing village where most people knew each other at least by sight. Inside he found Mr. Cruickshank crumpled in a heap at the base of his stairs. He had lost his footing descending the stairs and had fallen the rest of the way, cracking his head on the last step, he told Duncan groggily. Duncan got him to the sofa, propped his head up, and elevated his legs. Then he phoned the doctor, who arrived in no time. Duncan noticed his own hands were trembling. Please don't let anything happen to this man, he kept repeating inside his head.

"Yer goin' a 'ave some colorful batt'l scars to show for this, George. It'll give you something to brag about!" the doctor said. Blue and red and black bruises were flowering on Cruickshank's legs and crowding out the many brown patches on the thin skin of his arms. When the doctor loosened Cruickshank's trousers and pulled them down to view his abdomen, an enormous dark and angry purple patch could be seen spreading across his right hip, which, when touched, elicited a groan from the old man despite his resolve to "be a sturdy old bloke whatever the outcome."

The doctor phoned for an ambulance to get him to the hospital in Elgin for some x-rays and tests. Duncan rode with him, which he could see surprised and pleased Mr. Cruickshank.

Ineke picked Duncan up from the hospital and made up a bed for him at her house, Buckie being closer to the Elgin Hospital than Portsoy where Duncan's Wee Cottage was. When she made this case for staying at her place, he did not protest. He could feel his heart accelerate at the thought of staying with her …until the memory of Amy crowded out his excitement. He should be focused on his friend, George Cruickshank, he chided himself.

The tests showed Cruickshank had broken his hip, and the doctor ordered hip replacement surgery, which could be done at Elgin Hospital. Duncan contacted Cruickshank's sons and assured Mr. Cruickshank that he would take care of the shops while Cruickshank recovered. Perhaps they could pay a neighbor to take care of him in his house in Cullen? Duncan could drive to Cruickshank's each night to review with him the day's work, expenditures, and receipts.

He had never before seen Mr. Cruickshank so flustered. When he asked what was worrying him, Mr. Cruickshank blurted out his fear that with a bad hip and surgery, he would be unable to resist his sons' pressure to retire from the antique business and move south to live with one of them. "Leaving the business, I'm sar'tin, will be the end of me."

His distress alarmed Duncan, who determined to find a way to help this man who had assisted him when he was so low.

Cruickshank's sons traveled north to see their father and held a family meeting to decide what to do about where he would live in the future. They gathered in the cramped waiting room off the surgery wing of Elgin Hospital. Duncan was already there when they arrived and introduced himself. There were four sons. Andrew, the eldest, already gray at fifty, radiated a gloomy seriousness that worried Duncan.

Andrew took charge of the conversation, pacing the small waiting room as he talked. He reminded them that none of them could care for their father while he lived five or six hours away. Nor could their wives, most of whom were also working. A hip replacement necessitated someone to care for Da' while he healed and the North Sea was simply too far away. He saw no alternative to closing the shops and moving him south. It would be a squeeze, but he and Mary could take him in with them.

The room was silent. The other sons looked away shaking their heads. Jack, the youngest and smallest, spoke up. "We canna do that to Da'. It'll kill 'im sure."

The middle sons weighed in, straddling the options, unable to land firmly on a plan. It was clearly a decision no one was completely comfortable making.

Duncan felt increasingly agitated. He'd grown close to Mr. Cruickshank and he loved the old man who had given him a chance to reinvent his life. He didn't want to lose this relationship, and he didn't want Mr. Cruickshank to lose the work that kept him loving life.

Duncan had been sitting on the other side of the waiting room, outside the family circle. Now he asked if he could speak to them. Jack grinned and motioned for him to pull up a chair and join them. They slid their chairs together to make room, and the sound of sixteen chair legs scuffing against the linoleum brought a young nurse to the doorway checking to be sure everything was all right. Andrew reminded his brothers that the young American was the person who found Da', got him to the doctor, and contacted them all. "'E's been takin' care o' Da's shops fer some months now," Andrew told them. It was the first time Duncan had seen Andrew smile.

The waiting room had been painted a dirty yellow and machine-produced prints of obscure impressionists looked down from their high placements, all hung at the same level along each wall. Disheveled magazines lay on the coffee table in front of the circled chairs. Empty paper cups bearing the remains of the morning's coffee squatted atop piles of old brochures-- Understanding the National Health System, Why Washing Your Hands Matters, Preventing Infection--their preachy titles went on and on. A few paper plates balanced precariously on the end tables, displaying the corpses of half eaten sausage rolls. It was not a promising environment for making his case that the North Sea coast was the right place for this beloved old man, Duncan thought. He collected his thoughts for a few minutes and they waited him out. Then he spoke quietly, determined to do his best.

"Your father took me in not knowing anything about me. He taught me the business and made me his associate." His throat constricted, catching him off guard, and he paused for a moment before continuing. "He's told me he wants me to take over the business when he can no longer do it, but I don't think this is the time for that. I think the work will keep him going and help him recover. I will take care of him and the shops. I will keep him involved. I've been thinking about this a lot since his fall. I could even move into his house while he's learning to walk with the new hip. I can shop and cook for him, clean up after him, do whatever he needs done."

"You'd do all that for him?" Andrew looked surprised.

"Of course! He has given me a new life. I can certainly help him learn to live with a new hip."

The room was silent as the sons pondered his proposal. None of them knew this shy American. Could they trust him? Might he be intent on scamming their father? Andrew suggested they talk with their father about Duncan's proposal. When the others nodded agreement, someone suggested Duncan wait here while they did so, and the four men moved together down the hall to his room. Their substantial bodies filled the hallway as they moved in close formation to Mr. Cruickshank's room. Watching them Duncan felt regret pass through him, wishing that he had family who would come together like this if he needed care. No, don't go there, he told himself. Focus on now and on Mr. Cruickshank.

He fidgeted as he waited, trying to prepare himself for another loss.

They remained in Mr. Cruickshank's room for what seemed a long time. Finally, Jack poked his head into the waiting room and invited Duncan to join them "in Da's room."

Mr. Cruickshank was smiling broadly. "Aye, laddie, I'll have your proposal and be grateful to ye, aye, aye, aye!" Then he laughed, winced at the twinge of pain the laugh prompted, and spoke again. "From what my sons say, you gave a discourse to rival Maggie Thatcher herself. Ye been learning elocution and persuasive speech as well as antiques, it seems." His eyes softened. "I'm right grateful to ye, me friend."

With that brief exchange it was settled, and Duncan Allan's relationship with Old Man Cruickshank moved to another level. Both men welcomed the change.

Ineke sat at her kitchen table after Duncan phoned to tell her that he was at the hospital with the Cruickshank sons. Elleke was already asleep. For more than a year Ineke had been careful not to frighten Duncan Allan away by revealing her attraction to him. She could tell that he was wary of opening himself to anyone, and she intuited that he had a lot of healing to do before he could receive anything other than casual friendship. She had taken it very slowly, reminding herself to have no expectations. Frankly, she wasn't sure that she wanted more with him.

Duncan was unlike anyone she had known. Sometimes he reminded her of Pig Pen, the character in Charlie Brown that moves in a cloud of dust and debris that even a good bath can't wash away for long. But the cloud that followed Duncan seemed more threatening than dust and debris. She did not want another self-absorbed man like Jens. But was Duncan's depression self-absorption or the byproduct of neglect and lack of love? Even asking that question made her uncomfortable. "So, you're going to rush in and save him?" A voice inside her pushed her to be realistic. "One person can't save another. Relationships must be between equals." But, recently he'd been changing. There was a new playfulness about him that came out around Elleke, and his relationship with Mr. Cruickshank, how much he cared about the old man, showed he had some capacity for attachment. To be fair, Duncan was not at all like Jens. She sensed that Mr. Cruickshank and Elleke had provided Duncan something new to invest his life in, personally and professionally. She thought it a good sign that he wanted to commit himself to Mr. Cruickshank's recovery.

She poured herself a glass of wine and got out her journal, opening to a new page and writing at the top left PROS and at the top right CONS. Then she listed them:

PROS
- He and Elleke like each other. And he is good with her.
- I'm attracted to him now that he's looking more fit.
- It would be lovely to be in a nurturing, satisfying relationship.

CONS
- I don't know much about him. I would need to know much more.
- Is he capable of love?
- Can he let himself be happy?

When she finished, she closed her journal, put away the wine, and turned out the lights. It felt good to have laid it out like this. Time would tell if the CONS would be eliminated.

Ineke and Elleke had offered to be part of his recovery team after Mr. Cruickshank came home from the hospital with his new hip, which, Ineke calculated correctly, would mean they would also be part of Duncan Allan's. Elleke took very seriously her responsibility to help nurse Mr. Cruickshank, reminding her mother that a five year old can bring water, snacks, and fetch things for patients. Duncan phoned early afternoon to report that they had reached an agreement regarding Mr. Cruickshank's recovery care. Could

Ineke come to the hospital to meet the sons before they left for their homes in the Borders? He wanted to talk over the details of what would be needed with her as he'd never provided care for an invalid. She hadn't either, but didn't say so, flattered that he wanted her input. She collected Elleke from school and drove west to Elgin

At the hospital she met Mr. Cruickshank's sons and they talked briefly. Then Duncan excused himself to sort out with Ineke the details of Mr. Cruickshank's home care. They left Elleke in the hospital room chatting with Mr. Cruickshank and his sons. The two of them moved to the cab of Duncan's old truck. It was starting to grow dark, and Ineke could not see his face as he told her of his offer to care for Cruickshank, but his voice went a bit wobbly when he said he'd be moving into Cruickshank's house for the duration of his recovery. That surprised and pleased her. Yes, it pleased her very much. Forgetting her intention to not push him, she blurted out,

"I could help you move your things to Mr. Cruickshank's spare room."

Was the dry air responsible for that soft sizzle of static electricity in the closed car? When he replied, "Great," she exhaled audibly, embarrassed to realize that she had been holding her breath.

"They are dismissing him from the hospital tomorrow and I'll bring him home to his house in Cullen."

"I could meet you there, say at four? Maybe Elleke can stay with Mr. Cruickshank while we fetch your things?" Her voice sounded almost timid. At his nod, they climbed from the truck and walked back to the hospital room where Cruickshank and Elleke were in the middle of a game of Parcheesi.

The following afternoon after school they met at Mr. Cruickshank's home. Duncan had shaved off his beard and she found him quite attractive. Elleke preened at her mother's suggestion that she could take care of Mr. Cruickshank while they moved Duncan's things, and Cruickshank's eyes sparkled. They drove in Duncan's truck to the Wee Cottage. There Duncan gathered up his few clothes and books while Ineke made them tea. She carried a cup to him as he was packing his only suitcase and set her own cup on the rickety table.

"Is that all you have?" she asked, surprised.

He nodded and she smiled. So there was no need for help moving. Perhaps he, too, wanted this time together alone? She turned to retrieve her cup and, turning back, found herself face to face with Duncan, face to face and very close, for the cottage's main room wasn't big enough to swing a cat. He took her tea cup and set it with his on the table. Then his mouth latched on to hers gently and his strong arms held her close. She hesitated, remembering that she did not want to rush him, but when her mind caught up to her body, she realized that it was he who had kissed her. Putting her mind on hold, she kissed him back unambiguously. They stumbled to the narrow straw-mattress bed and fell into it, arms and legs moving in a dance as familiar as life and older than Molly McDonald's coupling with George Cruickshank on that same bed so many decades ago.

There in the Wee Cottage, while Elleke nursed the man she began that afternoon to call Granddad George, Ineke and Duncan found solace, together. Afterward, when they lay together on the bed, he said he was sad, remembering, but also grateful. Then he told her that he hadn't slept with a woman since his wife, who had betrayed him a year and a half ago. "It feels confusing and scary, but not as scary as I imagined it would be."

"You've imagined this?"

"Oh, yes. Lots of times. Beginning with the day we went to watch the seals," he said.

They had more in common than she had guessed and his honesty impressed her.

Elleke remembered the first night she had played nurse to Mr. Cruickshank, the fun they had had together. He would ask her to fetch things and make a big display of gratitude when she did. When Mom and Duncan finally came back to Mr. Cruickshank's with Duncan's suitcase, Elleke noticed something was different. She thought their skin looked rosier. Definitely their eyes were shining. It was another one of those moments Mom said happen in life when you see clearly something very beautiful yet fragile and know you must handle it carefully.

The two months of Mr. Cruickshank's convalescence provided opportunities for Ineke to spend time with Duncan while Elleke stayed with Granddad It was natural to eat together at Mr. Cruickshank's and natural to get their daily exercise walking together after the meal while Elleke entertained the patient. No more haunting the bake shop in Portsoy hoping to run into him.

Like Jens, Duncan was not a person to talk about his private life but, unlike Jens, he asked about her life experiences, feelings, and thoughts.

One evening walking together along the braes he asked about Elleke's father. She did not glow-coat anything, telling him that her husband found her boring, that she was blind-sided when he said he wanted a divorce, that she'd been angry and depressed learning there was another woman. She remained dry-eyed up to the bit about the other woman, whom he had married and with whom he recently had twin daughters. She didn't know why naming that upset her so. Maybe because if Jens had reconfigured his life with a new spouse and more children—after never wanting children when he was married to her—then, she must be the cause of her marriage failing, she must be the one at fault.

They were walking through a patch of gorse brambles that challenged the path along the cliffs. Her hands were scratched from pushing them aside. Suddenly she stopped, stood still, and began to cry. Duncan didn't speak. He stood behind her and began untangling the thorns that were taking root in her jeans and her wool sweater. He worked silently, persistently, breaking thorny shoots off the bushes to make it possible for her to escape their painful embrace. She just stood there, unheeding of the tears dropping from her chin onto her sweater, letting them come.

After a time they stopped.

A three-quarter moon slid out from its dense screen of clouds, bestowing the path with a bluish light. She noticed Duncan holding open the way he had cleared for her. His hands and face were covered in cuts and blood slithered down his right cheek from a particularly nasty scratch on his forehead. His thoughtfulness moved her. No man she knew other than her father had treated her with such care.

Now she thought about him, how little she knew of this man. One thing was clear. Somewhere in his life someone had taught him to be caring. It was, she thought, the most important lesson to teach.

"My Mother," he said, his voice barely audible.

Had she spoken her observation? Apparently so. Before the moon slid back into its hiding place, she saw in his eyes a look of sadness and yearning. The returning darkness blurred any visual clues, and she was on her own how to proceed. She reached out her hand and he found it. Together they moved tentatively forward on the path covered in darkness.

"I would like to hear about her," she said when they had walked more than a dozen meters in silence. She could hardly breathe, so intent she was not to get it wrong. "Please don't feel you must say anything," she amended.

Their legs moved in time, right legs forward together pulling their bodies along, then left legs swinging forward, relieving the right. When he replied his voice was soft and he sounded tired.

"She and my father died in a car crash when I was seven, skidded on ice and hit my grandmother's old oak tree. I don't talk about it, but I still miss her."

She wanted to ask him for details. She imagined how terrifying it must have been for him. She wanted to be a safe place where he could talk about it, but she sensed that he needed her attentive silence more than her questions. They kept walking.

Gradually over the next hour stories from his other life emerged, seeping out in small dribbles, a sentence at a time, while their rhyming feet found the path that twisted its way across the shadowy braes. When it was time to start back, she held him carefully and without passion before they turned and began walking. The moon lit their way. Apparently, it had decided to stick around until they were safely home.

Portsoy and Cullen, Scotland:

Elleke loved her life. Sunny and outgoing, she had invited people into her early childhood and invited herself into their adult lives easily and with a natural charm that brought her the return she wanted—attention, praise, smiles, and affection. It had worked with "The Scruffy Man," who was beginning to seem more like her dad than her actual father, who had built a new family with his replacement wife in Holland and never invited her for summer holidays.

Her ability to communicate with adults and invite them to be her friends paid off with Duncan and with Mr. Cruickshank, "Granddad George." She and Mom spent time with him several times a week while he was recovering from his hip replacement. Mom would cook and after supper she and Duncan would let Elleke "Granddad-sit" while they went off for walks.

That was when he began showing her some of the small statues he displayed in the windows of his house, treasures "my Molly" collected. Hand painted porcelain people, all beautiful with faces open to the world, showing delight. Granddad told her once that they reminded him of her and Molly. The girl statues wore ruffled aprons and long skirts that flowed out behind them, curved and billowing from the force of an imaginary wind. Their hair tossled and their faces shining, they smiled up at the sky or at a playful kitten the artist had shaped as though it was rolling on the ground beside them. One girl statue knelt on the ground tending to an injured bird.

The one she especially liked had red hair like hers and lay sprawled on her back, arms outstretched, knees two upside down Vs, eyes crinkled at the corners, mouth open in a hearty grin. Except for the long skirt and high buttoned boots, this girl could be me, Elleke thought. I have experienced this joy. Often!

Granddad George encouraged her to make up stories about Molly's statues and listened as she described what had happened just before the moment the potter captured forever. It became a ritual of their relationship. Since Molly had two dozen of these statues, Elleke's imagination and Granddad's listening skills were both well exercised.

When Mom apologized for how talkative Elleke was, Granddad laughed, placed his large hand gently on Elleke's shoulder, and said that his Molly was a talker, too, and he loved it. It was one of the things he missed most living without Molly.

By the time he was recovered enough to climb the braes, cane in one hand, Elleke's hand in the other, Mom and Duncan's evening walks had expanded to include spending all day Sunday together. When Granddad suggested he no longer required as much of Duncan's time, that Duncan need not stay the nights, Elleke and Granddad speculated whether Duncan would move back to Wee Cottage.

"Maybe he'll move in with us," she said.

"How'd that abide with ye?" Granddad was observing her carefully.

"I think that would be great," she responded.

"Me, too," he replied.

A few days later while Mom and she were cleaning up back at their house in Cullen, Mom had asked her the same question. When she said Granddad and she had talked about this and that she told him it would be great, Mom turned quickly from the dishpan full of suds and enfolded Elleke in her arms, setting off a volcano of soap bubbles flying through the air and landing on the floor in slippery clumps. They both laughed. Elleke wondered if the person who made Molly's statues had made one of a moment like this.

On the Wednesday after their soapy hug, while they were eating supper at Granddad's, Duncan announced that he was going to move into their house in Cullen since he was no longer needed at Mr. Cruickshank's. Anyway, he said, the Cullen house was closer to Mr. Cruickshank's, should Granddad need him. Mom's face flushed when he said this, but she was smiling. So was Mr. Cruickshank.

Elleke had believed since that evening that she was responsible for this family—Mom, Duncan, and Granddad. They had become family because of her, and she remained their center. She knew that they adored her and supported her uniqueness. Sometimes they reminisced about how she had brought them together and kept them together.

It was good for a kid to know that the people who loved her and who she loved were happy.

Cullen, Scotland: 1999

For several years Duncan, Mom, and Elleke lived in Elleke's house in Cullen. Granddad came for supper Wednesdays and Saturdays and sometimes went with them on Sundays for drives in the country.

On those drives they observed the seasons repaint the landscape that stretched over the high plains from the edge of the cliffs. From the perspective of the barley fields, you wouldn't know the sea was waiting below. All the eye could see was fields, alternately brilliant green, golden, tan, and pink according to the season. Mom said right after harvest the fields looked like masses of soldiers with blond buzz cuts standing in close formation.

Driving the countryside the four of them sang songs, counted sheep and cows, and listened to Elleke and Mr. Cruickshank's stories. When she was learning to read, they competed to see who could read the road signs first. They took turns naming things that began with the last letter of the item named by the previous person: "Apple" produced "elephant," produced "tiger," produced "reindeer," produced "rhinoceros" and so on. They tried to identify the makes of cars on the road. They made up stories, each contributing one sentence, the next person adding a sentence, and so on, spinning fantastic and imaginative tales. Elleke loved these drives

Her mom was especially good at making things fun. Before Halloween they would discuss what each of them would dress up as, and Mom would take the lead making their costumes. At the Halloween party in Cullen Town

Hall, their family was always praised for Mom's clever costumes.

Of course, Elleke had other memories that were not so good.

The summer she was eight, her father swept back into her life. The international priority envelope arrived in July. It held a brief letter and a round trip, non-refundable airline ticket to Amsterdam for the first two weeks in August. In light of her young age, Jens wrote, he had not before now wanted to remove Elleke from her mother, despite his legal right to have her for summer holidays. At eight she was now old enough to fly to Amsterdam, under the watchful eye of the flight attendants, and spend two weeks with him and his wife and twin daughters. Her ticket was enclosed. They would meet her plane on August first.

"I don't want to go." Elleke spoke with the certainty of a prosecutor making her summation. She dropped the ticket in the trash bin and left the room, her face confident, as though that was that. Ineke, observing, recognized Jens in Elleke's unquestioning assumption that life would fall into line as she intended. She was, indeed, Jens's daughter! Ineke went after her, aware that her child was about to have her first experience of the power of patriarchy.

Ineke sat on the bed in Elleke's room waiting for her silent, serious presence to register with the child. "Elleke, he has the right to have you during summer holidays. I know you barely remember him, but he is your father. Once you are sixteen, you may decide for yourself whether you want to continue visiting him. Unfortunately he didn't consult with us, but it is typical of your father not to consult, just to announce it, everything decided, case closed. I'm sorry, honey."

It was the first fracture in Elleke's perfect childhood.

She recognized the big man who met her plane from the pictures Mom showed her of when she was little. He was tall and carried himself with authority. He gave her a perfunctory kiss on the cheek and introduced his wife, younger and pretty, and "your sisters" who were four, fidgeting, and easily distracted.

Their Amsterdam apartment was in an old row house with a stair-step roof along a canal. Inside it was large, modern, and flooded with light. She had her own room and Marika, Vader's wife, made her welcome.

The two weeks dragged at first, but she liked Marika and her sisters were a distraction. Her father wasn't around much, except on the weekends when he took her to see his parents who lived in the countryside. Elleke didn't know what to think of her father. Marika said he was an important man and "successful." But when she spoke of him, her face looked tired. In Scotland, Mom and "Pappie Duncan" talked with her every day and were interested in what she thought. Here her father barely acknowledged her, talking with Marika over dinner while the children ate and spending each evening on his computer. In the course of two weeks she had no conversations with him.

Every day Marika let Elleke write emails to her mom and took her for walks with the girls-- to the parks, along the canals, to the Anne Frank House, the zoo, the Houseboat Museum. It wasn't a bad experience, but she was super glad to get home to Mom and Pappie.

One afternoon that fall Duncan came home from work just as she was arriving from her fourth grade class. He looked troubled. Granddad had fallen in his shop in Cullen, and Duncan had taken him back to the hospital to see what was wrong. All of them drove to the hospital where the doctor told them that Granddad had a condition that made him faint. She had not understood what it was, but she remembered a woman doctor in a white coat saying that he would not be safe in the store any longer. He could black out again at any time.

Driving back to Cullen after they visited with Granddad, they talked about what to do. Mom said if Granddad passed out, he'd almost certainly hurt himself, his stores being so crowded with sharp edged tables and chests with only narrow walking spaces between them. He could be badly injured.

Mom and Duncan had talked more that night after supper. Duncan had an idea. He'd seen a larger house in Cullen that was for sale and thought it would have enough space for all of them, including Granddad, to live in to-gether. There was a fourth bedroom that could become Mom's design studio. Granddad could putter with his clocks in his room while Mom designed her jewelry.

The next afternoon the three of them drove to look at the house. It was built of gray granite blocks. Like so many of the houses in the villages along the coast, the stones around the central doorway and its flanking windows were painted--dark red in this case. The second storey dormer windows looked out on the street that led downhill to the harbor. There was virtually no front garden as the house sat quite near the street, but the back garden, surrounded with stone walls, climbed uphill to a low hedge that ran across the back. Close to the house tall, scraggly rose bushes clustered covered in bright red hips, hard and round, place holders for next year's blossoms. There was an apple tree in one corner and currant bushes in another. Even amid all of the decline of autumn, they could see its promise. They liked the house.

Before he called the real estate agent, Pappie Duncan wanted to call Cruickshank's eldest son, Andrew. No point bringing the proposal to Grand-dad if his family wouldn't support the idea.

The phone rang in Ineke's house and Elleke ran to answer it. She didn't recognize the voice asking to speak with Duncan Allan. She passed the phone to Pappie and returned to drawing designs for each room of "our new house."

It was Andrew Cruickshank. "Me brothers and I, we bin talkin' what to do 'bout Dad. Dunno but it makes more sense to bring 'im here with family rather than load 'im on you." Duncan felt he'd been pierced with a sharp object aimed at his heart. It washed over him how much he depended on Mr. Cruickshank, counted on him for answers to all that he didn't know about antiques and Life. He sat down heavily, trying to prepare himself for losing the person who had become a surrogate parent to him over his years in Scotland. He must do something, at least try to prevent them from removing Mr. Cruickshank from him and Ineke and Elleke.

"Andrew," he began, "This may sound crazy to you, but your father is more of a father to me than I have ever had. He's taught me a whole new profession and encouraged me through my mistakes. He's been kind to me and I depend on him. My whole family does. It would be a terrible loss for us if you take him away." His words sounded lame to him, unpersuasive. He struggled to think of a way to make their need clear to this man who had the power to separate them from a person central to their identity as a family, but he couldn't come up with anything.

As soon as he said it, Duncan remembered that Andrew and his brothers had lost their mother and--by his remaining on the Northeast coast--their father. Certainly they had a need for their father that trumped his need for him? Mechanically he went over every possible option that might appeal to Andrew without offending him.

"Do you think if we bring him South to see you and your families each

Christmas and in the summer, that you might let him stay with us? We'll be sure he eats properly and take him to the doctor, and we'd not accept any money from him or you." He could hear desperation in his voice and worried that it would set off alarm bells for Andrew.

Andrew said nothing. Then he thanked Duncan for his offer and asked if he could call him back in the next few days. He needed to consult with the rest of the family.

After Andrew rang off, Duncan stood holding the phone for several minutes before returning it to its cradle. He was sweating, though it was November. He wiped his face with his pocket handkerchief before joining Elleke and Ineke at the kitchen table. "We'll have to wait and see," he said.

That night lying close together under the duvet he told Ineke how frightened he was that they would lose Mr. Cruickshank. "We'll cope with whatever we must cope with," she responded, stroking the firm curve of his shoulders. "We'll be all right."

It was several days before Andrew called back. His voice carried none of the heaviness of his earlier call. He seemed to be reading from notes, every sentence planned. "Firstly, we want you to know how grateful we are to ye for carin' for Da. We bin talking every night trying to settle on what's best. Our mither is buried there in Portsoy. We know Da likes to go to see her. He'd na be happy removed from Ma. We nae feel right aboot you takin' Da on fer no pay. Wid ye consider Da deeding to ye one o the shops sence ye be doin' the work now? Mebbe the biggest one? The one in Cullen? Ye cud still manage the rest and decide wither to sell 'em or keep 'em open."

Duncan knew Ineke was fretting how they would manage financially. This offer was generous and would relieve her anxiety. "An we be grateful to ye fer bringin' Da South to see us, if he hinna more health problems. We talked wi' Da aboot yer offer an' he was happy to move in wi ye. Duncan, ye be family to all of us now."

Duncan let out a whoop that brought Ineke and Elleke running. Then he laughed and apologized to Andrew for his undignified response. "I'm just so happy," he said lamely.

That night after prolonged lovemaking he held Ineke in the circle of his arms, her back against his chest, his face nuzzling her hair. His eyes took in the starlight that eased into the room through the open window. Gratitude overpowered him and he began to weep. Half asleep, Ineke stirred. "Are you all right?" she asked. His answer was barely audible. "I have a family."

Mr. Cruickshank insisted on selling the Banff store—"downsizing"—and contributing some of the money he got from the sale to the down payment for the new house. The house they were buying being empty, the purchase moved quickly. They sold Ineke's Buckie house soon after that and moved Granddad George's things into the downstairs bedroom across from the room Ineke would use as her studio. Duncan took on an assistant to help run the store in Buckie while he managed the Cullen and Portsoy stores. Elleke didn't even have to change schools.

Wichita, Kansas: 1999

When Little Duncan was nearly five, Amy opened Amy's Real Estate: A Woman's Touch, specializing in finding homes for wealthy Wichitans that were just what their wives were looking for. She painted her office on Douglas Avenue next to the old Mentholatum building a soft pink and installed tasteful, subdued floral chairs and crisp white linen curtains in one of the sitting areas and dark brown leather sofas, polished wooden end tables with brass lamps, and real wood venetian blinds in the other area that she painted hunter green. She thought her décor would serve as a psychological test of her potential customers. She could get an idea of their taste from which area they chose to wait in. It was unscientific, even wacky, but it was fun.

She enjoyed her work, did well financially, and was able to arrange her schedule so that Little Duncan was with her most days. In the evenings when she showed houses Mom took care of him. Amy loved being a mommy even more now that it wasn't all she was doing.

Her grief for her missing husband continued to play in her interior spaces like a muted, Adagio for Strings. She kept his voice on the answering machine and could not bring herself to get rid of his clothes. That subterranean grief prevented her from making friends, because she assumed friends would find her hanging on to these things inappropriate and unhealthy. As the years passed, she constructed her own tangle of realism and denial. Most of the time she commended herself for presenting a competent exterior to the world. Occasionally she wondered if her husband would recognize her.

Amy had been raised in the church and, though she did not want a church that spouted judgment and One Way, she recognized that she and Little Duncan needed a supportive community of people who would provide a place of safety and acceptance for them both.

One Wednesday afternoon Amy, with Little Duncan on his tricycle, took a longer than usual walk and passed a white frame church she had not before noticed. The marquee read, *God is Still Speaking.* That intrigued her. A woman not much older than Amy was exiting the building, and Amy asked her what God is Still Speaking meant. The woman was one of those people whose eyes invite you in. She laughed as she replied.

"Lots of people ask me that. I think for our church it means that God's love is infinite and doesn't exclude any one and that God is telling us that people, regardless of their religion, their sexual preference, their wealth or poverty, their nationality, are all equally loved by God who wants us to treat each other the same way."

"I like that," Amy said.

"Why not try us out? Are you busy tonight? We have family night tonight at six with supper and choir practice and intergenerational classes in music and pottery plus child care for the little ones." She smiled at Little Duncan. "You are most welcome to come."

As they talked two brown squirrels scampered up and down the sturdy oaks in front of the building and leapt from tree to tree chasing each other. The church woman reached in her pants pocket and brought out some peanuts. Squatting, she held out her hand. One at a time the squirrels came up and nibbled from her palm, then darted away to resume their play. Amy watched with interest.

"I'm Pastor Wendy, by the way," the woman said, wiping her hands on her pants and extending her right hand to Amy. They shook hands and Amy thanked her for the invitation. Then Amy said they needed to get home and turned Little Duncan's tricycle around, starting back toward Eastborough. She yearned to feel the warmth and acceptance that squirrel taming woman gave off. But it also scared her. If Pastor Wendy became her pastor or even her friend, what would she think of a woman whose husband walked out on her with no explanation, a woman who kept his clothes and his voice on the answering machine? Amy was working very hard to have people admire her spunk, not feel sorry for her. Pity would diminish her, reduce her to a stereotype—a desperately lonely woman grasping friendship wherever it was available. Pathetic. The last thing she needed. When she reached her house she stored the trike in the garage and followed Little Duncan up the steps and into the house. "Okay, Little Man, we can do this on our own," she told him.

After that day alarms went off in her head whenever that God Is Still Speaking church or Pastor Wendy sidled into her consciousness—which happened usually late at night when she couldn't sleep. She would see those soft eyes welcoming her to share who she was, what burdens she was carrying, and she would awaken saying out loud, *"No!"* She was not ready for that. Opening up to Pastor Wendy could dismantle the barrier she had consciously and carefully erected to incarcerate her fear that Duncan was gone forever, that she would never again know the joy of a loving, intimate relationship. She couldn't take that risk. She would get up from bed, get something to drink, and grab an engrossing book to keep her evangelistic ghost at bay.

Wichita, Kansas 2000

John phoned one night and broke down as he told her that Phillip had finally let go of life. He had held on for nearly six terrible years, his suffering so intense that John was ready to release him, knowing that his death was better than such an existence.

Guilt crawled up her spine and settled down in her brain. She had never gone to see Phillip, never gone to help John care for him, despite her blasé promise to come. She tried now to focus on her brother-in-law, to listen to him.

"Amy, I promised you I would come to Wichita and help raise Little Duncan and I want you to know that I have applied for a position at Wichita State." She could feel her heart beating and something akin to elation flooded her. That afternoon she had felt so alone, so unable to share her feelings with anyone. If John moved in with them, he would be her best friend. Actually, he already was.

John found a faculty position at Wichita State University which, while not gay friendly, was not hostile to closeted homosexuals, "closeted" being the important qualifier. John went back in the closet and moved from New York City to Wichita to live with Amy and Little Duncan.

He expected living in Kansas to feel like a living death. Kansas was, after all, a flyover state. Who in their right mind ever actually landed there? As he got off the plane, he forced himself to put on a positive façade, but his insides protested that he had made a terrible mistake. He briefly considered taking the next flight back to New York. Kansas was the state that was probably going to require the teaching of creationism as "science"! He walked down the exit ramp toward Amy determined not to let her see his regret.

She was looking well and appeared very happy to see him. Come on, John, he said to himself. You can fake it. The five year old stood beside her, observing him quizzically. "Are you my daddy?" he asked.

John picked him up and spun around with him. He noted a resemblance to his and Duncan's mother. Poor Mom, never to know her children as adults, never to know her grandchild. But how would she deal with his brother's abandoning his family? How would she deal with his being gay, for that matter?

During the past few months, while Phillip gradually let go of life, John had lingered in a limbo world, between life and death. He had asked himself if life was worth the pain and loss. But this moment, holding his brother's boy and seeing the look on Amy's face as she embraced him, tipped the balance to Yes.... At least for this moment.

Over the next month John was astounded to discover that he—who liked his clothes tidy and pressed, needed his evening cocktail precisely at six, and coveted time to himself--actually liked the rough and tumble play and the physicality of parenting. Hugs and sticky kisses before bed and romps on the carpet with his nephew on his back helped fill the void left by Phillip's absence. The child had been told he was "Uncle John," but in the absence of any Daddy, the boy treated John as though he and not Duncan was his father, showering him with affection. Being a surrogate dad to his brother's boy was not bad, John decided. And he learned that he could be clear with Amy and the boy when he needed time to himself.

John discovered that Wichita was not the desert he had assumed it would be. From a colleague at W.S.U. he learned that Wichita had a menu of gay bars and safe gathering places, and he began trying them out, though not without mishaps. On the edge of Old Town he found Jonathan's Coffee Shop. He nonchalantly entered, ordered, and approached a group of men sitting close together in the back listening carefully to each other. As he pulled up a chair, trying to look like he belonged, he heard one of them say that the hormones the doctor had him on were messing up his sleep. Was anyone else having this problem? It dawned on John that this was not a gay men's discussion group but a transgendered support group, which one of the participants confirmed when John whispered the question. John excused himself and retreated casually across the room to drink his coffee and head for home.

One night while he was "shopping," quite by accident he found the Cowboy Bar he'd been told about. The decor should have alerted him that he would not fit in here, but he was lonely and curious and undeterred. The bar was dark. Large heads of decapitated long horns loomed on every side. They looked heavy enough to bring the walls down. Their glass eyes stared ahead like they were working on a math problem. He congratulated himself for making no attempt to strike up a conversation with them.

Most of the men in the bar wore cowboy boots, tight jeans, and string neckties over their flannel shirts. A few sported Stetsons from Sheplers, probably a status symbol, he thought. Some were equipped with muscles that reminded him of the Brawny paper towel man. Others revolted him with the snug fit of their plaid flannel shirts that gaped from button to button and their muffin tops that obscured their silver belt buckles. I am a snob, he concluded.

He tried to make a connection with a nice looking, well-built man sitting at the bar who appeared to be alone, but the man looked at him as though he was crazy when he asked if the man liked Kurt Weill or Berthold Brecht. "Durned if I know either of them," he muttered before turning away. Overhearing the conversation, another man told him that most of the patrons of this bar drove trucks or taxis or loaded stock out at Lowe's and Home Depot and suggested he try another bar out East where he might find men more his type. The guy spat an elongated glob of tobacco juice as he said this, and John concluded that once again, he was better off returning home to Amy.

Eventually the community found him and welcomed him with down to earth Kansas hospitality. Still, most of the men he met were in couples. As grateful as he was for their reaching out to him, he was not ready to be part of a couple. He missed the sophistication of New York City, and, as much as he cared for Amy, he couldn't spend his evenings settled in playing house like they were characters in the sexless marriages of children's books. Playing house got old.

He was afraid that Amy didn't understand this. Both nights that he had come home early after disastrous attempts to meet other gay men she had welcomed him warmly. She poured his favorite wine and invited him to sit in the living room and share how his evening had gone. Did she think he preferred her company? That could become a problem.

To his surprise, Wichita, Kansans included some very good people, and offered opera, ballet, many theatres, an independent film festival, and dozens of outstanding restaurants serving food from around the world. Gradually he settled in to his new life and found himself beginning to laugh again. He credited Amy, his new Kansas friends and university colleagues, and the lively little boy Amy had started calling D.J. Sometimes he felt ashamed that he was recovering, but he guessed that Phillip's horrible, prolonged death left a vacuum inside him that could only be filled by new relationships.

For the most part, his relationship with Amy was comfortable and undemanding. They joked about their sexless "marriage" and tag-teamed child care. Some evenings they spent together playing with D.J. and being silly. One night he awoke at three a.m. with a revelation that felt very important. He was finding with them the home that he had lost so abruptly at thirteen. Most of the time that felt good, but was it enough?

Amy discussed with him what to tell D.J. about his father. Bless her, the woman insisted on the truth, whatever bits of it they knew. "You are named for your father who was a wonderful man who could do many things and who loved me very much. Then one day before you were born he went away and we don't know where or why. I hope you will meet him some day so that he will know you. Sometimes I feel sad that he's missing knowing you, watching you grow up, and being your dad. One good thing that came from Daddy leaving is that we got Uncle John, Daddy's brother, who loves you very much. What a lucky boy you are to have so much love."

It was their agreed upon script. They had a home, work to do that they each enjoyed, a darling little boy to raise and each other as best buddies. "Not bad for an arranged marriage," John joked. Amy, who had been reading Yates, quipped: "Things fall apart, but the center holds."

After John moved in, Amy shut the door to her memories of her husband, deciding that she had been noble and self-sacrificing long enough. It was time to move on with her life, the way John was moving on. She called the Goodwill to come get Duncan's clothes and erased his message on the answering machine, replacing it with her own cheery greeting. She and John lived in tandem, sharing expenses and house work and alternating who cooked supper. They were good friends. Sometimes she wished that John was not gay.

Cullen and Portsoy, Scotland: September 2001

Duncan nestled into his new life with Ineke and Elleke the way one comes in from the cold to a bowl of warm soup, a fire in the fireplace, and fresh baked bread. His enjoyment was sensual, eager, and without much reflection. Amy no longer intruded on his thoughts. He guessed he'd forgiven her. Ineke and Elleke were his New World, where he could let go of the pain of betrayal, let go of depression, and soak up the love and laughter of his resurrected life. Ineke told him he was a blessing in their lives, which helped him to live her vision of himself and let go of the Duncan who had wallowed in grief and despair.

He saw things now, noticed things like the Scottish sky with its beefy clouds muscling their way from horizon to horizon and the wall to wall carpet of colorful fields atop the cliffs. His eyes took in the crisp profiles of rooftops angling this way and that and the solid rectangles of stone warehouses beside the harbor, reminders of an earlier, prosperous time.

He noticed the human landscape, too, and wondered about them. The wiry elderly woman in a practical woolen jacket and skirt who pulled her grocery cart to the Coop and home again, avoiding eye contact or any sort of interaction, as though she had been alone so long she had lost the capacity for speech. He recognized in her his old self. One day when she was coming out of the Coop as he was going in, he smiled at her and said hello. The smile she returned was full of gratitude, and he wanted to reassure her that he understood her loneliness. But he decided that might alarm her and walked on into the store.

Everyday he watched an old red-faced man, hunched and hobbling, make his painful way along Seafields Street, taking his daily constitutional, as though this defiant act of sheer will would hold back the dark. Was he grateful for another day above ground?

Those wholesome looking young girls with scrubbed faces and tied back hair who waited on shoppers—did they dream of lives with other options? He enjoyed being teased by the shop girls with purple and pink hair and silver rings in their noses, lips, and eyebrows. They joked that he was the only person in Northeast Scotland who *chose* to come here rather than to *leave*.

Once he started noticing, he began to engage the old men in basic conversation, brief but enough to let them know that he recognized them. He smiled at the timid, silent old ladies and joked with the girls with the outrageous hair and metal-enhanced faces. He wondered where the young men were. Often now he returned to the cottage the end of his work day smiling.

There was a natural flow to life here on the North Sea coast, gentle and predictable. Not much drama, just folks taking care of themselves and each other, doing the best that they can, and paying attention to the life around them. It seemed he was becoming one of them.

Occasionally floating fragments of his other life visited him while he slept in the bed he shared with Ineke, jerking him awake. He rarely talked about these times. He would rise from bed stealthily so as not to awaken her and prowl the house until they moved on. Then he would slide carefully back into bed and sleep, banishing his fear that they lay in wait for him, at least for the moment.

Most nights lying next to Ineke, one hand touching some part of her, he felt gratitude wash over him and commended himself for fully occupying Now and this calm, good life. What most surprised him was living with an expectation of joy.

A little after 3 p.m. on September 11th Duncan returned to the Portsoy store from visiting a family in Keith who had an 1860 highboy they were interested in selling. He was still thinking about the piece as he entered the back of the store. He heard his cell phone ringing, and realized that he'd left it on his worktable. It was Ineke calling from the house. Her voice sounded shaky.

"I've been trying to reach you. A few minutes ago two planes flew into the World Trade Center's Twin Towers in Manhattan. Doesn't your brother work in Manhattan?"

"John." His stomach contorted.

"Can you close the shop and come home now? They're reporting nothing else on BBC News. We could get on the internet and try to find him." Her voice changed. "It's very scary, Duncan. Please come home."

"I'm coming now."

He turned out the lights, locked up the shop, and drove the short distance to their house in Cullen. He heard Ineke crying when he entered the house. She came to him and they held each other while the screen filled with scenes from Hell. Chunks of concrete and glass fell from the sky. Thick gray smoke billowed from the crumpled one-hundred-and-ten storey Twin Towers. Some people held each other weeping. Others darted about looking for safety, running this way and that like rats in a maze, their open mouths dark ovals that speckled the streets like madly proliferating copies of Edvard Munch's painting, The Scream. On the scene the BBC reported that thousands of people were fleeing the city on foot through the thick dust and debris that clogged the air.

They discussed how to talk to Elleke about this, but when she arrived home from school, her face distorted with worry, they learned that the school principal had already told the students about the disastrous events across the Atlantic.

They sat together on the sofa, mesmerized by the explosions and destruction filling their television screen like a monstrous video game with never before seen special effects. But this was real. They listened as the reporters described the attack at the Pentagon in Washington, D.C., and the downing of a plane in Pennsylvania. They didn't talk. There were no words.

The phone rang. Mary Bennie was collecting donations for the Red Cross to help the American victims, could they contribute? Of course, they would.

Duncan went to his computer in their bedroom and keyed in "Borough of Manhattan Community College." That was where John worked. The college's website was down. He pulled up a map of New York City, enlarged it, and located the College--not far from the Twin Towers. It had been seven years since he'd had any contact with his brother, but in the crisis of the moment, that didn't matter. It was essential that he find John. He sat at his computer obsessively trolling the internet for the latest news.

That evening's dinner was solemn. While they were eating Mr. Cruickshank asked Duncan about his brother. The three of them stopped chewing, forks midway to their mouths, and waited for Duncan to speak.

He said they'd been estranged since before he came to Scotland, but that John was a professor at a college in Manhattan that had, according to his research online, been affected by the attack, one building destroyed beyond repair. He told them that John was his big brother, the only family he had since he was seven. Elleke got up from the table and went to stand behind Duncan, her arm around his neck. "We'll find him, Pappie," she said.

For the next several days he spent hours in front of his computer scanning the lists of the missing and the dead. He found no John Allan, but it would be weeks before everyone was accounted for. Ineke suggested he do a Google search for his brother and see what came up. To his surprise he found no John Allan on the faculty at the Borough of Manhattan Community College. There were so many pages of John Allans to go through but on September 14 he located an article on a John Allan joining the faculty at Wichita State University. The article said he'd come from Manhattan Community College. It had to be him.

Relief swept over Duncan closely followed by a wave of sadness. If John had moved to Wichita, then he probably was living with Amy. It puzzled him why John had waited years before making the move. But the evidence was there for all to see. His brother left the city he loved and a job he enjoyed to move to Wichita to be with Amy and their child.

He exited the internet and turned off the computer. He told Ineke and Elleke and Mr. Cruickshank that John no longer lived in New York, so he was safe. He never again mentioned his brother John.

The Borders, southern Scotland: Christmas 2001

The first Christmas in their new configuration, they took Granddad to
Andrew's home in the Borders, the area where Scotland and England meet
and mingle. The sons and their families gathered there for the holiday.
Neighbors of Andrew who were spending Christmas in London with their
family invited Duncan, Ineke, and Elleke to stay in their house for the several
days they'd be in the area.

Duncan felt anxious about their time with Mr. Cruickshank's sons. Most
of the time he pretended that Mr. Cruickshank belonged to his and Ineke's
family, but with the sons around sharing stories of a life together that Duncan
didn't share, he felt himself an outsider, even a phony. His feelings made him
back off from interaction. He remained on the fringe of conversation, often
retreating with a book or finding a chair in the most remote area of the room
from which to watch the others. The absence of family from his life growing up returned to haunt him. It was hard sometimes to stay focused on his
present happiness when his past deficits yanked at him like he was on a leash,
demanding attention.

At Andrew's house he roamed the rooms looking for photographs of the
Cruickshanks in earlier times and found them, lots of them, adorning book-
cases and table tops. George and Molly and their boys at various stages in
their lives, Molly touching whomever she was near, George more reserved but
with a prideful look about him as he surveyed his clowning sons and clapped

a hand on his wife's waist. There was a picture taken by the seaside, the boys pointing at the seals basking on the rocks behind them. Another of them apple picking. Several of the family cavorting in the snow and several featuring birthday cakes loaded with candles.

Jack happened on Duncan peering intently at the photos and asked if he'd like to look at the album "Ma" kept. Duncan sat for the next hour entering the lives of this family through Molly's photographic record that she had carefully labeled in white ink on the black album paper. Some of the pictures were discolored. Those from the 1950s looked overexposed as though the new color film was still working out how to do this. He looked at photo after photo, noticing the details, where they were taken, the expressions on the faces, who was touching whom. He was trying to imagine the life of this family, the life that had slipped away from him the night of his parents' deaths.

As he turned the page, one photo jumped out at him, straining to escape the triangular black corners holding it in place. The mother squatted beside a small boy, his face turned away from the camera. He looked to be about seven years old. The woman—Molly--so full of life with her red hair and red sweater. The camera caught her looking intently at the child, face radiant and smiling. The memory triggered by the photo, by the red sweater and the beautiful, caring mother, felled him. He set the album on the end table, collected his down jacket, boots, and woolen cap, and exited the house by the kitchen door, avoiding the laughter that spilled from the front room.

He set off down the road heading away from town along the winding roads, paying no attention to where he was or where he was going. He pushed himself against the virulent wind that bore the first contingent of ice crystals, harbinger of the storm to come. They stung his cheeks and bounced off the shiny surface of his parka.

Mr. Cruickshank on his way to the toilet noticed the photo album open on the table to the spectacular picture of Molly and one of the boys, hard to tell which one. He smiled, glad to see her there in all her glory. Heading back to the front room he wondered which one of them had been looking at the album. A while later he noticed Duncan was missing from the family group and fretted privately about what had become of the young man he'd come to think of as his fifth child.

Duncan walked the dun colored hills until the early dark of late December hovered in the clouded sky. Then he turned around and started back, relying on instinct as he navigated his way toward Gallashiels, squinting to make out a cluster of houses ahead that he thought looked familiar, hunching his shoulders and leaning forward as he walked to conserve his body heat in the freezing half-light.

The ice had changed to snow that began to coat the roadway and pile up on the stone fences separating each house from its neighbors. Lights went on in the houses and their welcoming glow nearly broke his heart. All along the street grey stone houses with their stone framed gardens lit up revealing the people who belonged there engaged in the ordinary activities of family life at the end of the day. Here a young woman stood in her kitchen window looking down, her right hand moving up and down. Was she making preparations for supper? She turned her head to say something to someone to her left not visible through the window frame.

In another house children sat before a television watching cartoons. The boy jumped up and launched a pillow at the girl who threw it back at him before returning to the TV.

Another window silhouetted a man in an overcoat as he strode across the room, removing his coat and galoshes, his profiled mouth opening and closing. Who was he speaking to?

The vignettes visible through the lighted windows evoked in him thick and palpable nostalgia for his little family of Ineke and Elleke and Granddad Cruickshank.

He picked up his pace, wanting to get back to them, but the snow obliterated all clues to which way he should walk. He was thoroughly lost. It panicked him.

A young man wearing an oversized knitted muffler, its color indistinguishable in the nearly dark street, nodded and passed by him walking a small terrier.

"Sorry, but do you know which is the way to Andrew Cruickshank's home?" Duncan asked him. The man stopped, smiled, and gestured to the right.

"Walk fifty meters that way at the next intersection. It's the house with burgundy trim and a black Land Rover in the drive. I bowl with Andrew, so you asked the right person!" He grinned and turned back to his task. The terrier, using the stop to relieve himself, aimed a long stream of steaming water at the streetlight, making a yellow hole in the fresh snow.

Duncan walked faster, relief and excitement replacing nostalgia as he hurried along to the house that held the people he loved most in the world.

He knocked at the kitchen door, ruddy cheeked, his breath a small cloud around his face, like a comic strip character's word-balloon.

"Pappie! You're home!" Elleke ran to him and stood waiting to hug him until he'd stomped off the burden of snow piled on his head and shoulders. He had come in from the cold. He, like the people in the windows, belonged to someone.

That night he dreamed of Amy. He hadn't thought of her in some time but now he saw her with several small children baking Christmas cookies and decorating a tree. He tried to reach her but just when he got close enough for her to hear him, she and the children moved to another room, then another, and another. He pursued her but could not catch up with her. The dream disturbed him. Could he and Amy have had a family like Cruickshanks if he hadn't left? They'd been the center of each other's lives, but now there was only a chasm empty and deep. If she had a family, it wasn't with him. He awoke yearning to expand the Now family he had made with Ineke and Elleke.

Elleke liked being with Granddad's other grandchildren. Their third night there she announced that she planned to have a big family, at least four kids, she liked big families. They couldn't miss the look she threw their way. It was no secret that she wanted a sibling and did not approve of their not producing one.

That night after she was asleep they talked about Elleke's desire to have a brother or sister. Ineke was reluctant to add another person to their household. Her work was important to her and with Elleke nearly nine, it had been a long time since she had had to cope with diapers and the demands of babies. Duncan felt conflicted. He loved their little family, but he liked imagining adding another child, a child blending his and Ineke's genes.

"I can be the primary caretaker for a baby," he suggested.

Ineke snorted, finding this idea ridiculous. "How will you manage three stores and keep Granddad occupied alongside caring for an infant? You're being totally unrealistic."

It was the closest they had come to a fight and both backed away from any further discussion of reproducing, though Duncan still hoped it would happen. He wasn't sure why, but it felt important to him to have a child. He even contemplated sabotaging their birth control, a properly inserted needle in a condom, perhaps?

At the end of the Holidays they returned to their Cullen home. Duncan added solar panels to the house, and he and Ineke developed the back garden into a colorful sanctuary with bird baths in view of Mr. Cruickshank's window so he could watch the age old contest between fluttering birds and stalking cats. They got a dog, a black medium sized mixed breed stray who had begun hanging around. Elleke named him Needja, a transliteration of Need You. She figured that was what the dog was communicating as he hung out around their home.

Cullen & Portsoy, Scotland: 2002

The next time they took Granddad to visit the rest of his family, the long drive seemed to wear him out. When they stopped for lunch in Inverness, he didn't come out of the toilet for a long time. When Duncan went to check on him he was sitting on the floor beside the urinal breathing heavily. Duncan was furious that no one had alerted them to a problem. He had seen men enter and leave the toilet. Surely one of them would have noticed the old man. He was furious with himself, too, for not going with him, making sure he was safe.

Mr. Cruickshank blacked out again when they went for a walk on the coastal trail. Fortunately he was between Ineke and Duncan who caught him as he collapsed and got him to a bench and then back home to his pills and bed. Clearly his health was worsening. They could all see it. He asked Duncan to take him to the cemetery in Portsoy "to see my Molly." Equipped with a walker and with Ineke holding one arm and Duncan the other, they slowly made their way to the Cruickshank plot, where they helped him sit on the walker's seat and left him alone to visit his Molly. Standing several yards away, Duncan noticed Mr. Cruickshank's lips were moving and his face more lively than it had been in some time.

After Elleke's tenth birthday, he grew too weak to go outside and spent his days sitting looking out the front window at the sea or out his bedroom window at the birds. Sometimes he sat at the dining table looking through his magnifying glass at one of the clocks Duncan brought home for him to work on. Like Elleke, he enjoyed the Harry Potter books that everyone was reading. She would sit next to him on the sofa reading them aloud for hours. She could tell he really enjoyed that time. They had made it through four of the books, but as they began book five, Elleke noticed that Granddad could no longer pay attention for more than a few pages before dozing off.

His deteriorating health made them all sad and apprehensive.

One night at supper Granddad told them that he was "ready to go" and that his four years as part of their family were a very special blessing in his life. Elleke cried when he said that. She did not want him to go away. It was very unclear to her where he was going and why he had to go at all.

In the weeks that followed he grew progressively weaker. One evening Duncan heard his voice, unusually husky, calling Duncan into his room. There was an urgency in his tone.

"Laddie, I be wantin' to talk with ye," he said. Duncan pulled the side chair close to the bed, sat beside him, and waited. It distressed him to see the decline in his friend. Recently Granddad had been unable to come to the table for supper, and they had to borrow a wheelchair from National Health to get him to the bathroom. Their days of walking the braes together were over and that made Duncan very sad.

"I think ye knowt what's happening with me, but from your scarceness, me guess is you dinnae want to face it. There be things I need to say to you, lad, now, whilst there's time." His Scottish accent had grown more obvious of late.

Duncan couldn't look at Mr. Cruickshank. He sat slumped forward, elbows on his knees, eyes studying the pattern in the carpet. The old man continued.

"When my Molly took sick, I dinnae ken what I'd do without her. I need you to know what I never have told anyone. When she left, I walked the braes and wept and wept. One day I walked to the edge of a cliff and screamed at God, so angry I was. I considered lettin' meself fall on the rocks below or walking into the sea till it covered me. But I cud nae do it. Maybe I was a coward. I dunno know."

Duncan had lifted his head and was staring at Mr. Cruickshank. They'd never talked about their private sorrows. He was stunned that this wise, stable man had ever known such despair. The thumb and forefinger of Duncan's right hand fondled a 50 p coin, rubbing back and forth across its solid surface the way the new man he'd hired worked his worry beads. Except for that soft rubbing sound it was very still in the room.

"Eventually, I went home, drove to me shop, and went back to work. I managed to get through my days--most days--without ending up in a puddle on the floor wailing for my woman. But I was sore miserable. Then you entered the shop in Portsoy. A wraith you were, lookin' like you'd been underwater too long, barely functioning. Something told me to give you a chance. And to my surprise, you gave *me* a chance at a new life." His eyes glistened and he reached for Duncan's hand. "I'm right grateful for ye, Laddie, right grateful."

Tears crept past the barriers Duncan had erected, sliding out of control down the slopes of his cheeks. "I don't want you to go," he said.

"You'll be all right, son. I'm sairtin."

The following morning Mr. Cruickshank's breathing was labored and the color had bleached from his face. His hands on the blanket were brown and pink spotted and cold to the touch. Duncan called Andrew and urged him to gather his brothers and come. Then he drove to school to fetch Elleke so the three of them could be with him as he left this life.

Ineke and Elleke sang the Scottish songs he had taught them. They talked about the good times they had shared as a family and the joy he had brought them. Elleke left the room and returned carrying Molly's porcelain figure of the girl lying on the grass smiling at the sky. "There she is, Granddad, and she's so happy."

He opened his eyes enough to take in the child laying her head on his shoulder, red curls shining in the lamplight, and the other red haired child, caught forever in this moment of delight. His lips curled slightly and they heard him sigh. Ineke said it was a sigh of contentment.

The brothers arrived about midnight. They gathered around his bed, Andrew on the side chair Duncan had occupied, Jack sitting on the bed, holding his father's hand, and the other two on the ladder back kitchen chairs Ineke and Duncan carried in for them. After Elleke kissed Granddad goodnight, Ineke and Duncan guided her out of the room. "Now his other family needs him," her mom told her. "Why don't you sleep with us tonight?"

In the early morning, while the sun was still hiding, Andrew knocked on their door. "He's gone," he said.

Later, looking back on his last conversation with the old man, Duncan realized he'd not told him that hiring him had saved *Duncan's* life. When he told Ineke how regretful he was, she assured him that George Cruickshank already knew.

That morning when the three of them entered his room to pay their final respects, Elleke knew at once that her Granddad was no longer there. His body lay on the bed, but his face, whose moving wrinkles and shifting expressions she had loved to read, was vacant, and he didn't look like himself. Once while he was still speaking, he had whispered to her that he wanted to be with 'Molly. It was their secret. Now when she asked her mom where Granddad had gone, Mom told her that she didn't really know, but she suspected he was with his Molly and happy. So Elleke, too, was happy in a way. Mom and Pappie Duncan were sad. She could not remember seeing them cry before.

All the Cruickshanks came to Cullen, staying in Granddad's house which had been closed up for the past four years while he'd been living with them. The funeral was at the Church of Scotland in Portsoy, twenty minutes from Cullen. Granddad would be buried in the same plot as his Molly in the cemetery in Portsoy that sloped downhill to the sea.

The day was cold and rainy, but the clouds parted and the rain stopped briefly during the service. The church was full, people from across the Northeast coming to pay their respects to one of their own who the rector called "a man of principle and integrity."

After they sang a hymn, the rector invited people in the congregation to speak, starting with the family. The sons went first, telling stories of their growing up, stories that George Crickshank's second family—Elleke, Ineke, and Duncan--had not heard before.

An elderly man rose painfully and limped to the front of the church leaning heavily on his cane. He looked out at the group assembled. As he began to speak, his voice was raspy and everyone leaned forward to hear him.

"George and I were friends from primary school, really more rivals than friends. The day I saw him leaving the Wee Cottage in Portsoy with the fair

Molly, both o them aglow and laughin', I figured I'd lost that contest." Most people smiled at this and Ineke squeezed Duncan's hand, though there were some shocked gasps from the Brethren sitting together in the rear half of the church.

"Over the years there were other contests--who could put away the most ale and whiskey in our twenties, who produced the most sons in our thirties—ye can see he won on that one!" He grinned at the four Cruickshank sons and a wave of chuckles moved through the congregation, overpowering the disapproving looks of the Brethren.

"Then George decided to cut back his ale consumption and did, which I figured made him a better man than I. Lately our competition was over who'd live the longest. George, me friend, I beat ye on that one but it's a right rough win fer me." His voice wobbled but recovered. "Ye bin me good friend fer eighty years and I miss ye mightily. Save a place fer me. I promise not to pinch yer bonnie lassie."

While he'd been speaking the old man looked surprisingly hearty, even animated, exercising his comedic skills that had not gone rusty from lack of use, but as he finished and started shuffling back to his pew, the vigor and energy fell from him, his shoulders curled inward and his skin seemed to shrink away from the ridges of his cheeks and chin. He looked frail and feeble.

His humorous tribute seemed to touch many in the church. Now as one they held their collective breaths watching him maneuver the steps down from the chancel and hobble slowly up the aisle. When he safely took his seat, the congregation exhaled collectively. You could hear the aaaaaaaah.

Then, to Ineke and Duncan's surprise, Elleke stood and walked to the front. Her face was wet but she was smiling.

"My Granddad George taught me many things. He taught me how to tell the age of a clock and the names of the wild flowers that grow along the braes and how to make up funny stories. Best of all, he taught me how important it is to be curious about things and people. Granddad, I know you were ready to move on, but that hole in your heart you said you had since your Molly passed, well Mom and Pappie and me, we bear that hole now without you." She unfolded a piece of lined paper she'd been gripping while she spoke and scanned it, then refolded it, explaining to the congregation, "Just have to be sure I didn't leave anything out." She flashed a quick smile. "I didn't." With that she moved back to her pew. Pappie Duncan shifted his knees to the side so she could get past to sit between them. "I'm proud of you!" he whispered.

The service closed with the congregation rising to sing together in four-part harmony the old hymn, *Abide with Me*. By its end, the four sons, Duncan, and three teenaged grandsons had moved to the casket, four on each side. They lifted it gently and carried it from the church to the hearse, which drove slowly down Seafields to Church Street and Rose Lane and pulled up at the cemetery. There the men of the family lifted the casket and bore it through the wrought iron gates to the Cruickshank plot.

A lone bagpiper preceded the casket piping the hymn and the congregation, following behind the casket, hummed and sang along.

It was a chilly day and a slow rain resumed falling when they were almost to the plot. It wet the faces of the mourners and swelled the grass that carpeted the steeply sloping ground. Grave stones large and small lay in rows facing the harbor. Walking across the grass to the Cruickshank plot, forty pairs of feet moved in tandem, a forward step that sank slightly into the waterlogged ground, another forward step that necessitated pulling the back foot up from the boggy grass. Each step made a sucking sound, muffled and melancholy, a dreary percussive rhythm to accompany the heart-piercing sound of the bagpipe.

The ground over Molly's grave had been opened by the town councilmen and, after the clergyman read a passage from Corinthians about the lasting power of love and another from Ecclesiastes about everything having its season, a time to live and a time to die, they lowered the casket carrying the remains of George Cruickshank into the ground to rest atop of the casket of his dearly loved wife. The rector gave a benediction, and the mourners greeted each other, hastily, on account of the rain, which had picked up its pace. The service was over.

The brothers and their families had invited folks back to the assembly hall in the basement of the church for refreshments. After that Ineke, Duncan, and Elleke returned home.

Wichita, Kansas: 2005

The phone rang in the house in Eastborough. D.J., passing through en route to his room, picked it up in the living room on the third ring, expecting a call from his best friend about meeting to play video games. It wasn't his friend. Some woman was calling for his mom. She asked him in a voice that made clear that she knew nothing about children if he would please take a message for his "mommy" and asked if he was sure he got everything right. The woman even spelled out "dinner"! When Amy got home from work, D.J. told her about the dumb lady who had called, ranting to his mother about the way adults treat children, "as though we have no brains, no memory, like I wouldn't give you her stupid message!" Then he stomped off down the hall to his room.

"I get it, D.J., but what did she want?" Amy called after him, having a hard time suppressing her laughter at his forgetting to give her the message, just as the woman had feared he would.

He walked back into the living room. "She wanted you to come to dinner to meet some 'friend' of hers, some guy. She went on and on about him and how 'special' he is." He mimed a parody of specialness and walked back to his room.

Amy sank into the plush purple sofa and shook off her shoes. Another matchmaking "friend." Again. She reached for the scrap of notebook paper on which D.J. had printed the woman's name and number. Would her "friends" never get it? However unconventional the way I live, my life serves me well. I live with my best friend, a gay man, in the largest city in Kansas where, despite the oppressive conservatism, progressives do thrive. I avoid straight men like the plague. I've been clear about that to her and all of my acquaintances who invite me to come to dinner to "meet the loveliest man." I reply to all such invitations briefly, logically and intransigently, "With D.J. and John, why would I want any other man? Not interested."

Most of them stop inviting me. But not this woman. She is the self-appointed matchmaker of Eastborough and butts into other people's business like a zealot on speed. The woman needs to get a job!

Annoyed that she would have to call the woman back to say she could not make it, Amy sat on the sofa and stewed. Her eyes scanned the living room. It was one of her refuge spaces in this house, but something had changed. The landscape painting that had hung over the mantle ever since she and Duncan had moved in was gone, replaced by an gigantic abstract, thick brush strokes of primary colors smashing this way and that with an incongruous bright white rectangle on the lower right. God-awful! The painting clashed horribly with her beloved purple sofa and her leaf green armchair. She reached for the arm of the sofa to help herself up and winced as the head of a needle punctured her palm. Someone had stuck a needle into her sofa to secure several 3" x 3" squares of fabric, each of them a primary color. Who was invading her space? What the hell were they doing to her beloved room?

It must be Cliff!

Cliff had joined their family that fall. He'd moved to Wichita from San Francisco to buy and run a club in Old Town, which was where he and John had met. Apparently it was love at first sight.

Before long John brought Cliff home, where he stayed, moving in with his classy, camp furnishings. It seemed that every day he had replaced something else of hers. The bedroom he shared with John went from soft blue to glistening black with a white fur bedcover and mirrors covering one wall. Amy had tolerated that change. It was, after all, their room. But as Cliff's Nouveau Gay high fashion furniture expanded like a bad dream into the adjacent rooms— chartreuse family room, fuscia bathroom—she felt increasingly uncomfortable and irritated. It wasn't that she was uncompromisingly committed to her conventional décor. It was that he didn't consult her. His changes were *fait acomplis*. She tried to sit on her feelings, telling herself that the most important thing was that John loved Cliff and she wanted him to be happy.

Now she peered around her occupied living room, discovering that he had removed numerous items of sentimental value to her. Her anger swelled. Her fingers itched and her toes stung as she noticed that where her wedding photos had been, modern metal frames without pictures leered like a family of empty-faced robots. "What's going on? Does this man have no respect for boundaries?" She said it out loud and D.J. opened his door to ask if she was all right.

At first their new configuration had worked fairly well. Cliff worked late at the club and slept in, whereas Amy and D.J. were in bed by nine and up at six. They saw Cliff only on weekends. However, John seemed distracted and they saw less of him. D.J. complained about that. Within three months Amy was burning out. Not only had her space had been taken over, but her primary adult relationship was on life support. She had to admit it, she was jealous of Cliff. And she suspected he did not approve of her way of raising her son. They never discussed it and Cliff kept his mouth shut when she was around, but he couldn't totally suppress his conviction that she was smothering and overly indulgent with the boy. She'd overheard him say as much to John. It was a source of tension between the two men as a couple.

She stood and walked to the mantle. Cliff's painting was heavy, but she got it down and carried it to the hall closet, forcing it back behind the winter coats, where it was barely visible. She unpinned the fabric swatches from the sofa and put them in a metal baking pan that she took to the patio where she poured on lighter fluid and set them on fire. That felt good, though for a moment she had second thoughts. Cliff would be furious with her. Still, he's living in my house, she told herself. Bye-bye upholstery fabric.

When John walked in the door that evening, she asked him if they could talk. They sat on her purple sofa facing the glaringly empty wall over the mantle. A dust line marked the space where her painting had hung. In her mind that lighter rectangle marking the missing painting seemed to blink like a neon sign, enraging her. She knew that if she attacked Cliff, she would force John to choose between them. A man in love would see only one choice, and clearly John was a man in love. Attacking Cliff was not a good option. She knew, too, that her anger could drive John away. She sat on the sofa like she was afraid of falling off, tight, tense, and brittle.

John asked where the missing painting was, referring, she assumed, to Cliff's monstrosity. She asked where her missing painting was, trying hard not to let her voice sound steely and working at it so fiercely that her vocal cords tightened and her pitch rose suspiciously. John calmly moved to a new subject--Cliff's concerns. Amy could tell he, too, was being very careful, as he wrapped his remarks in overall praise for how she was coping with all the change that came with adding a new person into their household. She saw through his Ode to Amy and called him on it.

She stood and walked to the kitchen island where she stored wine in a cabinet below the counter. John was saying that he felt triangled, torn between his allegiance to his sister-in-law who, he stressed, was doing the best she could in a difficult situation, and his desire to keep his partner happy. She asked, "Merlot or Riesling?" And when he said "Either," she pulled out the Riesling, her favorite. She deliberately took two water glasses from the cupboard and carried them and the wine to the low table that squatted in front of the sofa. Then she poured an inordinate amount of wine into each glass and passed one to John. She didn't give a damn that when he served wine he would never use a water glass, always choosing the proper wine glass, one size for red, another for white.

"John, you are my best friend, even my only friend. I want you to be happy. But this is my home and altering my color scheme, changing out my furniture is something I deserve to be consulted about, not surprised by a done deal."

He avoided looking at her. She knew he hated conflict, but, damn it, the conflict had not been introduced by her.

D.J. came out of his room and into the living room. "What happened to the painting, Mom?" he asked. Then, with no transition, "When is supper?"

"Uncle John and I have to talk just now, honey. There's a pizza in the freezer if you can't wait for an hour."

She wasn't facing him but she could imagine the look on his face. Adults suck, he would be thinking. She heard the opening of the freezer and a rustling as the ice crystals on the items she had packed into that space slid against each other. The microwave ticked through two minutes, and its bell announced his pizza was hot. She heard him open the microwave and then close it, open a drawer and close it, open the cupboard and close it. Then she heard the slap-slap of his feet heading down the hall. She welcomed his interruption. Time to let herself cool down.

She glanced at John, who looked pale and was fidgeting with the cuff of his shirt. He finally spoke.

"I've been talking with Cliff about all of us finding a duplex where we could each have a side to ourselves. I think that would provide us both togetherness and the privacy we each need. Would you be willing to look at some duplexes with us, Amy?" It was a compromise proposal. She could not imagine any of them being excited about such an arrangement.

It irritated her that John had not responded to her question about where her painting was, but she decided not to push it. It irritated her that his eyes avoided hers. She cautioned John that there were few if any duplexes in Wichita comparable in size or perks to this large home. "But I'll see if I can locate some," she said doubtfully. They sipped their wine, neither of them saying anything.

When John stood saying he was ready for bed, she wanted to scream at him, "Don't you know how much I count on you? Don't you know I couldn't stand it if you leave?" Instead, she wished him a good sleep and retired to her bedroom.

She didn't sleep most of the night. How would she cope with another forced dismantling of her life? She went online and through Zillow located two possible duplexes, one in Midtown, one in Riverside and a third, very unlikely, in Plainview.

On Saturday morning the three of them set out to look at the options, each of them irritable and unusually quiet. None of the places were sizeable. All were fixer-uppers with considerable work to be done to bring them up to code, much less to Amy's and Cliff's standards.

Looking at the duplexes, she found herself feeling more and more annoyed. She did not want to leave the house she and Duncan had designed in the early years of their marriage, the house she redesigned after the fire, the house to which she had brought her new baby ten years ago, the house that had harbored them in the stormy years after Duncan vanished, the house John had moved into, where the three of them had made family together. Grimly she completed the litany...The house that Cliff moved into and "destroyed." That was too harsh and not technically accurate. "Altered negatively" was better.

That evening back at the house she asked for time for the adults to talk and dispatched D.J. to the family room to watch a movie. They sat at the dining room table, sipping wine, Cliff and John waiting in awkward silence for her to begin. She was calm and logical at first.

She said that this was her home and had been since she had married John's brother fifteen years ago. She loved this house. She appreciated very much the role John played in her and D.J.'s lives. She thought she had been very generous welcoming Cliff to live with them. She had told them both that she was glad that John had found a new love. She'd tried to be supportive, but, "Damn it, this isn't fair." Her words were getting away from her, like an accelerating train moving wildly—inevitably--toward a crash. She tried to decelerate. Her voice tensed and changed key.

"Cliff, I know you and John need more privacy so you can lead your own lives. And I sense you are not happy living here. I've come into the family room when you were saying something to John that you didn't want me to hear. I'm not dumb, I see where this is heading and I need you to know that... *I'm not moving from this house that I love.*" Her declaration flew from her mouth loud and defiant.

"Shit!" John mumbled.

Cliff, feeling attacked, jumped in to defend himself. "You're a very nice lady, Amy, but I doubt you'd tolerate what I have put up with here—my husband always trying to please and take care of you and D.J., D.J. raised like a free range chicken, allowed to enter any room, get into any drawer, say what he likes, eat anything anywhere in the house. Do you realize how often that kid has devoured the ingredients I had bought for one of my special dinners? Do you realize he has gone into our bedroom, rifled through our drawers, torn open condoms and sassed me when I caught him at it? This is no life for a couple to share. I cannot do this any longer." He turned to John. "And I won't move into a duplex with Amy and D.J. a wall away!"

"At least there is one thing we agree on," Amy said, her jaw clenched. She could not stand this pompous man and his criticism. He had no inkling of what raising children and working full time and managing a household required. Why did he have to come along and complicate—no, *ruin*—their life together?

As angry as she was, when she turned to John, sitting with his head in his hands, she felt sorry for him. But regretting John's pain didn't stop either Amy or Cliff from letting loose powerful words in the living room that was contested territory. Again she spoke.

"Cliff, do you even care that John and D.J. are like father and son?" She wanted to ask if he really cared about John, but held back, knowing that would be over the top. All she could see was her losses already in a pile so high it terrified her. She felt a premonition that devastating loss was about to hit her life like a tidal wave...again.

John declared his need to take a break and suggested he and Cliff go for a walk. They would talk again Sunday evening. Their leaving the room was a relief for each of them.

Only John and Amy met Sunday evening. D.J. was at a friend's house. Sadly and with some regret, John told her that he and Cliff would find another place to live. He would still remain an active part of D.J.'s and her lives, but he could no longer live under the same roof if he wanted to sustain his relationship with the man he loved.

Amy nodded her agreement with his decision, hugged him, and said little. She heard the front door close as he left the house. Then she fell apart.

Over the next several months her grief at John's departure from their daily lives exceeded her grief at Duncan's leaving, though she didn't know why. She had successfully restructured her life to make a nurturing environment for her son. She'd rolled the boulder up the hill, as Camus would say, only to have it escape her and roll with accelerating speed back to the bottom. Did she have the energy to try again to haul their lives back to the top? She considered seeking out Pastor Wendy, but when she stopped at the church, the marquee announced a welcome reception for the new pastor, a man.

Though not a conventional couple relationship, being devoid of sex, her friendship with John had felt like a marriage of a sort, the kind old people happen into that is grounded in companionship and comfort. Her low grade depression returned and she called in sick to her office so she could avoid seeing people.

D.J. appeared oblivious to the dislocation of their household caused by Cliff and Uncle John moving out. He continued his life playing soccer, accompanying her to the store and the library, and spending time playing video games alone or with his friends. The major change was that he and Amy went out for dinner more frequently now that Uncle John and Cliff were no longer sharing the cooking.

On the third Saturday morning after Uncle John and Cliff moved out, D.J. was in the kitchen making pancakes, a tradition Mom had revived after John's departure. As he stirred the eggs and milk into the flour, salt, and baking soda, he was thinking about the last three weeks. He remembered the day when Cliff caught him in Cliff and John's newly black and white bedroom. Cliff had screamed at him for being in there and called him a spoiled, snotty little kid. Well, he didn't like Cliff, either, and there were lots of nasty words he could think of to describe him. He was *glad* he was gone. But he missed Uncle John. Even though Uncle John dropped by the house each Sunday evening, things had changed between him and Mom.

Uncle John took him out for ice cream last week so they could see each other without Mom overhearing their conversation. Baskin and Robbins was crowded so they took their cones to the park and sat on the beat up push merry-go-round that the little kids were avoiding. The sun was warm and the ice cream began melting so they postponed talking while they licked. Near them a woman who had been running with her two golden labs poured water into a large bowl for her dogs. The dogs began licking in sync, their tongues going in and out like Uncle John's and D.J.'s, which struck D.J. as hilarious. Unfortunately, lately when he had recounted something like this to Mom, she didn't laugh. He was learning to keep his observations to himself.

After they finished their cones Uncle John asked how school was going and worked his way around to asking how Mom was doing. When D.J. said she was in a bad mood most of the time, Uncle John was quiet. "Your mom needs to get out and meet people," Uncle John said. "I think she's lonely."

There hadn't been much more to their conversation, other than Uncle John apologizing for Cliff. But D.J. felt scared thinking about Mom being lonely. Was that his responsibility? Well, he was lonely, too. If he didn't know how to solve that for himself, how could he fix it for Mom?

Mom had been clingy with him since Uncle John left, and it made him uncomfortable. Being "the man of the family now" had its drawbacks. He'd noticed that boys his age were beginning to pull away from their mothers, to complain about them to their friends, but he had a feeling that she would not be able to take it if he pulled away. And, he loved her. He used to think she was the best mom in Wichita. Recently, not so much. He still allowed her to hug him and tuck him in at night, but he made her promise to limit Public Displays of Affection to when they were in their house without his friends around. She thought that was fair. Yes, he guessed she was a good enough mother to him.

It was just that he felt odd. No one he knew lived like he did, but then no one he knew *talked* about life with their single mom. Maybe there were a lot of kids like him keeping quiet.

He wondered if he could tell Uncle John that sometimes Mom irritated him. She would treat him like she and he were a special couple living together in a bubble apart from the rest of the world. That made him very nervous. Secretly he hoped she would find someone else to build her dream world with.

He had already decided that he wouldn't stay around Wichita when he grew up. It was too much pressure having to take care of her, even though he realized that at this point technically, it was her taking care of him. He sometimes felt he was on a space station where he couldn't escape Mission Control.

He'd been distracted and forgot to flip the first set pancakes, which were scorched on one side. "Something's burning," Mom sang out from the bathroom over the noise of her hairdryer. "Damn it," he said quietly. Mom would be upset if she heard him. He threw the pancakes in the trash and poured four more onto the griddle.

Then there was his homework. Mom was getting on his last nerve the way she pushed him on that. He wasn't a stellar student. He wasn't sure why. Living alone with Mom in the big house he had plenty of privacy, and she was readily available to help with homework, as she told him so many times that he had tuned her out. It just was hard to focus. Again, he didn't know why and tried not to think about it. He just did the things ten and eleven year old boys do, playing with friends, riding his bike, shooting hoops, playing video games, and trying to avoid the girls in his class who were "developed" and eager to get his attention.

One of the kids in his class had asked him to come over and spend the night. But the parents were not home, although they had told Mom they would be. The kid took him into his parents' bedroom and opened the bedside table drawer. There was a shiny revolver, not a toy, a real one. The kid took it out and asked if D.J. wanted to hold it. Reluctantly, D.J. had taken it in his hands.

"Heavy sucker!" He had said passing it back.

"Next time you come we'll take it out in the yard and try it out," his friend had said. D.J. felt both excited and scared thinking about that. He certainly was not going to tell Mom.

He flipped the pancakes when they bubbled and a minute later slid them onto two plates adding butter and syrup and finger sausages. Mom was coming out of the bathroom carrying a box. He was still preoccupied thinking about his friend's gun. After they began to eat and Mom praised him for a great breakfast, she opened the box to show him what she had bought at Cabelas.

"I figured with just us here in this big house we need some protection from burglars," she said, lifting a small pink pistol from the bubble wrap. "Of course, you know not to ever play with this, D.J. Guns are terribly dangerous. I'll just keep it next to my bed just in case of an emergency."

If Mom has a gun, what's wrong with me trying one, especially if it would keep us safe in an emergency, he wondered.

Cullen, Scotland: September 2005

Ineke sat at her worktable in front of the window, before her on the table her narrow nosed pliers, small pots of turquoise and coral sorted by size, and puddles of silver wire in varying thicknesses. She was working on a pendant for a necklace. She curled silver around half-inch pieces of turquoise, which she'd mounted on silver backs, and worked the silver so that it held the turquoise tightly in place. Then she laid out the pieces as she planned it to look when she'd finished, silver shoots growing out of thicker silver stalks that curled like new fronds of fern, the turquoise peeking through the silver. This was not her usual medium but she was making the necklace for her mom who was coming with Dad from Holland for Elleke's thirteenth birthday, and Mom loved silver and turquoise. Yes, this was quite nice. She connected the pieces, soldering them and wiring them to a band of silver that would encircle the neck. Her last task was to attach tiny spherical beads of coral diagonally in three parallel rows from the band through the pendant, the barest suggestion of rain.

She still marveled at the designs her fingers made of their own volition, nerve endings responding to images received from somewhere outside herself. Like radio frequencies. Or holograms from satellites. Was creativity just a developed sensitivity to invisible pulses that rode the air from some cell tower in space?

Her back hurt from sitting so long at attention, every muscle focused on the delicate work of her hands. She moved to the sink and filled the electric tea kettle. When it whistled a full boil, she poured it over fresh-ground coffee and let it steep before lowering the press to squeeze out flavor from the sodden grounds. She could nearly see George Cruickshank as he used to sit across from her in the chair by the window that opened to the back garden, watching the birds and waiting for their shared "tea" time.

Her mind drifted. She was worried about Elleke. She'd mentioned her concern to Duncan last night as they lay in bed, but the poor man was so exhausted that he was out like a light, while she nattered on about that boy. She heard him snoring contentedly in the dark and realized that he'd never heard a word she said!

She stood by the front window looking toward the harbor. Her eyes followed the rooflines of the houses, inverted Vs zigzagging down to the sea, their cylindrical chimneys silhouetted against the bright September sky. She liked the way the houses seemed to lean on each other. Halfway to the sea, the nineteenth century brick railway bridge ran parallel to the coast, bisecting the town, its graceful arches soaring like runners taking hurdles. She could make out walkers treading the path where trains had once run. She sighed, feeling sentimental. She loved this place and her life.

She saw Elleke walking along the road from the bus stop, swinging her book bag. Ineke heard the soft padded footfalls of Needja, the dog, coming to stand beside her to welcome her ginger haired daughter. She bent over and scratched behind his ears. "Good Needja!" she said. When she looked back at the street, she saw that Elleke had stopped and was in conversation with the boy who was visiting his grandparents two doors up the hill. He was considerably older than Elleke, starting university in Edinburgh at the end of the month. A handsome boy. Her mother radar switched on. It was working overtime these days with a thirteen-going-on-nineteen-year-old daughter.

Needja's ears stood up and his tail stopped swishing. That a boy, Needja, always on duty protecting them. She patted Needja's head, and he looked up at her gratefully and leaned against her thigh. When she looked back up the street, neither Elleke nor the boy was in sight. She opened the door and let Needja out. He raced to the house two doors up and she heard Elleke greet him.

"It's okay, Needja. Calm down. This is Byron, my new friend."

Ineke heard Needja barking. The house beside hers, being set perpendicular to the road, blocked her view of Elleke. She *could* see Needja who appeared to be racing around Elleke. She trusted his instincts. She stepped out of the house and called, "Elleke! I need you right now." It was not like her to interfere. Generally she trusted her daughter's good sense. But something in Needja's behavior alarmed her.

Elleke called that she was coming. Ineke saw her coming down the sidewalk toward their house.

"Mom, why are you doing this?" Elleke was scowling.

"I need to talk to you." Ineke held the front door open and her thirteen year old stomped into the house, dumping her book bags on the sofa and slumping down beside them, a sour expression shadowing her face.

"That boy is too old for you. You're not even thirteen. You cannot go out with…"

"I wasn't going out with him. He was showing me the new puppy his Gran got. Come on, Mom, I'm not going to get pregnant looking at his puppy."

Ineke felt chagrined. Was she over-reacting? Her daughter's argument was reasonable. Perhaps he wasn't a dangerous person. But her own vivid memory took charge now, flooding and paralyzing her. She tried another tack she remembered her mother using. "Pouting like that a bird will mistake your lower lip for a perch and peck at your nose."

Elleke's eyes flashed.

Ineke recalculated and tried again

"Elleke, when I was thirteen I resisted my Mom's warnings about older boys. And my mom was right." Ineke stopped speaking. Should she be more specific if Elleke was really only interested in seeing a new puppy?"

"I am not you. And I can take care of myself. You always tell me I make good decisions. Can I go to my room now?" Face frozen, Elleke stood and reached behind her for the strap of her backpack. "I have homework to do." She went to her room.

Ineke did not know what to do, so she nodded, walked back to her work space, and returned to her design. She heard Elleke's door shut and then the bass pulsing of her music drifting through the heavy oak and down the hallway. Like an instant replay, a memory from when she was thirteen swallowed her. She wanted to banish it but couldn't.

There had been a guy, three years older and very sophisticated, she thought at the time. Cool. He even smoked weed and offered her some when he walked her home from school. She remembered feeling drawn to the "grownup" experiences he invited her to try. Once he stopped her as she was walking home from her bus stop. He asked if she liked David Bowie and invited her to see his collection of Bowie's CDs. It had felt supremely rebellious and exciting, as well as scary, and she had said yes.

He'd taken her to his room and told her to sit on the bed while he fetched a special CD. She remembered sitting on his bed, trying to arrange the skirt of her school uniform so that it covered her legs. She remembered sniffing her underarms when he left the room and blowing her breath into her hands to see if it smelled bad. She remembered her heart beating too fast. She'd wanted him to kiss her, to carry her into a grand romance that would expand and occupy every space around her. She was also nervous, uncertain how to behave with this "older man."

She'd sat upright on the edge of his bed, waiting for him to return with the special CD, Bowie's *Station to Station*.

He entered the room and she wondered why he closed and locked the door behind him. He smiled at her as he approached the bed, but his smile looked different, tainted with an intensity that she had not seen before. It scared her. He pushed her back on his bed and loomed over her, his mouth descending on hers, his tongue pushing open her lips, ramming against her teeth. She didn't want *this*. This was not romantic. She struggled to turn her face away from him but his mouth bore down on hers. She tried to pull down the skirt of her school uniform, but he grabbed both of her hands and pinned them to the bed while his knee forced her legs apart and pushed fiercely against that part of her body no one but her touched. Horrified, she had tried to call for help but the weight of him, the pressure of his mouth against her mouth, his knee against her crotch, rendered her able only to make guttural noises of protests that she was certain no one could hear. She didn't know what he was doing. She only knew he meant to hurt her and that he would not be stopped.

She kicked her right knee against his leg and kept moving her face back and forth to try to escape his mouth. She tried to kick him with her other knee and must have been successful as he cried out and doubled over, his hands leaving her wrists and grabbing his groin. She felt a surge of energy as he released her wrists, and her arms pushed him away from her with a strength that surprised them both. He rolled onto the floor, his face stark with pain and rage. She lunged for the door, turned the key, fortunately in the right direction, threw open the door and fled down the steps and out of the house. Only when she reached her family's apartment did she realize that she'd left her book bag on the floor beside his bed. Ashamed and humiliated, she told her mom she'd left it on the bus. She never told anyone what happened that day.

She sat at her work table in their house in Cullen twenty years later unable to control the shaking of her hands, terrified that her daughter might experience what she had experienced or worse. The impossibility of protecting this child she loved so from such terror overwhelmed her, and she sat immobilized while darkness devoured the fragile light of late afternoon.

A while later Duncan turned the key to the front door of the dark house on Blantyre Street, calling, "Ineke, is everything all right?" He turned on the lamp beside the sofa. Its golden glow transformed the room into a place of safety that spread like sunlight into the adjacent rooms, nearly reaching her work space where she sat covered in shadow. She stood and moved uncertainly toward the light, trying to reconstruct her face so that her terror would not show. As she came into the living room, she saw him still standing by the front door. The concern on his face undid her. She moved toward him and into his arms that opened to receive her. He pushed the front door closed behind him and simply held her, waiting for her to speak. When she stopped crying, she did.

"When I was Elleke's age, a boy tried to rape me, and now I'm so scared for her. I don't know how to protect her."

She didn't see Elleke who had come out of her room when she heard Duncan's voice and was standing in the doorway. Ineke felt her daughter's arms hugging her from behind. She was enclosed by the two people she loved most, encircled and protected.

Elleke spoke quietly into her ear, "Mom, I promise you I will be very careful to protect myself. I will be safe."

In the weeks that followed their little family seemed especially close. Elleke and Duncan were both making special effort to take care of her, and Ineke was grateful.

Wichita, Kansas: January 2006

Amy came home from work early one Friday. D.J. was at a friend's for the evening. She collapsed into the purple sofa, kicked off her shoes, and let the feelings come. Last week she'd buried her Mother, who, despite the onset of dementia, was the person she counted on to always be there, whether or not Amy took advantage of her availability. They'd grown closer over the years since Duncan's departure. Still, the depth of her grief over Mother's death surprised her. She was now orphaned, alone in the world, without family, other than her son. That was hard. There. She owned it.

Her relationship with John had changed after he and Cliff left, no longer best friends, although she knew in a pinch she could call him and he would be there for her. But their frequent contact and comfortable interactions were a thing of the past. With Mother gone, there was no one she talked with every week other than D.J. and the folks at work.

She'd kept Mother's ashes in her bedroom, unable yet to relinquish this last part of her. Now she stood and walked back to her bedroom to fetch the brown cardboard box. She carried it to the coffee table in front of the sofa and sank back into the sofa staring at the box. "How did you manage, Mother, after Dad left?" She spoke aloud what she had never asked her mother when Mother could answer the question. The room was silent.

How do others cope? Do women alone present to the world the appearance of successful coping because it is expected of them? The way they bring food to the homes of ill friends? The way they must frantically clean house before company comes so that the chaotic places of their lives remain hidden? But intimacy relies on honesty. Do we sabotage our chances for intimacy by misrepresenting ourselves, hiding our loneliness? Her questions were disturbing.

Her primary goal since Duncan left was to raise their son well. Her own needs would have to take a back seat until he was grown. And maybe that would be too late. After a certain age—about her age now—women rarely had the chance to remarry.

She dismissed this thought, returning to her commitment to providing her son with a father figure. When his contact with John dwindled, she'd signed him up with a mentor from Big Brothers Big Sisters. That seemed to help some, the two being relatively compatible, but in a way D.J.'s new relationship highlighted the absence of any special friend in her own life. She'd found herself wondering if D.J.'s Big Brother might be a potential friend for her. Then D.J. told her that his Big Brother had a wife and three grown children and was being transferred by Raytheon next month. She decided to text John with that information and ask him to resume his weekly contacts with D.J.

Today she'd taken a couple about her age to look at houses. Second marriage for each of them. They seemed so happy together. Was she making a mistake turning down invitations to meet men? Should she look into one of those online dating services?

Mother was being uncharacteristically silent, her ashes content just to listen.

Amy remembered something Mother had said when she was just starting down the irreversible road to losing her mind: "Don't look for attachment, honey. Do what you love and you will be so radiant that attachment will find you." She'd so often dismissed Mother's advice over the years that she'd paid little attention at the time. Now she was glad it had rooted in her memory anyway.

What do I love to do? My work. Cooking. Eating good food. Having D.J.'s friends over. Gardening. Going to the theater. Meeting people from other parts of the world. Discussing books and ideas with other women.

Most of those things she was already doing, other than the last two. Funny, while she and Duncan were together she'd have added "making love" to the list, but she'd gone without that so long, she thought she could understand how nuns managed celibacy. She could do something about her deficits. And, if Mom was right, she could look for a book group and a way to meet internationals and expect radiance and attachment to show up soon. Well, after D.J. was grown. She opened her laptop and posted on Facebook that she was looking for a book group and a way to meet internationals. She felt better. Nothing like being pro-active.

Cullen, Scotland: February 2006

Elleke celebrated her thirteenth birthday by making a trip to Edinburgh with Mom, Pappie Duncan, and her Dutch grandparents to visit the Harry Potter sites. Duncan had taken on reading aloud the Potter books with her after Granddad died, and both he and Ineke shared Elleke's fascination with the battle between good and evil played out at Hogwarts. When they got back from Edinburgh, Mom organized a major birthday party at the Salmon Bothy in Portsoy inviting the students in her class. Mom decorated the room in a Harry Potter theme--broomsticks and hockey sticks, steaming cauldrons filled with Elleke's favorite foods, dry ice releasing smoky mist. They played Quiddich on the lawn of the caravan park and in the evening a group of them spent the night at Elleke's house, staying up till three spinning stories of what would happen to Harry's friends who survived him. The party was a great success.

Ineke did not seem to recover her usual energy in the weeks that followed. She sometimes complained of feeling tired, of odd aches and pains, and of an upset stomach. Later Elleke would remember this as the time everything changed. Her childhood ended abruptly after that amazing thirteenth birthday party.

Cullen, Scotland: April 2006

Ineke lay in bed half awake and whoozy. A sharp pain in her abdomen brought her to full consciousness. The bed was still warm beside her where Duncan had lain until a short while ago. She tried to focus on the sounds she heard coming from the other part of the house, lowered voices punctuated by light laughter and the pinging sounds of spoons clinking on the sides of bowls as they lifted porridge to their mouths. Porridge cooked on the stove in milk, nothing more comforting, she thought. Her mind drifted back to when she and Duncan first got together, when he ate porridge three times a day. She had asked him why.

"Oatmeal's my comfort food," he had said.

"You must need a lot of comforting," she had joked.

He had turned to look at her very seriously. "Yes, I do," he had said.

Later, after they had been lovers and friends for many months, he had looked at her again with those deep set dark eyes and said they needed to talk. He said he loved her, something he never expected to say to a woman ever again in his life after his marriage ended so painfully. He loved her. And he wanted to be with her until he died.

His intensity left her breathless and a mite apprehensive. She knew that she felt the same about him. Actually, she had known it longer, even though she, like Duncan, had to scale walls of past pain and betrayal before she could let in love.

She felt very connected to this man who had been so deeply hurt by life. She vowed to herself and to him that she would protect and sustain him for the rest of her life. She had tried to lighten the moment by pledging to ply him with porridge until death do them part. He had pulled her to him and had held her close, overwhelmed by his feelings. "I never expected to be happy again," he'd told her.

Gradually he had grown stronger, more comfortable in his skin and with others. She knew that she and Elleke were a major part of his healing, along with Mr. Cruickshank. The Cullen community had helped, too. People there had accepted them as a family, and welcomed them to the many village events. Of course, there were a few busybodies. The woman who cleaned the church, someone told her, was openly disapproving of their not marrying, but on the whole people didn't pry or judge. They had reinvented themselves as a family of choice, created rituals and traditions, common values, ways of reminding each other that they belonged to each other. They worked well together, and she was grateful for that. Her mom and dad were obviously happy about her relationship with Duncan, too, as they'd told her often.

Professionally, her art had made her a Name in the world of high end jewelry, her designs bringing in a sizeable income in dollars, Euros, and pounds, as it was marketed on the Continent, in the U.S., and across the U.K. As Duncan put it in his American English, "You're at the top of your game."

Still, this morning she felt uneasy. Foreboding slipped between the whoozy spaces in her brain and she felt apprehensive.

She must get up. Usually she was the first one of the family to rise. She'd have breakfast waiting for them and sometimes had already perched on the high stool in her studio where in the early morning light of April, augmented by a halogen lamp, she would be wielding her tweezers, stretching and shaping the gold and silver wires and experimenting with where the precious stones looked best.

Not today. Not yesterday either or the day before. Gradually she found herself more and more weary, less able to climb from the warm sheets into the cold air of springtime along the North Sea, less ready to get to work, more bone tired. But she kept pushing herself.

After two weeks of dragging, Duncan, who had been noticing, insisted she see the local doctor. The doctor thought she might be anemic and put her on iron supplements. Two weeks later she was back, feeling even more depleted, and the doctor ordered blood work and sent her to a specialist in Elgin. Duncan was worried.

The specialist in Elgin ordered an MRI and then, to be certain, a biopsy of her pancreas. He said he was by nature cautious and wanted to check out all the possibilities. They needn't be alarmed. Yet.

They made two more trips to Elgin, Duncan assuring her that doctors in bigger cities like Elgin or Aberdeen had access to the latest technology that the doctors in these small coastal villages couldn't afford. He was glad they were testing so thoroughly. She could tell he was worried.

Because her symptoms were vague and chronic, she had to wait for the MRI and biopsy. Duncan wanted to take her to a private doctor, but she didn't want to spend the money. After all, she was a very healthy person, had been all of her life.

It took several weeks for all the tests to be done and coordinated and analyzed. Today the two of them were driving to Elgin to get the results. Ineke shivered, unclear whether from the morning chill or the fear that nibbled at the calm, confident, contented face she usually presented to the world. Duncan let her out at the entrance to the specialist's office and parked the car. Walking back to meet her he almost didn't recognize her. She was leaning on the in-take counter as though she hadn't the strength to stand up, one hand on her stomach, her face frozen in fear. Seeing her like this stunned him.

Dr. Ghosh smiled at them as she invited them into her office and asked after Elleke before getting down to what she had found as she reviewed the tests. Her face shifted to serious. "I'm afraid the news is not good..." Ineke did not remember the rest, only the feeling in her stomach, as though wet rags, sodden and heavy, were filling her gut and pushing bile into the back of her throat.

Driving home Duncan helped her understand what the doctor had said. They were both in shock. Dr. Ghost advised them to call her parents to come and help. Ineke should think about what she wanted for Elleke once she was gone and be sure those arrangements were made. "This disease can move very quickly."

Call in her parents? *Plan for Elleke's life after she was gone?* She could not incorporate what the doctor was telling them. No. No! She would fight it.

They would fight it.

They made an appointment with another specialist in Elgin for a second opinion. He maintained a private practice rather than working as part of the National Health Service. They got in to see him at the end of the week. His verdict was the same: aggressive stage four pancreatic cancer with, if she was lucky, several months left. Too late for clinical trials.

On the drive home to Cullen, Duncan and she took turns crying. The one not crying was responsible for watching for cars and trucks. Vehicles on the A-98 moved dangerously fast.

"We could simply cross the lane in front of one of those eighteen wheeler lorries and go together," Duncan had suggested. When she looked over at him, she could see he was serious. Her love for this man overwhelmed her. How could their shared life be about to come to an end so prematurely? They'd had only a decade together. They were young, vigorous. They ate right, exercised, cared for each other. Finding each other had been such a · blessing. How could they be separated? She fantasized gathering their things and fleeing to the end of the earth where this awful diagnosis could not find them.

"Ineke, I can't let you go. How can I live without you?" His voice keened his despair. His eyes were on the road that spread out gray before them. On either side the rich spring greens of gorse and bramble bushes and the tender pink buds unfolding on branches reaching into the road celebrated the advent of spring. April along the North Sea was unbearably beautiful, but knowing what they now knew, its promise was barren and bitter.

"I can get morphine tablets. We can both take them. We chew them. Too many can kill you."

She felt his eyes pulling her, claiming her, holding on for dear life. She laid her hand on his thigh. Already the weight of her hand in this familiar gesture felt lighter, as though she was disappearing, changing form.

"My love, we can't do that to Elleke," she replied. Elleke. What would become of her daughter with no mother to guide and love her along life's zigs and zags, to help her navigate the dark nights of the soul. A searing clarity went through her like lightning. "How we handle this will be the most important lesson I—we—can teach Elleke."

In that moment she knew that her dying must tie together all that she had left to teach her daughter about how to live. She must work out how to include it all in this teachable moment of her dying no matter how foreshortened or protracted. "How I die will override everything else she has learned from me," she said aloud.

Duncan was looking at her, his face distraught. She suspected he knew that from here on she would be singularly focused, until that was no longer possible. He had already begun to lose her.

Ineke suggested they wait to tell Elleke, who had the lead in her school play that weekend. She needed the next few days to think things through while Duncan was at work and Elleke at school. On Thursday she called her parents and asked them to come for an extended visit. She called a friend who made independent films asked if he would help her make a film for Elleke and one for Duncan. She called her distributors and said she would be unable to fulfill the Christmas orders. She located online the Dutch government's forms for transferring custody of a minor. Tending to so many details exhausted her.

Duncan found her in bed when he came home early that afternoon and crawled in next to her, holding her gently, curled together like two spoons while tears poured out of them both.

By the time Elleke came through the door with her standard cheery greeting, they were recovered enough to invite her to come cuddle with them, an invitation Elleke later thought she should have picked up on; few thirteen year olds cuddle in the bed with their parents.

Saturday came and Elleke received flowers and a standing ovation from the enthusiastic audience, including her proud parents, Pappie Duncan and Mom, who seemed a bit over emotional. The particular play, after all, was a comedy!

Sunday morning over a hearty Scottish breakfast Duncan had prepared, they told Elleke what the doctor had said.

They all cried.

Elleke went to her room where she paced back and forth and swore under her breath using every bad word she'd ever heard. "Damn fuck Motherfucker shitty asshole. Crap fuck it God-damn it." The words felt wimpy and there were not enough of them. She screamed into the air, *How could you do this to me? I'll never forgive you, Mom, never.* Needja fled to hide under the bed. "It's not fair. I still need my mommy." She thought she heard the back door close and Duncan's voice, low, the words indistinguishable. She made out something like, "She needs to be alone for a while."

Alone! God damn it, motherfucking son of a bitch, that's the problem. I will be alone. The realization buckled her knees and she fell back on her bed. She turned to face the wall, hugging her curled knees and wept. Her wrenching sobs and gasps for breath brought Needja out from his safety zone. He stood beside her licking the back of her right arm, the only skin his tongue could reach without getting up on the bed, which was not allowed. Elleke cried until, depleted, she fell asleep. When she awakened, Needja was cuddled beside her, his head resting on her hip.

After they told Elleke, Ineke felt completely worn out. Pain moved across her abdomen in waves alternating with nausea. "I need to get my pills," she told Duncan, who brought her a glass of water and her pain killers. They sat in the living room listening to the sounds of rage coming from Elleke's room followed by her weeping. Ineke wanted to go to her daughter but hadn't the energy. So she sat, keeping vigil a room away. When all was quiet, she pulled herself up from the sofa and walked to Elleke's door, turning the knob silently and looking in. When she saw that Elleke was sleeping and Needja on guard, she closed the door and moved with some discomfort back to the living room where Duncan sat on the sofa watching her.

"Are you up for a walk on the braes?" he asked.

Her pain meds had started to kick in raising her expectations. "Let's go to where we watch the seals," she said. It was the place they had gone with Elleke on their first outing together ten years ago and many times since. Duncan helped her into the car and drove to the overlook. Slowly they walked to the bench where they always sat to marvel at how the sun slid over the hills and rocks as it journeyed toward the horizon.

"We've been very lucky to find each other," Ineke said. "Many people go through lifetime without finding such joy." Her voice was soft.

"Are you afraid?" he asked her.

"Afraid of what will happen to you and Elleke. Scared that there won't be enough time. I want my spirit to at least roost in some tree and watch over you. *I don't want to leave you.*" She held on to Duncan weeping inconsolably. When her tears were no more, she wiped her eyes and turned his face to hers. She looked at him intently.

"I don't believe this is happening to us because God is capricious or mean spirited. I feel like God is weeping, too, Duncan, as strange as that may sound....I have known since I was very small that everything dies, that death is part of life. We get the joy of being alive and we get the pain of letting life go, even as the cycle begins again for the one just born. But even though I know that, I'm not ready to leave, not ready at all." She stood up from the bench and raised her arms like a preacher giving a benediction. Then she screamed, "I DON'T WANT TO DIE! I DON'T WANT TO LEAVE YOU!" and the hills undulating across the cliff tops echoed back her scream: "leave you! leave you! leave you!"

She sat back down, sighed, and grinned. "Guess I told them! I feel better." From the look on Duncan's face, she could tell his heart was breaking.

A while later they walked back to the car, arms around each other.

Some time later Elleke awoke, grabbed her hoodie, and left the house, striding toward the old Seafields estate with its miles of walking trails. Mom had cautioned her that the area was posted as private land—No Trespassing--and that it was easy to get lost there if you left the path. She went anyway, breaking off small branches and ripping apart leaves as she walked. Needja padded behind her.

In her mind she listed all the things that were unfair about Mom being so sick. *I already lost Granddad, which is enough loss for a child. I need my mom to be there when I graduate from secondary school. I need her through college. I need her when I marry. I need her to be granny to my kids. I NEED HER TO BE HERE!* She screamed this last and then screamed it again as loudly as she could.

She could not imagine the world without Mom. *Not my mom!!!!!*

When Duncan and Ineke got back to the house, they found Elleke sitting in the garden furiously throwing stones at one of Mr. Cruickshank's porcelain statues, the one of the red haired girl lying in the grass, her favorite. It was clear that she was trying to break it. Her face was distorted with grief and anger.

"I won't get over this, Mom. I HATE it. I want you to be here when I graduate from secondary school and college, when I get married and when I become a mother. I NEED YOU TO BE HERE!!!!!"

Ineke had no words to reply, and Elleke heaved a large stone at the statue. They heard the crack as the stone connected and severed the head of the red haired girl.

That evening Ineke forced herself to sit at her worktable with her magnifying glass and tweezers gluing the statue back together.

"Why are you doing that, Mom?" Elleke asked her.

"I won't let you destroy her. I know you'll regret it." Ineke was intent on gluing the last chip in place and Elleke watched her trying to work her creative magic.

"Even fixed you can tell she's broken."

"Even broken you can tell she is happy," Ineke replied. She placed the repaired statue out of reach to dry and opened her arms to her daughter. She felt exhausted.

During the next few weeks each of them was preoccupied by the same question: Why must their life as a family end so soon? When Ineke's parents arrived and they shared their desolate news, the heaviness of despair sat more solidly on the occupants of the house on Blantyre Street. As Ineke grew weaker, Duncan, her parents, and Elleke were all needed to help with her care, but it was clear to each of them that their remaining time with her, split among the four of them, meant no one would get enough of her and time was running out. She slept a lot now and relied more and more on her pain pills.

The six weeks that followed were full of pain. Locked in their grief, Duncan and Elleke could not help each other. It took all of Ineke's energy to get through the things on her Must Do list and manage her physical distress. While Duncan was at work and Elleke at school, her mom and dad cared for her, monitoring her energy so that the calls coming in from friends from university and through her work didn't wear her out. Day by day they watched helpless as her energy diminished.

One afternoon Ineke's filmmaker friend showed up with his camera. Making the film was her secret, and she made her mom and dad swear that they would not tell. She had been working on what she wanted to say. It could not be much as she ran out of breath and words fairly quickly now. She had planned to make two films, one for Duncan and one for Elleke, but she didn't have the stamina. Instead she spoke to them both on the same film. Mom and Dad helped her get up to the top of the viaduct overlooking the sea. She was seated on their favorite bench there, the spring wind tossing her hair, the North Sea behind her. She looked tired and was thin, but the smile she flashed to the camera was her trademark irresistible grin.

She began speaking once her friend signaled her that the tripod was holding the camera still despite the wind off the sea. "I am proudest of two important things I have done with my life. The first is raising you, Elleke, to be a loving and independent person who brings happiness to others and knows that the world is her friend.

"The second is helping you, Duncan, discover that you are an amazing and caring man who can experience happiness and joy and that your life has meaning....

"My time here is ending sooner than I want it to, but yours will continue." Here she paused and drew several breaths to gain enough strength to keep speaking. "It will be tempting for both of you to become bitter people who don't trust that life is good and worth living fully. Resist that temptation." Another pause. "Don't ever forget how lucky we have been to have each other and Granddad Cruickshank and our friends and family." She paused again. Her camera man asked if she needed to stop. She shook her head and kept going.

"I ask you to take care of each other, encourage each other, remind each other that you are loved. I am counting on you to do this. I will do whatever I can to help from whatever comes after this life, but I am counting on you, Duncan, to look after Elleke, and you, Elleke, to look after Duncan."

The camera zoomed in to her face. Her eyes shone but her voice was frail. "Duncan, hold onto caring and connecting—your ability to connect with Elleke and me and to care for Mr. Cruickshank brought you out of your despair and gave your life meaning. It is what will save you now.

"I love you both more than I can ever express and am so lucky to be loved by you. That's all for now." Her shoulders sagged with the relief of having completed this legacy.

She had her friend make two copies of the film to be given to Duncan and Elleke three months after her death. She could not know that three months after her death Elleke would be living in Holland far from Duncan and the Northeast coast, living unhappily with her father and his wife, while Duncan would be barely existing in the Land of the Lost.

Cullen, Scotland: July 2006

They carried the cardboard box with her ashes up to the braes where they had walked so often along the coastal path. Each of them said some words and then took turns shaking the ashes from the box, watching them form a gray cloud that lifted on the wind and was carried down the cliffs and out to sea. She had clung to life beyond the doctors' expectations and when the end came, they all were ready to let her go. There was so little of her left. Her haggard face, yellowed skin, thinning hair, hoarse voice, bony hands, and almost weightless body—they did not want to remember her like this. It angered each of them and left them spent and isolated in their anger. So they were ready to let go. And weary. So weary.

Her parents left a few days after the makeshift funeral, looking aged and worn, faces pinched, hands constantly moving, plucking at things—pieces of lint on the carpet, fuzz on a sweater, stray hairs in the sink—or tapping against table tops or coffee cups as though communicating in Morse code their loss. They all felt like survivors of a war they had lost, survivors going through the motions of picking up the remaining pieces of their lives. Survivors with haunted eyes and sleep-deprived bodies and an inability to smile.

Elleke and Duncan rattled around the house in Cullen, looking for the ghosts of Granddad Cruickshank and Ineke in every room and finding only memories already blurry. "I can't remember what Mom looked like," Elleke told him one morning at breakfast. "I don't want to forget, but I can't remember."

They rarely said much to one another, their love for Ineke and their yearning for her took up all the space between them. Duncan roamed the house at night, unable to sleep for the ache in his heart, walking room to room as though he might find her hiding in the shadows. Passing Elleke's room he saw her, lying on her left side, profusion of auburn curls fanning out helter skelter over her pillow, right arm reaching out to the other side of the bed for her mom. It helped, somehow that he and Elleke were together in this pain, bonded. He could keep going. Ineke had made him promise this, for the sake of their girl.

One Saturday morning three weeks after Ineke died, the doorbell rang at eleven o'clock. When Duncan opened the door, a man filled the doorframe, a tall, robust man obviously used to taking charge. "I'm here to collect my daughter," he said with a smile that Duncan read as condescending. He towered over Duncan, waiting impatiently to be invited in. Numbly Duncan took a step backward, which was all the invitation he needed. "Elleke," the man called out in a voice that boomed, "It's your Vader come to bring you home."

Duncan's brain clicked into gear. He had to stall this man, who must be Jens. He had to prevent him from taking Elleke away. He offered coffee, which Jens accepted. He tried small talk, where did Jens live? In Utrecht. How was his family? Well. How many children did he have now? Two.

Then he said, "Ineke and I filed adoption papers for Elleke. She wanted—me, too—Elleke to stay here with me. I've been her pappie for most of her life." He could see by the flush blooming across Jens' face that he was offended. No, he mustn't do that. He tried another tack but before he got the words out, Jens' large voice resounded authoritatively. "Your legal process was not completed when Ineke died. Elleke is my child. My wife and I will raise her in Utrecht with our girls as is proper for a Dutch child. Please get her things together. We leave on a flight from Aberdeen at five."

Elleke stood beside the double doors to the kitchen facing the two men, the one so big and powerful, the other small and lost, seeming to shrink in the presence of this stranger. "I want to stay here. I don't want to leave." Her words were those her mother had hurled at the sky from the cliff the day they heard her prognosis confirmed by the second doctor. The truth cut through Duncan like a knife blade: What Elleke wanted made no more difference than what her mother had wanted. Jens would take her away. Parental rights. Nothing he could do.

He walked to Elleke and held her. They both cried, conscious that Jens had stood up from the sofa and was frowning at them, disapproving of this show of emotion. "Come, now, Elleke. Gather your things. I have a taxi waiting to take us to Aberdeen," he said. When they didn't stop holding on to each other, he cleared his throat impatiently.

"I WON'T GO WITH YOU. I PROMISED MOM I WOULD STAY WITH PAPPIE DUNCAN. YOU CAN'T MAKE ME GO!" She rushed to her bedroom and locked the door.

Jens followed her trying to force open the door, and, when he couldn't, knocking loudly as he said, "It is not your decision to make, Elleke. You are my child, and, according to the law, it is I who decide where and with whom you live. This display of emotion is futile. Get your things together. The cab is waiting. We cannot miss our plane."

Duncan called Jens to come into the living room and leave her alone. "Surely your busy life doesn't allow much time for another child. Here she has friends, her home, and me. I love Elleke and will take very good care of her. You cannot disregard Ineke's wishes."

Jens dismissed his words. "The law is the law, and the law says you have no right to her. Now, where is her suitcase?"

Frantic, Duncan made every argument he could think of, but he was speaking to a man used to winning.

"You do know that I can prevent her from having any contact with you if I choose to?" Jens' face was dark red and threatening. "It is in your best interests to cooperate, or do I need to call the constable?"

At these words, Elleke emerged from the bedroom, her face swollen and blotchy. She went to Duncan and put her arms around him. Their despair hung heavy in the room.

Needja sat beside Duncan leaning against his leg, looking up at them. Duncan realized with dismay that Jens was taking everything away from him that bound him to his life with Ineke and Elleke, everything except the empty house. He kissed Elleke's forehead and the top of her head, holding her face in his hands. His tears dropped onto her cheeks. "I can't stop him from this," he whispered into her ear. "You take Needja. He will look after you. We will write. I'll call. I love you very much, Elleke. That won't ever change."

Then, feeling his face falling away, he moved to bring their two big suitcases from the hall closet and helped her fill them.

In the end, Jens refused to bring Needja, something about allergies to pets and having no carrying cage and the airline assessing extra charges for animals.

It had begun to rain, the gentle spitting mist so common along the North Sea. Duncan, holding Needja's collar, stood in the doorway as Jens hurried Elleke from the house. Her face had no plasticity. It was merely a mask of grief and anger that he feared she directed at him for not being able to stop this severing of her life. She climbed into the taxi and didn't look back.

"I need your address and phone number," he yelled out, running after the cab. But the cab sped away as Needja began to howl and the mist turned to a pelting rain.

Cullen, Scotland: Autumn 2006

Two things kept Duncan going after Jens separated him from Elleke:
One, his promise to Old Man Cruickshank that he would maintain his stores
and two, Needja, the dog Jens would not allow Elleke to bring with her. He
stumbled through the weeks, his grief like a cancer consuming him. He
rarely went to the store in Buckie, giving it over almost entirely to the assistant he'd hired. He continued going to the shops in Cullen and Portsoy most
weekdays, although he kept abbreviated and irregular hours. Some days he
worked on a clock or repaired a piece of furniture that was missing a strip of
molding or needed its gilding touched up. The rest of the time he sat at his
work table for hours staring at nothing and circling an endless spiral that took
him lower and lower.

Weekends were roughest. So many hours alone stretching out before him.
He tried to structure his time. Friday nights he would go to a pub in Portsoy
beside the old harbor that he and Ineke had never gone to. No one knew
him there, and he could down four pints of Guinness sitting in a dark corner,
eat a burger or baked "jacket" potato, and then walk back up hill to his Wee
Cottage. He began taking Needja with him. If he got completely nackered,
he could count on the dog to lead him home.

Saturdays he walked with Needja, climbing the braes and walking the
coastal path, sometimes west to Sandsend and Cullen, sometimes east to
Whitehills and even on to Banff. Exhausting his body seemed to help him

get through the nights.

He located their copy of the adoption papers they'd submitted too late and found Jens' address. He wrote Elleke every day, but when he read over his letters before posting them, they sounded too morose to be helpful to her. He tore most of them up, sending greeting cards he bought at the pharmacy instead. The child didn't need the drama that was consuming him. She just needed to know he missed and loved her.

One rainy Saturday several months after Elleke had left, he and Needja trod the dead grass along the path east to Whitehills, careful to avoid the slippery mud churned up by earlier walkers that sucked at his shoes and clung to the hem of his jeans. Those boggy areas were treacherous when it was wet. One misstep could carry a body over the cliffs to the boulders below. Avoiding the muck was not easy on those stretches where gorse bushes lined both sides of the path and reached out their long thorns to lacerate whatever touched them.

He remembered early in his relationship with Ineke when the gorse thorns had caught her while they'd been walking, how she'd stood very still while he untangled her slacks and sweater from the briars' painful embrace. He could almost see her standing there in the moonlight while he carefully removed each thorn from her clothing. She had looked at him so gratefully, so caringly.

Now he let the gorse scratch his legs and catch on his jacket, let the blood, diluted by the rain, run from the tears the thorns made in his hands. He wanted to feel this pain. He considered letting himself slip over the edge of the cliff onto the rocks below. He considered jumping.

Needja's teeth held one leg of his jeans, pulling on it, on him, pulling him away from the gorse, onto the grass and the barley stubble that was hibernating until spring on the south side of the path, away from the sea. Needja wouldn't give up on him. Duncan reached down and rubbed the dog's head gratefully as Needja licked the nasty gashes on his hand, blood and rain both.

When they returned to the Cullen house, he built a fire in the ancient fireplace and sat before it nursing an ale, lost in thought. He remembered George Cruickshank telling him about his desolation after Molly died, how he didn't want to live for a long time. He felt a rush of gratitude to the old man for sharing this with him.

The following Saturday Duncan and Needja took the coastal path in the opposite direction, westward across the braes. In the crisp, clear November day bits of color lit the autumn landscape—blond fields of barley stubble, white and mustard yellow lichen adorning gray and brown cliffs, the iridescent sea. The sun spots on the water were so bright he had to squint against them. Dazzling white clouds danced overhead tossed about by the wind. He remembered Ineke saying this place made her a believer in giants and nymphs and gods. She claimed she could see them cavorting across the colossal stage of sky, playing out dramas worthy of Wagner above the earth while sea gulls and cormorants, resting on the rocks for a chat, made an inattentive audience. He smiled, remembering. The woman's way of seeing had opened new passages in his mind and led him into a surprisingly nourishing world of imagination.

Now he observed something he'd not noticed before, though he'd walked this path hundreds of times. The huge rocks growing from the sea and soaring to form the cliffs were not only different in color. They were different in how they dealt with the North Sea. Some leaned out, jagged edges profiled against the water as though daring it to limit them, fiercely resisting its power. Others leaned toward the land, as though seeking refuge under the cliffs from the relentless beating of the sea. Defiant resilience or self-protective retreat? Both options seemed in that moment to be messages from rock and sea intended for him.

"What do you think, Needja?" He spoke aloud, then, startled by the sound of his own voice, looked around to see if anyone had heard him. Seeing no one within earshot, he focused on Needja, awaiting a response. The dog merely sat and watched him, brown eyes soft and attentive, determined to keep him away from the cliffs' edge.

Duncan turned back to the path and resumed walking. Needja padded along beside him. He was thinking that he was glad he hadn't missed this day.

Sundays he began riding the bus into the countryside. Nowhere in particular. Anywhere would do. He'd catch an early bus and ride as long as he wished, then exit, walk the fields and villages until he tired, and catch another bus back home. After several weeks the bus drivers who worked Sundays greeted him as a regular, smiling their "Eh-yah" (hello). He wondered what they thought of him.

Most of the riders were frail elderly, some men but mostly women, navigating the steps up to the bus with their canes. Some greeted the driver, others looked out from masked and undecipherable faces. He wondered if they were grateful to be alive.

The old folks seemed to dress up for their bus rides, unlike the occasional young people who would hop on, usually in pairs or groups, heading who knows where, wearing jeans and T-shirts that peaked out from their parkas bearing slogans he thought must shock the pensioners.

Not much open on Sundays to draw young folks. He wondered why they bothered. Then there was himself, long haired, privacy-phobic, forty-something. An outlier. No doubt about that. Actually, he didn't give a damn what any of them thought of him. Riding the bus on Sundays had become his ritual. It gave him things to notice and brought him out of his funk, at least for several hours.

His correspondence with Elleke was sporadic. She wrote daily the first few weeks, then weekly, and he wrote back, though he hadn't much to say. He could see where this was headed. Jens had made his claim on her, and Jens was her father, regardless of who Elleke called Pappie. Best let the child re-establish her ties to her father, painful as that was for him. He gradually restricted his letters to her—once a month, then every other month. Not that he didn't think of her. Lord, no. He thought of her every day, trying to imagine how she was changing as she transitioned to becoming a young woman. Maybe he'd never know.

Cullen & Portsoy: 2007

After a year of rattling around the house in Cullen and daily bumping into exquisite memories that fed his desolation, Duncan decided to close the house and move back to the Wee Cottage in Portsoy. It was enough space for him and Needja, and bringing it up to code, installing insulation and new wiring, a modern bath and an adequate kitchen, would give him projects to occupy his evenings. He congratulated himself for making it through the saddest year of his life. He told himself if he'd managed this, he could keep going.

During that first year he talked to Ineke, told her how much he missed her, how deep was his grief, how superficial his coping. She didn't talk back, though there were times he thought he felt her presence, especially at first. After the first anniversary of her death, that sense of connection tapered off no matter how intently he reached for her. Eventually he stopped trying to reach her except in his dreams.

His life became singularly unremarkable. He went through the motions of staying alive, but his emotional circuitry felt disconnected. He spoke infrequently, a few words to the clerks at the Coop grocery or to the bartender at The Shore Inn or to the rare customer who dropped by the antique shops. His voice when he heard it sounded unfamiliar, egg shell thin and so soft people usually asked him to repeat himself. Repeating himself--an apt description of his life now, repeating the rituals that enclosed his days and the few sentences that were all he used now. He waited without expectation.

Amsterdam, Holland: Spring 2009

At sixteen Elleke had grown into her new body with relative comfort. She was tall and leggy like her mom had been and shapely, and she carried herself with confidence, shoulders back, head up, red curls set in motion by her long stride, warm brown eyes smiling a welcome to those in her perimeter. She attracted attention without meaning to.

She liked school, earned first class grades in all of her courses, and had twice been elected president of her class. Like when she was little and captivated Pappie Duncan and Granddad Cruickshank, her openness and interest in others drew people to her.

There was a purpose behind her academic achievement that she confided to no one. She was planning how to reconstitute her Scottish family, despite the damage Death had done to its two survivors. She researched universities outside of Holland that offered degrees in archaeology and anthropology, fields that especially interested her. She discovered several in the United Kingdom, including the University of Glasgow and the University of Edinburgh.

Her father was adamant that she would attend the University of Utrecht, his alma mater. When she broached the possibility of studying in the United Kingdom--strategically using "UK" instead of a "Scotland" to avoid igniting his jealousy of her relationship with Duncan—he ranted about how attending university in the UK would cost nearly twice as much as attending a university in Holland. But she had done her homework. If she was a star student, universities in the UK would want her enough to pay for her education. In that case, scholarships would make her financially independent of her father, meaning she could choose the university she most wanted to attend. She could go back home.

It was two weeks before Duncan's birthday and she'd bought a card to send him. She enclosed a breezy letter telling him about high school and reminding him that he would always be her true Pappie. She sealed the envelope and asked Marika, her father's wife, for a stamp. Marika offered to take the card to the post office for her before supper, so that she could get to work on a demanding history project. She left the card on the table, thanked Marika, and returned to her computer.

She heard her father call to Marika as he came into the dining room after work. Each evening he reentered the house as though life there could now begin. His announcement, "I'm here" resounded like a general's call to attention. She imagined her twin half-sisters running from their rooms and lining up in front of him like the Von Trapp family in *The Sound of Music*.

She heard his voice grow louder and more agitated than usual, and then the outside door slammed and all was quiet, except for the low mumble of the news that Marika kept on the television in the kitchen while she cooked dinner. Elleke didn't think more about their exchange.

Her father was not an easy person to get along with, and frequently she felt sympathy for Marika, having to adjust to his mood swings and petty jealousy. Having missed his military manner of parenting for ten years of her life, Elleke generally treated him politely but without fear, unwilling to let him bully her. And she got away with it, although she hadn't a clue why.

The next morning was Saturday, when she was expected to clean her room and both bathrooms and take out the trash first thing after breakfast. As she emptied the waste basket into the recycling bin, her card and letter to Duncan tumbled out onto the kitchen floor. It had been ripped in two. She pulled out both halves and tucked them inside a book she was reading, then completed her chores. She waited for an opportunity to talk to Marika when no one else was near.

On Sunday when her father was visiting his parents, she approached Marika, who sat in the sunroom reading. "I found this in the trash," she said, holding out the two halves of Duncan's birthday card and her letter to him.

Marika looked distressed and embarrassed. "I am so sorry, Elleke. Your father saw it on the table where I'd placed it next to my purse so I'd not forget to mail it. He read it—he shouldn't have done that—and tore it in two. He yelled that I was your collaborator and that he wouldn't have me helping you stay in contact with 'that man.' He ordered me to give any letters you receive from Duncan to him. I am really sorry, Elleke. You know how stubborn he is."

Elleke held in her fury until after supper when she could talk with her father alone. She didn't want to bring Marika into it. She sat on the sofa next to his chair and pulled out the torn card and letter.

"Did you do this, Vader?" Her voice was subdued. She needed to stay calm to confront him. When he looked at the card and then at her, his eyes acknowledged that he had.

"You will not have contact with that man. I am your father and you will obey me. You can forget about going to any college in the U.K., too. I forbid it." His voice had a hard edge that would have cut her had she allowed it. He turned back to his newspaper.

She stood and walked toward him. With both hands she removed the paper from his fingers. Her face was livid. "'*That man*' raised me for ten years. While you were making your replacement family, he directed his love and attention to being a father to me. You have no right to demand this, no right to read my mail, no right to destroy something I got for him. You don't know how to be a father. You only know how to make demands. I will never forgive you for this."

She turned her back on him and walked out of the room, locking herself in her bedroom.

She taped her letter and the card back together and found an envelope they would fit in, which she addressed to Duncan. She added a brief note before sealing it. "Sorry, my father did this, but he cannot stop me loving my Pappie Duncan." She drew a big heart around the words with a red marker.

The next morning she mailed Duncan's reconstructed card from school.

Wichita, Kansas: September 2009

D.J. and his mom were in the kitchen Friday afternoon. D.J. and Uncle John had a regular date most Saturdays, when Cliff was working. But D.J. did not want to go with Uncle John tomorrow. He told his Mom that Joey Nguyen, his best friend, had invited him to go to the state fair in Hutchinson. They would see the Demolition Derby. He'd gone to the fair before and seen the rodeos and some rock concerts, but never a Demolition Derby. Time was running out for letting Joey and Uncle John know what he was doing the following morning.

"Mom, you call him, pleeeease."

"Maybe Uncle John could go *with* you and Joey."

D.J. groaned, an exaggerated, exasperated, drawn out groan typical of a fourteen year old. He could imagine Uncle John in his dapper clothes walking around the fair with him and Joey and Joey's folks. They'd be their own freak show! Uncle John would try to be a good sport, maybe offer to treat them all to a ride on the camel. He'd probably control his response if the guide stopped the camel and Uncle John climbed down onto a chunk of camel shit, but his distaste would be obvious from the roll of his eyes and he'd be bitting his lip to keep from saying something sarcastic.

He'd probably like the sheep shearing and the birthing house sponsored by Kansas State's Agricultural Program, the only air conditioned building at the Fair. There you watched pregnant horses, cows, sheep, and pigs give birth, surrounded by nervous parents and gawking children with snotty noses and dirt streaked faces. Mom always said the parents brought their kids to the birthing exhibit to see in living color what they hoped never to have to talk about with their children. He remembered the steady buzz of ooos and ah-hhs from the audience as the poor animals strained to do their painful work in this theatre in the round. He remembered an almost-mother horse look-ing over her shoulder at him with an appeal in her eyes that he interpreted as saying, "How can a good looking thoroughbred keep a shred of dignity in these circumstances?"

There'd be an indulgent parent—usually a woman with a bachelor's degree--explaining reproduction to her three year old. Hadn't Mom done that with him? He remembered how embarrassed he'd been as she went on and on describing how the male pig's corkscrew penis straightened out before he slid it into the female to make a piglet. Factual and calm, she'd been. He remembered the other families standing around turning their attention away from the pig in labor to stare at his mom. Didn't she know this was Kansas? People don't talk about things like that in public. That part of the Fair would probably interest Uncle John.

Imagining Uncle John at the state fair in these circumstances made D.J. chuckle. He was enjoying himself.

It'd take a lot of self-control but Uncle John would probably keep quiet about the death defying deep fried Snickers bars and Twinkies. Even when the sirens sounded and the helicopter landed in the pasture where they parked the horse trailers to evacuate some three hundred pound woman who'd ingested one too many of these delicacies. Even then, Uncle John would remain under control. He'd keep quiet about the women in tight shorts and strapless stretchy tops, fat overflowing their push-up bras in the back and the front. Could they possibly think they looked "hot"??? D.J. carried a vivid picture of these women from previous trips to the fair. The marbled fat of their thighs was a sight to behold if you had the stomach for it. It moved as they walked, to the right and then, reversing direction, headed left like a hyped up glacier. Regular as clockwork, right then left, right then left. Someone ought to figure out how to patent that action. They could put the sleeping pill industry out of business, he thought, grinning at his own ingenuity. Could the women feel their mass of fat colliding like a pile up on the highway when it switched direction? He wondered.

Uncle John was a fitness junkie. He worked out an hour every day, determined, despite being over fifty, to keep his movie star abs. He could not abide fat and usually he said so. But he wouldn't say anything around Joey's family. For one thing, the Ngyens were not fat. Why were Vietnamese people all slender, D.J. wondered?

No, asking Uncle John to go with them to the fair was not an option. Not even if he might foot the bill for a ride in the helicopter, this year's new attraction.

He realized Mom was watching him, holding the phone, waiting to hit the speed dial. "It's your responsibility, honey." She passed the phone to him and stayed right where she was until he made the call.

No one answered. Uncle John must be out. That made it easier. D.J. left a cheery message on his answering machine, even suggesting that maybe they could get together on Sunday instead. He knew Uncle John and Cliff had a commitment to do things together, just the two of them, on Sundays so he felt safe covering himself with that message.

There was another reason he wanted to cancel with Uncle John this week. But he couldn't tell anybody.

Amy puttered about the kitchen Saturday morning after D.J. left for the Fair with the Nguyens. She had an open house from two to four, and she gathered her props in her large rectangular wicker basket: potpourri in jars with candles under them to scent the house, cookie dough in a refrigerated tube to squeeze onto her shiny baking sheets and pop in the oven just before two to give the house that inviting smell of cookies fresh from the oven, a brilliant bouquet of mixed flowers in a simple glass vase for the dining room table, a dozen roses in assorted colors with plain bud vases that she'd distribute throughout the house, her business cards, and copies of the house particulars.

She really liked her work. Every open house was an opportunity to invent a new story for her own future, imagining herself living in each space, sometimes with additional children coming to lavish kisses on her, all homey and loving, sometimes as a svelte single woman with lots of friends with whom she'd travel the world—soaking up sun on cruises to the Bahamas, walking the cobbled streets of picturesque Greek villages, climbing the ruins of the Roman Wall, oogling the army of life sized terra cotta soldiers in Xian, China. Rarely was there a man in her storyline. She had to confess that sometimes she added them for a night of passionate sex, but she'd write them out of her fantasies after the sex, moving them out by the next morning.

Now she paused as she wrapped sheets of plastic bubbles around the vases to keep them stable in the car. Why weren't there men in her concocted futures?

Maybe because she was a realist? Certainly she'd met no one who interested her in the nearly fifteen years since Duncan had disappeared.

Could it be because she liked being single? Certainly she'd grown into this life, literally grown, if she was honest about it. Gone up two dress sizes. Still, in Wichita she remained a good looking woman, everything being relative.

Carefully she lifted her basket of props and carried it to the small table at the front door where it would sit until she backed out her car and loaded it. She still had an hour before she had to leave, so she returned to her purple sofa and opened her laptop, deciding to check D.J.'s Facebook page. She'd allowed him to have a Facebook account on the condition that she could access it. Maybe she was too controlling, but on this condition she wouldn't budge. D.J. had protested but given in. He'd figured it was better to be on social media observed by Big Mama than to have to explain to his classmates why he wasn't there.

She looked first at his friends, chuckling to herself at the selfie photos they'd posted, posing with an abandon she never would have had at fourteen. Fourteen! Her age when she met Duncan.

She went to D.J.'s messages and scanned through them. Nothing alarming. The usual daring come ons from girls asking what he was doing, if he wanted to hang out, asking if he could help them with homework—D.J. helping with homework made her laugh out loud. Her son was not the scholarly type.

Then she happened on a message from his friend Adam. "I hate the way they make fun of me and I won't take it anymore. U R the only good person at Robinson. Call me and help me pay them back bigtime." Adam's message was bizarre and alarming. She wondered if D.J. had read it.

She wasn't sure what to do. She didn't remember an Adam among the kids who D.J. occasionally brought home to the house. She didn't remember him talking about an Adam. What kind of payback was he referring to? There had been half a dozen school shootings already this year, though nothing like the big one at Columbine in Colorado when D.J. was four. Should she call the police?

She heard the "da-da-da-da-daaaa" of the alarm on her phone that she'd set so that she'd get to the open house in plenty of time. She had to leave now to have time to set up. She decided she'd talk to D.J. when they both returned tonight.

She lugged the basket to her car and set it in the trunk, wadding blankets around it to keep it upright. She set the house alarm and locked the door, checking her face one more time in the mirror as she exited. Not bad for forty-five, she thought, as long as I keep my clothes on. Then she eased her Lexis down the drive, keeping it at twenty through Eastborough where the cops are vigilant and the fines pricey. When she reached Route 54, she let it climb to sixty, loving the feel of its power as it accelerated.

D.J. returned at eight that night, sweaty, sunburned, and tired out. September was still clocking temperatures in the eighties in Kansas, which made the fair hot and exhausting. Amy urgently needed to talk to him about Adam's message, but she decided their conversation would be more productive after he'd had a good night's sleep.

She left a note for him on the island in the kitchen where he normally ate breakfast, which he found when he pulled himself from sleep and made his way, yawning and stretching, to find some food. The note said not to go anywhere; she needed to talk with him and would return by 11:45, after church.

D.J. was glad his mom had found a church. Every time she made a connection with someone or some organization, he felt the press of his responsibility for her happiness lighten.

He'd had four texts from Adam while he was at the fair yesterday, the last asking to get together this afternoon. He texted Adam that he'd get back to him after he did something for Mom. Then he turned on the TV. Nothing. She'd be home too soon for him to get into his World of War game. He guessed he'd shower and get dressed so he could leave for Adam's after they talked.

Amy sang out "I'm ho-ome!" as she came into the kitchen through the garage. She set her purse on the island, bumping into one of the dangling pots and pans and setting them off bumping into each other and clanging. The racket reminded her of D.J. as a toddler sitting on this very floor spinning lids and banging pots. Parenting had been easier in those years!

She'd brooded over what to say to him all through church, barely following the words to the hymns, the scripture readings, the prayers of the people.

Normally she attended to the latter as they provided the latest news on the parishioners' lives, Mrs. So-and-So newly diagnosed with stage 4 ovarian cancer, Mr. Fill-in-the-Blank asking prayers for his grandson severely injured as he was biking along Route 70, etc. She'd gone because the church newsletter she'd found that morning in the wastebasket next to the printer said the sermon title was, "You Shall Know the Truth and the Truth Will Set You Free." That sounded relevant. After years of shutting down when anyone engaged in God Talk, she was slowly learning to set aside her kneejerk dismissal of anything to do with religion. Her default response was, she believed, her most lasting inheritance from Mother and Mother's Bible Belt beliefs. But for the past year she'd been attending a large church not far from their home where she could remain fairly anonymous.

The sermon had been helpful. It reinforced her inclination to go straight to the point with D.J.

She poured herself a cup of coffee, adding a dollop of real cream—she needed all the help she could get for this conversation, calories be damned—and heated it in the microwave. Carrying it carefully, she walked down the hall to D.J.'s room and knocked on his door. "Can we talk now, honey?" she asked, trying to sound warm and the opposite of anxious.

He opened the door, wearing his baseball cap and jeans and HEART T-shirt. She guessed HEART was one of the bands performing at the fair. The cap told her he was planning to go out.

"I'm going over to Adam's, Mom. Can it wait?"

Her eyes latched onto his like a guard dog on an intruder. "No, it can't. Where shall we sit?" Then, intuition trumping anxiety, she asked, "Want some lasagna while we talk? I made it last night for you."

"Sure, Mom, but why are you acting so weird?"

"Okay. Let's talk in the kitchen." She turned and walked back down the hall feeling anxious, and her coffee sloshed dangerously near the top of her mug. She barely averted spilling it. Whew. She set her coffee on the counter and removed the lasagna from the refrigerator, cutting a sizeable square for D.J. and putting it in the microwave. Then she got out salad greens to make him a salad. She was buying time.

"*Mom!* You have to turn *on* the microwave! And you *know* I don't like salad. What's going on?" He was sitting with his left buttock cheek on the bar stool, his right foot on the floor supporting him. He looked precariously perched, freeze-framed between sitting and rising, but she silenced her inclination to comment. She set the microwave, put away the salad fixings, and, when the bing sounded, removed the plate and set it before him with a fork, a hunk of garlic bread and a glass of milk. She pulled out the bar stool across from him and sat down, her eyes on his face as he devoured the lasagna.

"D.J., I checked your Facebook yesterday and saw a message from Adam that scared me."

He stopped chewing, his eyes wary as they rose from his plate to meet her indomitable gaze. No question he knew what she was referring to. She waited for him to speak, though the silence was uncomfortable.

"Adam's messed up. He takes a lot of bullying at school for being a nerd and a Goth, and a bunch of kids have been calling him 'queer' and 'gay.' I try to stick up for him, but they turn on me, too. At least they can't call me a nerd!" His face shifted to a grin. She heard his father in his self-deprecating humor.

"When Adam says he's going to get them back, do you know what he means?" She couldn't erase the tension she felt from the set of her mouth or the way her irises went deep and liquid. She didn't want to scare him, but…, Damn it, this was scary stuff.

D.J. took his own sweet time answering, popping a bite of garlic bread into his mouth and mechanically masticating it to pap. She guessed he was grabbing for time to figure out how to answer her. Don't rush him, she told herself.

He set his fork on his plate and wiped his mouth on the back of his hand. She'd forgotten to give him a napkin. He stared at a crumb on the counter, his eyes glazed. Finally he looked her in the eyes. "He has a gun, Mom."

She leaned on her elbows, resting her face in her hands, and cupping them over her mouth and nose. Her eyes focused on the lone geranium shoot sitting in water in a whiskey glass in the window over the sink behind him. She'd been trying to get it to grow roots.

"Has Adam told anyone what he plans to do?"

"He hasn't really told *me*. Just hinted in that Facebook message. Maybe he'll tell me something this afternoon. I'm scared, Mom. Adam's into some crazy shit—whoops, I'm sorry, Mom." He didn't swear in front of her. Not until now.

"We have to protect the kids he wants to hurt." Her voice was insistent. "We can't let him take that gun to school."

"But if I say something, he'll be in serious trouble."

"He's *already* in serious trouble, in life threatening danger." She reminded him of the school shootings, young male students with guns shooting their classmates and turning the guns on themselves.

"He says he'll be a hero if he pulls this off. No one will make fun of him ever again."

"D.J., *you'd be an accomplice to murder. They'll put you away, maybe even try you as an adult....*" The kitchen was silent except for the clunk-clunk of the icemaker.

"What do you *want* to do?" She was trying to let him know he was not alone, trying to help him come up with his own way out of this terrifying nightmare. But the problem solver in her could not remain leashed. "We could go to the principal, the police, or we could start with Adam's parents. We could call them now so that they can get the gun and keep him away from the school, get him help, get him to talk to the school counselor."

"Mom, I think he has more than one gun. And Mrs. Costello's a nice lady but I think this is way beyond her skill set."

Amy felt panic seize her gut. It traveled out to her arms and legs, leaving them weak and floppy. She reminded herself that she was the adult, but she could barely contain her terror. "You can't go to Adam's. You can't. Maybe we should bring Uncle John into this to help us figure out what to do."

"He'd tell Cliff and it would be all over Wichita by tonight. No."

D.J.'s phone binged. A new text had come in. Adam. Asking when he was coming.

"Text him you've been grounded." It was a command and he complied.

D.J. suggested, "Maybe we can call his folks and ask them to come over. Tell them it's an emergency? Then they can call the police or take his guns away themselves." He looked at her for her response.

She jumped on his suggestion, pulling her phone from her purse and dialing. Good thing she'd required he enter the phone numbers of all of his friends' parents in her cell. The phone rang and rang, then went to voice mail. She hung up and tried again. Nothing. And again. She was afraid to leave a message but more afraid of going to their house. On her fifth try, she asked them to call her immediately. It was an emergency.

They sat watching her phone, waiting for it to ring. D.J. said they were probably at Adam's sister's piano concert. Amy was imagining Adam's family lying in sticky pools of blood. God! What should they do?

Adam's parents didn't call.

At six o'clock, tired of pacing the kitchen, stomach acidic from all the coffee she'd been drinking, she got on her computer and located the name of the principal of Robinson, but there was no number, only a work email. She tried Information, using the house phone so as not to tie up her cell, but the principal's number was unlisted. D.J. was playing video games. She wondered at how calm he was.

By seven, the only incoming call was from someone who had come to her open house and had questions about possible financing, if they made an offer. She was too distracted to answer sensibly and begged off--"a family emergency"--she'd call him tomorrow. She turned on all the lights in the house and hovered on the bar stool reading and re-reading the same pages of the #1 New York Times best seller.

At seven thirty, she went to D.J.'s room. His door was open, which was unusual, and his curtains drawn. Maybe he needed open access to her as dark cloaked the house and obscured the unknown dangers lurking outside.

"I think we have to call the police." She looked at the back of his head seeking affirmation.

"Okay." He didn't turn around.

When two officers, one man and one woman, arrived at their door, Amy ushered them into the living room and called D.J. to join them. Together they recounted Adam's anger and distress at being bullied, his having more than one gun, their futile efforts to reach his parents, and the ominous words he had posted on Facebook. The officers made notes, asked questions, and assured them they would look into it now, before school started tomorrow morning. As they were leaving Amy asked how a fourteen year old could own guns. "Aren't background checks required?"

The woman cop told her that in Kansas anyone can buy a gun online or at a gun show without a background check. "Very easy to get them. The Kansas House's considering passing concealed carry legislation, maybe even open carry. Getting guns is a piece of cake here. I hate to say it, but we've been waiting for something like this to happen in Wichita, Ma'am."

Waiting! Waiting for her son and other people's kids to be gunned down by a desperately unhappy classmate? A surge of fury ran through her, and she squeezed her hands into white knuckled fists.

"You want us to get back to you, Ma'am?"

"Of course I do!" She was shaking as she closed the door behind them. When D.J. made some joke about her performance being good enough to get her on *Law and Order,* she cuffed him, then pulled him close and held on to him. She needed to feel his gangly body, warm and alive.

The woman officer called about nine thirty. Amy called D.J. and put the phone on speaker so they both could hear her.

She said Adam's parents had returned home to find him pacing the house ranting and furious. He'd heard Amy's voice message and was acting crazy. Not knowing how to handle him, his mom called the police and asked them to send their psychological team to the house. The department was short staffed and the psych experts off duty at the time, so the two officers who had interviewed Amy and D.J. went instead.

When Adam saw the flashing lights of the police car, his panic had seemed to escalate. His dad opened the door. The officers could see Adam behind his father holding one of his guns. He was cussing a blue streak and swearing that they would not take him. They tried to talk him down but he walked toward them, coming outside to the sidewalk and waving the gun around and yelling at them to go away. They'd *had* to fire. She was very sorry to tell them this. He was a smart kid, from all reports. She guessed it was a case of "suicide by cop." His family's taking it pretty hard.

Amy didn't remember anything after that.

Except that D.J. was glaring at her.

He began hitting the kitchen counter again and again till his hands were cut and bleeding. *"It's my fault,"* he kept repeating. *"It's my fault he's dead. I betrayed him."*

She stood by the sink, unable to move, unable to think, unable to speak.

After what seemed like a long time he stomped off to his room and pulled the door shut behind him. She could hear the lock slide into its nest in the door.

She heated a cup of soup for him, cream of tomato, his favorite, and made him a tuna fish sandwich, seeking to supply some normalcy, a part of her knowing that Adam's Facebook message ended their previous Normal. She knocked on the door to tell him what she had made for him. When he grumbled that he wasn't hungry, she returned to the kitchen and ate it herself.

At least he was safe. Alive.

Amy went with D.J. to Adam's funeral. They slipped into a seat close to the rear of the church. St. James was crowded with mourners, half of them from Robinson Middle School, by the looks of them. Kids. Some had hair streaked with unnatural colors, neon pinks, blues, and purples. Many of the girls wore brightly painted fingernails with intricate designs, sometimes a different color on each nail. There were a few Goths dressed all in black, hair spiked with gel to make it stand straight up. A few wore intricate tattoos. Lots of artistry being expressed, she thought. Observing fascinated and distracted her.

The pastor began the service noting the sadness of the occasion, always terribly sad when one so young dies, leaving the survivors with so many questions and regrets. The young congregation had been shifting in their pews, fluid and moving like a living organism, asking each other for tissues, whispering, heads close, putting backpacks on the floor and then retrieving them to put in or take out something else. But when the pastor spoke these words, their movement stopped and they watched him with intensity, even desperation, Amy thought. To her surprise, Adam's father came forward to speak, which produced a murmuring in the congregation. How could he bear to do this?

He was a tall man, tall and thin. The contours of his face were chiseled starkly by his grief, dark circles under his eyes and the space beneath his cheekbones hollowed and haunted like a moonscape. He told them about Adam, the violinist, the child prodigy who from an early age took things apart, "and together the two of us would figure out how to put them back together." Adam loved to read, especially fantasy fiction, which he also tried to write. He had a dozen stories he'd written about a character from Ancient Egypt who time-traveled to the present and hated it, wanted to return but couldn't find how to make his escape.

The church was completely silent as Adam's father ploughed bravely on. Amy felt a terrible sadness as the father painted a vivid portrait for them of his unique and gifted son. His next words were riveting.

"Adam was different, wonderfully different, but being different exacts a price. He was teased, even bullied, and school was very hard for him this past year. I know that each of you, each of us, is different, too, and that is hard." He took a deep breath and continued. "Adam can't pursue those things he loved now. He won't grow up to use his gifts to improve the world. But our family wants very much for his death to help others—especially you Robinson students and your families." He was fishing something out of the pocket of his sports coat. It was grass green and squiggly. He held it up and while he was talking slipped it onto his right wrist.

"As you leave here today, we ask you to take one of these bracelets with

Adam's name on it and to wear it to remind you that you and everyone you meet are unique—*different.* When you're feeling down, if someone is mean to you or bullies you, let your Adam bracelet remind you that you are not alone, let it help you talk about what you're experiencing with your family and friends, let it give you the courage to report the bullies and stand up to them." He lowered his head, nodded twice, then moved back to his seat on the front row where Amy could see between the heads in front of her a woman put her arm around him and hold on to him. Was she Adam's mom?

A number of Adam's teachers and classmates spoke after that, short comments like, "I'll miss you, man" from the guys and tearful remarks from several girls. Amy was surprised at all the tributes and tears from what D.J. had told her about how Adam was treated at school. She nudged D.J. to encourage him to speak, but the anger on his face made clear that it was best he not speak. They left immediately after the service ended, picking up their green bracelets and walking briskly to the car to avoid having to talk to anyone.

She started the ignition and backed out, paying close attention to the horde of young teens pouring from the church. When they were moving along a main road, she told him she was sorry she'd made him angry.

D.J. threw her another stormy look. "It's not you, Mom. It's all those kids and even a couple of the teachers. *If they'd said any of that to him before, he'd still be alive.*"

That evening her cell phone rang. It was Adam's mother returning the answering machine message Amy had left on Sunday-- just four days ago.

"You left a message for us Sunday afternoon. You said it was an emergency. I am so sorry we haven't gotten back to you before this. We've been dealing with a lot as a family lately. What were you calling about?" Her voice was soft and sounded vulnerable.

Adam's mother still didn't know. No one had told her. Amy knew that the police and the press were keeping the cause of Adam's death quiet, wanting to spare the family and to prevent other kids from attempting copycat shootings. Now Amy explained why she had called, that the emergency had been what Adam planned to do the next day at school to pay back his abusers. She heard his mother weeping softly. Maybe she shouldn't have told her. Then the phone went dead.

Two days later a letter arrived from Adam's parents addressed to D.J.:

Dear D.J.,

We want you to know how grateful we are that you were Adam's friend. He told us about you. Thank you for standing up for him. Thank you for caring about him when some of the other kids were cruel to him.

We are also grateful that you and your Mom tried to tell us what was going on with our son. He had to be stopped or many more young people would be dead, Adam among them.

Please know that you did the right thing.

Sincerely,

Gerry and Julie, Adam's parents.

D.J. showed her the letter, but said he didn't want to talk about it. Both Amy and D.J. wore their green rubber bracelets with Adam's name in white encircling their wrists for several months.

Two months later, Amy drove along route I135 south from Emporia through the Flint Hills. She loved this drive through what was to her the most beautiful part of Kansas: treeless high plains lanced by cracks and crevasses that caught and held the afternoon shadows. You could see the arc of Big Sky from horizon to horizon.

She needed the Flint Hills today. She'd been preoccupied by her worries about D.J. since Adam's terrible, unnecessary death. Her son seemed to be coping. He brought home Cs and Ds and spent a lot of time with his rock band, if you could call them a band. Thinking of them made her smile. Three fourteen-wannabe-eighteen year old guys with overactive hormones trying to attract girls by performing their funky music. Most of their melodies started with three notes thumping down the scale, bong, bong, bong, like the start of Three Blind Mice, and the lyrics were variations of "the girl who left me." But she gave them credit for trying and was grateful to have them practice in D.J.'s room. Having them there meant she knew where D.J. was, which relieved her anxiety. That was well worth the cost of a perpetual supply of pizza and soda. He still didn't like salad but recently had asked for apples. Apparently a girl in his class he liked brought apples each day, and D.J. had decided they were cool. One step at a time to healthy eating, she figured.

She was concerned by the smell that wafted out of his room when they took her up on the pizza. She wanted John's advice how to handle that topic with D.J. Weed was illegal and by some studies could fuzz your brain's functioning. With D.J.'s grades, it was obvious his brain cells couldn't afford to be fuzzed; they needed all the help they could get to stay focused.

D.J. didn't see Uncle John much now. It seemed a mutual easing up on the accelerator, like neither one knew what to say when they were together. John was busy and, as an academic, she knew he worried how D.J. could have a future if he didn't get more serious about school. She couldn't tell him that D.J. disliked school, that twice she'd found him at home when he was supposed to be at school. He would disapprove if she confided that D.J. had mentioned he might switch to the technical school. It wasn't that she liked this option. It was that she felt powerless to alter how he felt. If she pushed too hard, he might drop out altogether, and after school smokes might develop into something much more serious.

She scanned the horizon, so definite that line separating earth and sky, yet also misleading. In fact, the horizon was constantly moving. Like parenting. You think you know how to raise a baby and they turn into a toddler, a young child and they become a teen. None of her parenting strategies seemed to work for long. She had never been certain how to approach her son, and Adam's ghost reminded her that parental misjudgment could be lethal.

She wondered how different D.J.'s life would be if his father had stayed around.

She was driving past a reservoir, made before she was born, when the state of Kansas flooded several valleys that had originally been Indian burial grounds to make reservoirs. Sixty years later the skeletons of trees still poked their barren branches through the water, forlorn reminders of what might have been. "I can't do anything about what might have been." She spoke aloud to the air inside the car. "We've done pretty well, the two of us, overall." But D.J. wasn't finished yet, and the next four years were crucial.

She squinted and tugged the visor down against the afternoon sun that glared through her windshield.

Utrecht, Holland: Spring 2010

Elleke lost the battle over which university she would attend. But attending her father's alma mater in the fall of 2009 and studying archaeology and anthropology there pleased Jens so that he eased up on his need to control her. He paid her expenses, and she understood from Marika that he bragged about his eldest child attending Utrecht University. It was a compromise that worked for her, at least for now.

The University included a sizeable international student population. English was the medium of instruction and scholarships for internationals were plentiful. That fall Elleke made friends with Amagdi, a Palestinian from Jordan who was also studying archaeology. They both signed up to participate in a dig in Lebanon for their off campus spring "study away." Jens was too busy advancing his career to pay much attention to her plan.

In March they boarded a plane for Beirut. There a bus would carry them to the site of the dig.

On the plane she opened *The Guardian* to read that Israel with its ally, the Mubarak government of Egypt, was preventing aid and supplies of every kind from entering Gaza—school books, paper, pencils, erasers, medical supplies, and construction materials. The Israeli blockade was said to be strangling this small strip of Palestine, "the world's largest refugee camp." People there were hungry. The article said that Gazans relied on international food relief for their food supply and that Israel was preventing international food aid from entering Gaza.

Elleke knew little about Gaza, but Amagdi had family still living there, he told her. She asked Amagdi lots of questions about his family, whom he hadn't seen in years. Even if he could go home for a visit, he said, Israel would never allow him to return to Holland. Maybe it was like her own situation, being unable to return to Scotland? Whatever. Right now they both would focus on what they were learning of the Hellenistic period from the ruins they would be excavating and from their favorite professor who was leading the dig.

Bergama, Izmir, Turkey: Spring 2010

The lead archaeologist on the dig was Dr. Mustapha Essen. He approached the work with indefatigable enthusiasm. He never complained of the hot sun or the long days squatting hour after hour in the rectangular area cordoned off by rope that marked the boundaries of the find. He modeled patience and tenacity, regardless of leg cramps and back ache. He also modeled how to make interesting the meticulous work of brushing the ground with small brushes, sieving the dirt loosened, and chipping ever so gently with narrow nosed trowels to uncover buried objects. Talking with him they learned so much about the period they were uncovering, the Attalid dynasty, 281–133 BCE. They also learned about Professor Essen's other passion, contemporary Middle Eastern politics.

One afternoon the sun was particularly hot and the air loaded with red dust. It was gritty between her teeth and irritated her nose hairs so that she struggled to breathe without sneezing. Professor Essen suggested they take a break and rehydrate. While she and Amagdi guzzled water he spoke of the situation in Gaza. Later Amagdi told her he was certain Professor Essen was trying to express solidarity with him, knowing Amagdi was Palestinian. For whatever reason, Essen said he found what Israel was doing to the people of Gaza unconscionable, denying food and humanitarian supplies to almost two million people, half of them under fifteen and most living in refugee camps, barely surviving.

"Did you have family injured last year in Israel's Operation Cast Lead?" he asked Amagdi. Elleke felt embarrassed that she had no idea what Operation Cast Lead was. She didn't want to show her ignorance so she kept quiet and listened closely.

"I had cousins hit with white phosphorus," he said, his face grim. "Doctors from Norway were there volunteering when Israel first attacked. My cousin Miriam was in the hospital for several days. It took that long to pull out the needle-sized slivers of white phosphorus that entered her body and kept burning. The doctors had to use tweezers to remove them." Amagdi was shaking his head. "My other cousin they couldn't save. How can anyone use such weapons on children? Operation Cast Lead killed over three hundred people, mostly children, and Israel's bombs leveled UN facilities where food relief was stored."

He stood up and walked away from the worksite. They could see him pacing back and forth. After a while he came back, his face set, picked up his trowel and went back to work.

Professor Essen said it was a crime against humanity, what Israel was doing to the people of Gaza.

None of them spoke after that, the only sound the soft click of their trowels gently tapping shards of something hard they carefully worked to unearth. Elleke wondered why people take such care with inanimate objects buried for hundreds, even thousands, of years but use white phosphorus and explosives on living beings. Her head hurt.

One evening in April over their packets of prepared meals Professor Essen said he'd been thinking of joining an international flotilla being assembled by human rights and peace activists from Turkey, his home country. He said the flotilla would include over a thousand volunteers from one hundred and forty two countries who were going to try to bring humanitarian supplies into Gaza via the Mediterranean Sea. Because Egypt's military government was allied with Israel, neither country allowed supplies to enter Gaza through their land borders. Possibly they could get supplies in via the Mediterranean Sea?

Elleke looked up from her meal and stared at him, an idea percolating. Amagdi did the same. "Could we go with you?" she asked.

"Maybe." Dr. Essen's smile indicated he welcomed her question. "I had an email this morning from a colleague who's helping organize the flotilla. They plan to depart from Turkey the week we finish working here, so we *could* probably join them. If you're serious, I can check it out."

After Professor Essen went off to his tent to sleep, she and Amagdi stayed by the campfire talking about the situation in Gaza. It was growing dark and she confessed to her friend that she had never heard of white phosphorus weapons before their earlier conversation. Amagdi said they were banned by the UN, but Israel still used them. It frustrated her to know so little about what went on in other parts of the world. At the same time, knowing was disturbing. Now that she knew, she felt responsible for doing something.

She debated asking Jens for permission to join the flotilla and decided he would probably say no. She decided not to ask. If it was possible for them to go with the flotilla bringing in supplies to the people of Gaza, she would simply go. She'd inform him later. She would deal with his anger then.

Several weeks later Elleke, Amagdi, and Professor Essen were three of 581 passengers on board the ship *Mavi Marmara* steaming from Istanbul, Turkey to try to break the naval blockade Israel had imposed along the Mediterranean coast of Gaza.

The Eastern Mediterranean: Late May 2010

The *Mavi Marmara* had sailed out of Istanbul to reconnoiter with other ships from Greece and Turkey. Once massed, the flotilla set off, heading southeast toward the coast of Israel, aiming for the twenty-five mile strip of land called Gaza. They were careful to remain in international waters. They had informed the Israelis of their intention to deliver humanitarian supplies to Gaza.

The ship was quiet, most everyone asleep, readying their bodies for the morning's work of entering Israeli waters, breaking the Israeli blockade, and delivering supplies to Gaza.

Elleke couldn't sleep. She was sharing a cabin with three other women, all of them Turks, all of them, thankfully, English-speaking. She had awakened about three a.m. and had been unable to get back to sleep. After an hour, she decided to walk the circumference of the deck, hoping exercise would help. She left the room without awakening the others, climbed the stairs to the deck, and stood looking up, awed by the star-spattered sky. The heavens were saturated with darkness, making the stars stand out like white burning coals.

She heard something humming in the moonless night. Must be the engine. The noise grew louder, and she looked around trying to identify the source. Something dangled from the sky, actually many "somethings." They looked like giant spiders descending on black threads they'd spun, supersized and scary spiders, crawling down the threads, dropping to the deck, and moving across it like a sci-fi film.

Terror gripped her, stopping the scream that pushed up from her gut.

Suddenly a siren pulsed loud and shrill. From the stairway behind her the men of the flotilla surged onto the deck from below, running toward the spiders, flailing at them in a perfect storm of confusion, of gun shots, screams, and voices yelling in several languages.

She stood paralyzed by her fear. Then she felt an arm on her shoulder. An older woman wearing a coatdress, her headscarf tucked into her collar, had ahold of her arm and was gently pulling her away from the chaos, speaking reassuringly in words Elleke could not understand, guiding her to the stairs, away from the fighting. *What was happening?*

When the two women reached the dining room below the deck, one of the women gathered there told them that the spiders were Israeli commandos who had descended from helicopters onto the deck, armed and with their faces blackened, to capture the ship. That explained the humming. "But we're a peace movement. We're not carrying arms," another woman said in dismay. The women in the dining room murmured in agreement. They appeared stunned and confused. When it became clear that none of them had more information to help them understand what was transpiring above them on the deck, the women in the dining area grew silent, faces staring and blank, awaiting the outcome of the fighting overhead. It didn't take long.

Armed commandos threw open the door to the dining room, automatic weapons pointed at the women. One spoke in American English ordering the women to their cabins, proclaiming this ship was in Israel's waters and they were all under arrest. They would be brought into port and taken to prison. They would not be harmed if they cooperated.

The commandos locked them in their cabins.

Elleke sat in her cabin with three other women, trying to piece together what had happened. One of her cabin mates had gone on deck at the sound of gunfire and reported that she'd seen at least nine people from the flotilla lying in pools of blood. She said they were not moving. Elleke kept swallowing, trying to keep ahead of the saliva that filled her mouth, swallowing as though her life depended on it. Where were Amagdi and the Professor? Were they safe? She did not voice her fears, figuring they were all as scared as she was, each wrestling with their own terrors.

An hour or more passed.

They heard the ship's engine accelerating. When they looked out the porthole of their cabin, they could see lights in the distance growing nearer.

After a while, the ship cut its engine, and they heard male voices calling back and forth. Had they had reached a port?

In a short time the commandos returned, voices authoritative and brusque, ordering them out of the cabin and off the ship, onto the beach. "Take only what you can carry."

Dawn had begun to lift the dark, and as they walked down the gangplank, they could see soldiers in camouflage on the shore pointing big guns at them. One of the women whispered, "Made in the U.S. of A." Elleke thought she meant the guns. The soldiers used their guns to direct the *Mavi Marmara's* nearly six hundred passengers to nondescript white vans waiting for them. In groups of fifteen they boarded. When the vans were full, those on the beach continued standing in line while the vans pulled away. Elleke was in the first batch of those arrested.

There was little they could see of the port where they had disembarked. The vans had no windows so they sat in the dark squeezed together, no one saying anything.

When the vans stopped, she heard more shouting, and the side door of the van slid open to disgorge them. They moved forward in single file following orders and entering what appeared to be an office building. They shuffled through the dimly lit entryway, down concrete steps to a darkened hallway with barred doors on either side. A female soldier directed the women to the left. Doors clanged open and, after four women entered, clanged shut. "Where are we?" one woman asked, her voice strident. Elleke admired her courage. There was no reply.

The next several days sitting four to a cell in the cramped, chilly concrete rooms intended for one occupant, Elleke and her cellmates got acquainted. The women in her cell all covered their heads with scarves, they were all Muslims, all Turks. She asked about them and they asked about her. One was a university student, like Elleke, and one a psychology professor. One was a stay-at-home mom with three daughters and a son whose mother was staying with the children while she and her husband participated in the flotilla.

They didn't match her image of covered women. They were informed—indeed, they taught her even more than Amagdi had about the struggle of the people of Gaza. They were vocal, independent-minded, and compassionate. Two of them spoke Arabic as well as Turkish and English. They commended her for participating in bringing relief to Gazans and expressed their worry about her, being so far from home and among strangers. They told her they would consider her a sister.

The women speculated that they were being held in an Israeli military prison somewhere south of Tel Aviv. What would happen to the tons of building, medical, and school supplies on the *Mavi Marmara* intended for Gaza?

They reassured each other that certainly the world would be outraged by Israel's invasion of ships from sovereign countries that were in international waters! It was frustrating to hear no news of the world outside their cell.

On Day 2 Esme, the university professor, suggested they take turns teaching each other something each one knew. She'd read that Nelson Mandela and his friends had done this in prison on Robben Island, turning their prison into a kind of university. It would help the time pass. The others thought this a good plan. So it was that Elleke learned about Turkish cooking and the holiday of Eid and the five pillars of Islam—the testament of faith, prayer five times a day, giving to those in need, fasting during Ramadan, and making a pilgrimage to Mecca. In turn she taught the women in her cell about the North Sea coast of Scotland, digging for ancient remains, and the University of Utrecht.

Day 3 they talked about their families as they sat in a circle on the floor of the small cell. One woman told about her younger brother who suffered from diabetes who she loved very much and worried about constantly. Another spoke of her Nene, the grandmother who had raised her when her mother died of breast cancer. So vividly and caringly did her granddaughter describe her that Nene seemed present in their cell. Their third cellmate, the mother of four, spoke of her husband with such tenderness and respect that the others, all unmarried, told her that her words left them yearning for such a nourishing primary relationship. When it was her turn, Elleke spoke of her mother, of Ineke's creativity and her bravery as she faced death.

The conversations knitted connections between them and fed their hunger for home. Esme, the professor, said their sharing was a holy time, a blessing amidst the fear and uncertainty of their imprisonment.

While it was still dark on the morning of Day 5 a guard entered their cell to remove Elleke, saying something about the Embassy of the Netherlands insisting upon her release. It happened very fast and the guard would not permit them to exchange contact information. As she left her new friends and moved through the dark hallway away from these women and the intimacy they shared, Elleke remembered Mom's kaleidoscope moments. Surely this had been one of them.

A woman from the embassy signed for her release, securing her passport and the few belongings she had with her on the *Mavi Marmara*. She escorted Elleke to Tel Aviv airport and handed her a ticket to Amsterdam.

Within a few hours Elleke was back in Holland, disheveled, dirty, and exhausted. She saw her father striding impatiently back and forth as she emerged from customs. The look on his face would curdle milk.

Portsoy, Scotland: June 2010

Duncan and Needja returned from their Saturday walk on the braes invigorated. The gorse bushes along the trail were radiant with yellow flowers, and purple thistle and blue bells waved in the wind, summoning the bees. It was a lovely day.

He opened the door of Wee Cottage to discover a photograph of a cruise ship lying on the floor. He leaned down and picked it up, surprised at receiving what he saw was a postcard from Turkey, his only piece of mail in many days. It was from Elleke. He recognized the artistic upward flourishes she added to the last word in each sentence. The card was postmarked Istanbul. "Pappie," she wrote, "I'm on this ship taking supplies to Gaza. Don't tell Jens, please. More later. I love you so much! Elleke."

When he moved to Scotland fifteen years ago, Duncan had left behind his interest in international news. In Wichita, advising people on their investments, he'd needed to know what was happening in the world, but in this alternate universe of seventeenth century fishing villages and antiques made by people long dead, international news mattered little. If anything it added to his depression. He had readjusted his interests and tuned out politics. Consequently, the postcard made no more sense to him than if it had been mailed from Mars--except that it was from Elleke.

Their correspondence since the torn and taped birthday message had diminished to only an occasional note or card, and missing her had worn him down over the years they'd been separated. He disciplined himself not to think about her, other than the daily blessing he sent her way each morning upon awakening.

He got out his laptop and waited through its bells and bings while it worked its way to the internet. He keyed in "flotilla to Gaza" and was surprised to see ten or more pages of sources. He carried the laptop to his bed. Pillows propped behind him, he sat reading for a long time, his feelings shifting from curiosity to concern to panic. The most recent articles he found told of the Israeli military capturing a flotilla of six ships headed to Gaza carrying humanitarian aid and hundreds of volunteers from around the world. Israel's military had raided the largest ship, the *Mavi Marmara,* at 4 a.m. on May 31, with armed Israeli commandos lowered from helicopters to its decks.

He felt his skin go cold and clammy and could see the blood pulsing against the inside of his wrist as his heart became a jackhammer. Her postcard was dated May 29. She was on that ship! He read on.

The Israeli commandos killed nine people who were part of the flotilla, including an American citizen. One of the volunteers on board filmed the attack with a cell phone and posted the footage on YouTube.

He clicked on the links and watched, horrified. Then he watched again. He enlarged a still photo of flotilla volunteers in their orange life jackets giving a press conference. He scanned the faces looking for her. Nothing.

He madly searched for more information. He found photos of millions of people around the world protesting Israel's action. He read that the government of Turkey, outraged, had recalled its ambassador and canceled planned military exercises with Israel. The UN Security Council had called a special session on the attack because it occurred in international waters where military actions are banned by international law. Israel had seized the relief supplies as well as the participants, who, it claimed, had started resisting the commandos with knives and a gun. Israel defended its actions by saying it was protecting its citizens from Hamas, the elected government of Gaza. Israel said Hamas threatened its existence by firing rockets into Israel.

Israel had brought the six captured ships and nearly six hundred flotilla participants to Israel's port of Ashdod, near Tel Aviv. He found one photo of some volunteers on the beach there, awaiting the arrival of the rest of their group. He noticed a young red-haired woman sitting among them, slightly off camera. Could she be Elleke? Damn! Why hadn't he been following any of this? Now, when it mattered, he was lost in the details.

He could find nothing about what had been done with the participants.

Duncan tried to reach Elleke by email, snail mail, and phone. He wanted to respect her instruction not to tell her father, but he needed help finding her. He contacted the U.S. embassy, only to be told that, since she was a Dutch citizen and not a blood or legally adopted relation of his, their hands were tied. "Israel deported all but fifty of the six hundred plus people it arrested. She's probably safely back home, sir," the young man at the Embassy told him. He roamed the internet looking for stories and names of people who were on the flotilla. The flotilla was no longer "news" and stories about it in the press had dwindled.

A week after he received Elleke's postcard, he could restrain himself no longer. He called Amsterdam and asked the woman who picked up the phone if he could speak with Jens.

"May I tell him who's calling, please?" Her voice sounded wary.

"This is Duncan Allan, Elleke's stepfather. I am trying to locate her." He stopped, unclear how much to say to her.

"She is back at the University, Mr. Allan. I think it best that you not talk with Jens right now. He is very upset with her. I don't know if you know that Jens was elected to Parliament as a member of the People's Party for Freedom and Democracy. Elleke's adventure with the flotilla has had repercussions for Jens. But at least she is safely home. You don't need to worry about her."

He sat down, his relief palpable. "I've been trying to reach her but no one responds." He probably sounded pathetic.

"Jens made her change her phone and email and apartment to keep the press from contacting her." The woman hesitated and he had the impression that she was not alone. When she spoke next her voice was very soft, almost a whisper. "I'm Elleke's stepmother, Marika. I'll send you her new contact information. I must go now."

That was the end of the conversation.

Elleke was safe! He missed her acutely and longed to hear her voice and listen to what she had experienced. But knowing she was safe would have to suffice for now.

Marika kept her promise and sent him Elleke's new addresses. He emailed her immediately telling her how proud he was of her courage. Questions spilled from his fingers onto the computer monitor. He heard back within a few hours.

Dear Pappie:

The flotilla was the most important thing I have ever done. I grew up in that week, came to know evil and good in new ways. Prison was difficult, but being there with so many other women strengthened me. It also cost me.

My father is very angry with me. He's into politics now and good friends with the man expected to be our next foreign minister. The man is married to an Israeli and very pro-Israel. Father insists my behavior has jeopardized his career. He forbids me to be involved with the Palestinian cause or he will withdraw all financial support for my university degree. I've decided I must obey him until I graduate in December 2013. After that I plan to take my stand.

I want to see you, but, you can imagine that Vader totally opposes my relationship with you. I've given up trying to convince him. I don't forget you and won't, but until I graduate, I must obey him. I am sorry that our contact must decrease for now. I will come to see you after I finish university.

Much love,
Elleke.

He could wait until then, he told himself, but as the next three years unfolded with no word from her, he retreated into the hermetic life he had lived when he first arrived in Scotland. Before his ten years of happiness. Without nourishment his hope dried up and the Arctic winds carried it away.

Portsoy, Scotland: September 2013

He sat solidly in his captain's chair at a desk in the front left of the appallingly crowded Portsoy store, where he could observe all areas of his shop while being barely noticed by shoppers. Not that there were many of those.

He was surrounded by clocks. Dozens of clocks from all eras hung on the walls crowding each other and reaching all the way to the ten foot ceiling. Clocks ticked softly or click-clacked. Some chimed each quarter hour. Because he did not care, the clocks went off when they wanted to. Twelve o'clock could go on for a good fifteen minutes.

Highboys, wardrobes, tables, and buffets consumed the floor space, leaving narrow pathways from the front to the back of the store. Every surface sported small porcelain figurines, lamps, and objects that defied description. Few people entered his shop and most, if they did, regretted it within minutes. The shop grabbed your attention and subdivided it, then subdivided it again and again as the plethora of objects drew your eyes from one to another. The visual confusion was compounded by aural overload--especially when the higher numbered hours of the day set the clocks coming, coming, coming like a cacophony of loud orgasms from unknown and resented strangers in the next room at a seedy motel. That experience was enough to drive the most dedicated shopper out of Cruickshank's Antiques.

Add to the sights and sounds the owner himself with his wary, hooded eyes that roved the room like the Grim Reaper. He made no effort to engage new customers in conversation and most left the shop within minutes.

In the three years of no contact with Elleke, Duncan became an unpleasant man, silent, miserable, and easily provoked. Since Ineke's death he had held onto the hope that they would reconnect as family, but now that hope seemed to be a misguided fantasy. Elleke must have moved on with her life.

This loss was too much. He retreated to the anti-social behavior he'd adopted when first he came to Scotland--only now his shaggy shoulder length hair, his thick, unruly eyebrows that looked like someone had rubbed them with good Scots wool to make them stand up, and his untidy facial hair were freckled with white. The locals who had observed his unraveling felt sorry for him and smiled encouragement to him, despite his lack of response. Newcomers viewed him as a grouchy recluse. His eyes behind his half-spectacles scanning constantly, avoiding direct contact with anyone, made them uncomfortable. When the odd shopper asked him about his merchandise or about the village or his years there, he abruptly brushed them off.

"I don't believe in talking about personal matters. What's here is marked. Look at the tags and you'll have no need to bother me." The accent was not Scottish, though he'd added a Scottish lilt to some of his words. Maybe American? Whatever, he seemed the least likely person to operate a commercial venture. More likely to dissuade than to invite purchases.

One afternoon an older couple on holiday from the States entered the shop sporting open faced smiles characteristic of retired couples enjoying their holiday and each other. Their expressions clearly irritated him. He'd cultivated a fierceness that kept him apart from other people, unapproachable and unknown. He clearly had no intention of relinquishing his control of what transpired inside this—*his*—space.

The American woman, however, was a slow learner, although she never would admit it. She prided herself on having the knack of getting the most reclusive of persons to tell her their story. Now she pried from him some basic information, using her usual tactic of fast fired questions that she counted on to break down her target's resistance. He released answers reluctantly and with a bad tempered scowl.

How long had he been here? *"Twenty years."*

Where did he live before? *"Elsewhere."*

Did he like it here? *"People hereabouts leave each other alone."*

Then a sleeper that brought him close to a revelation: What brought him to this fishing village on the North Sea coast? *"A woman."*

"I've heard that in Scotland church attendance has dropped off by a huge

percentage during the past twenty years. In your experience is that true?"
Now the woman had gone too far.

This question brought him to a boil. *"In my experience church attendance is hoodoo. But then you Americans are bamboozled by church and archaic notions of God, even when the rest of the world knows better. In my experience God is a joke and anyone who believes otherwise is ignorant and imbecilic. Now, have you finished your shopping?"*

His eyes stopped darting back and forth and closed on hers, ferocious and angry. Finally the woman got it; she had met her match. She remained civil, said a stiff goodbye, and they left his store and went on their way, enjoying the sunshine and putting the unpleasant antiques dealer out of mind.

The next morning when the couple had coffee at the home of a resident of the village, the American woman asked the Scots woman if she knew the antiques dealer up on Seafield Street.

"Ah, you have met Duncan!" she replied. "Duncan is our #1 example of how this village provides refuge to all sorts of people. Did he chew you out for entering his shop?" Her eyes twinkled.

"Sort of. He intrigued me. There must be a back story to explain his rudeness," the American replied.

"I'm sure there is, but I'm equally sure no one will ever hear it from him. He arrived here nearly twenty years ago."

"With a woman?"

"Heavens, no! He came alone and lived like a hermit, rarely coming out of his Wee Cottage all winter. He took his time sorting out what he could do to earn a living, I guess. He ended up apprenticing himself to an elderly man well respected in these parts, George Cruickshank, who had an antique business but could no longer handle the work of hauling and lifting. Eventually the old man retired and Duncan took over his shop. He had a woman and a darling child for a time, but the woman died and the child was taken from him. He's an odd one, he is, but I guess we are all a bit odd up here. Maybe that's what brings us here to the end of the world where there is nothing between us and the Arctic but the sea."

That night Duncan's loud groans half-awoke him. The dream was back. It recurred regularly when he first made the move "across the Pond" all those years ago, but over time its frequency had diminished so that its reoccurrence now was doubly disturbing. He had thought he was recovering. Yet here he was, drenched in sweat, sounds jumping out of him from somewhere deep inside, clashing and colliding in desperation. He was fleeing for his life through a dark wood with the trees reaching out to impale him. Birds flew at his face squawking, blue, black, and white magpies mostly, very large and intelligent birds. He kept on running, crashing, stumbling, falling, scratching his arms, his face, getting up again as he realized that there was no escape. It was terrifying. He was totally out of control, disoriented and lost.

He reached for the bottle on his bedside table. It was more than half gone. Consuming too much liquor was another development of the past few years. He poured what remained into the glass and tossed it back, savoring the hot path it made from his throat to his belly. He showered, changed clothes, and lay back down on the bed, seeking the solace of sleep. Instead, that woman with her damn questions appeared in his mind's eye. Now his dream shifted to the woman and a dozen who looked just like her circling him and throwing out questions he did not want to think about, much less answer.

He reached again for the bottle, but it was empty. He got up and searched for another, but he had no more. He turned on the television to some mindless reality show which only infuriated him. How could people diminish their tragedies like that, spilling them out for an audience that cared nothing about their pain, only about being titillated and entertained. He brought his hand down hard on the television, nearly toppling it, turned it off, and returned to bed. Sadness took him over, and he lay on his stomach, face in the pillow that muffled his sobs. Some hours later his bladder gnawed him awake. He decided a shower might relax him. He stood extra minutes in the shower with the water scalding hot. When he finished, he saw in the mirror that his skin was raw and red, which gave him some relief.

Aberdeen, Scotland: October 2013

The young man pulled on his jeans and topped them with a faded T-shirt and a wooly sweater he'd bought at the Charity Shop. He stepped into his boots, swilled a cup of coffee and was out the door. His mother had bought him those Red Wing boots as a special present for his eighteenth birthday. So like her to buy him what she knew he would love and couldn't afford, despite the thousands of dollars she had poured in vain into trying to get him "on his feet" and productive. She had been his best friend for most of his life, consistently encouraging him and supporting whatever he wanted to do or not do with his life. Mostly it had been what he wanted not to do. He'd dropped out of high school, dropped out of technical school, given up on a dozen jobs within the first three weeks, and broken up with every girl who tried to get close. Still his mother loved him and assured him that he would figure it out, would find his way.

He'd tried forming a rock band, writing songs for his buddies and him to play at occasional gigs, all of them volunteer and most of them unsuccessful. Audiences would listen to their first song and maybe to the first half of their second, then walk away one by one till his band was left playing to an empty house. Well, not exactly a house. A room with four or five tables, all vacant.

He had tried construction until a hammer came down on one of his fingers and it swelled up and turned black under the nail so alarmingly that he had to heat a paperclip with a match and force it down through the nail, releasing a spray of blood.

He tried cooking for an upscale Mexican restaurant at Waco and Tenth in Wichita, but the grease was so hot he worried that he would set the whole place on fire. It also spattered and burned small red dots into his hands and forearms. He hated smelling like fried food, so he quit.

Next, at his mom's suggestion, he got a job at the nursing home. But lifting old people on and off the toilet and cleaning up the shit they could no longer control was too much for him.

Last spring his Uncle John suggested he try working on an oil rig in the North Sea. Uncle John had told him, "Once you are out on the rig you can't just walk off the job, since you are surrounded by the sea and roughnecks who don't tolerate weakness. These guys consider changing jobs every few weeks the sign of a lack of character." It sounded like the best possible situation for a young man who ran through jobs faster than girlfriends. Sounded adventurous to D.J. Hell, it would get him far from Wichita, which definitely appealed to him. If he failed at working the rigs, no one back home needed to know it.

Typically, Uncle John researched oil drilling sites and made contact with a manager there who he knew through Wichita-based Koch Industries, the largest private oil company in the world. That guy suggested Aberdeen, Scotland, one of the richest locations in the English speaking world for off shore drilling, and set him up with someone there who was hiring. Uncle John even bought him an air ticket. Dear Uncle John.

That was six months ago.

D.J. made friends readily, being a generally nice guy, generous to a fault and the opposite of arrogant. The work was strenuous, but having no option but to stick it out helped. He made friends with several Scottish guys his age who became his drinking buddies. Mom would be unhappy if she knew he went to the pub every night when he was off the rig, but this was Scotland where every red blooded man hung out at the pubs. When in Rome, and all that.

D.J. liked living far from home much more than he'd expected. You worked hard but, as his buddy said, they were young and "thrawn" and the pay was better than anything he could get back in Kansas. *And* he wasn't wiping up shit!

One of his new Scottish friends proposed they use their next two weeks off to travel by bus west along the North Sea coast and on up north to the Orkney Islands. They'd buy a bus pass and hop off whenever the spirit moved them. The guy's extended family was well known in these towns, owned the major furniture and fine housewares business across the Northeast, with Cruickshank stores in most of the coastal villages. They would end up in the Orkney Islands, visit some archaeological sites and local fishing museums, do some hiking, and take a ferry from the islands back to Aberdeen at the end of their two weeks. The proposal sounded like fun to D.J. On the first of October the two set off, traveling on Stagecoach Bus 35 and planning to stop in Portsoy, Cullen, Buckie, Elgin, Inverness, and Wick before taking the ferry out to the islands.

His friend Drew talked a lot about his grandfather, apparently a good guy who had established antique shops in some of these towns. Never quite measured up to the financial success of the furniture and housewares branch of the family, but Drew said his granddad had been known and respected in the area. Drew wanted to pay his respects at his granddad's grave.

D.J. wished he had a grandfather. Mom's father died of alcoholism in his fifties and his unknown father's father in a car accident, even younger. Must be nice to have happy memories of a wise old man who taught you skills and encouraged you to follow your dreams, he thought.

They were riding the bus their first day away from Aberdeen and the rigs. He'd only half heard Drew going on about how his father and his uncles had all moved south to where jobs were more plentiful for career advancement. (Drew was a talker.) The moves meant that the old man was left to fend for himself in the under-populated Northeast of Scotland where the cold of winter demanded rigor and stamina rare in old people. Drew said something about an American who had turned up and taken responsibility for the old man in his final years, even moved him into his own house when he got too sick to work. (D.J. tried hard to focus on Drew's overlong story.) It seemed every holiday someone in Drew's family would offer a toast to the American—whose name Drew couldn't recall—for giving their elderly loved one care when he most needed it. It irritated Drew that none of them had stayed in touch with this man to tell him face to face how much they valued his relationship with his granddad.

When they stepped off the bus on Seafield Street in Portsoy, Drew asked the driver which way to the cemetery. As they walked downhill toward the harbor, he continued his monologue.

"I want to find the man and thank him. Granddad had a shop here in Portsoy as well as in Cullen and Buckie. After we find his grave, maybe we can find the shop here and see if anyone knows what's become of him."

The cemetery sprawled down a steep graded hill stopping before it reached the sea. It was large and the stones were bigger than any D.J. had seen back home. It resembled a natural amphitheater facing the water. Easy to picture the hundreds of people buried here observing whatever comes next from the best seats in the house! He chuckled at his own humor.

They walked down the path and opened the wrought iron gate. They leaned their back packs against the rear wall and Drew strode across the soft grass downhill, stopping to read some of the stones.

"What are we looking for?" D.J. asked as he followed him.

"Cruickshank, Molly McDonald and George."

D.J. noticed that the slabs were engraved with a lot of writing—where the person was from, their career, the names of family members with dates of births and deaths. The women were named by their maiden names as well as their married names. He'd never seen that before. He asked Drew, "Why are there so many people named on each stone?"

"Because they're all buried there on top of each other. Family come back together in death. Except where someone was lost at sea or moved to America, New Zealand, Australia, India, Africa—one of the colonies--or was killed in one of the wars. Even then they're named on their parents' stone."

D.J. began reading the stones. There it was, carved in stone, so-in-so and his wife and his sons and daughters and where each died, all named and claimed forever as family by careful carving on hard granite. He felt a rush of loneliness. "So your dad and mom will be buried here, too?" He was thinking that all he had was his mom back in Kansas, his only family, other than Uncle John. It was hard to think of Cliff as family; their relationship had never recovered from his childhood invasion of their bedroom.

"Not everyone follows the tradition any more. Lots of people are cremated now, but even then their names are usually added to the stone...Here it is!" Drew squatted in front of a large gray stone with CRUICKSHANK centered across the top of the slab, then "Molly McDonald, beloved wife of George Cruickshank of Cullen and himself" with their dates. There was plenty of space left on the stone. One day Drew could be buried here with his granddad and the rest of the family. D.J. felt jealous.

Next to the large stone sat a small one, the size of two bricks, bearing one word, "Ineke" and the dates, 1965-2006. D.J. wondered why it was so small and whether Ineke was a Cruickshank. Dang, she hadn't lived very long!

There was a pot of flowers planted in the ground between the two stones. Despite it being October, some of the flowers were still blooming. Drew said they were poppies, the flowers of remembrance.

D.J. turned away to allow Drew privacy if he wanted to say a prayer or something. He settled himself on the soft, spongy grass, and looked out at the sea. Almost immediately he realized that sitting on the grass had been a mistake. It had rained before they arrived and the grass was not only cushiony but full of water that he could feel seeping through his jeans. Damn it. Oh, well. Too late now.

He looked at the cliffs that grew almost straight up from the sea, like giant, slumbering creatures curled toward the shore. There was so much color in the moisture laden world he surveyed. The greens of the grass and bushes and trees, the blues and grays and greens of the sea that kept moving sluggishly back and forth. He was a Kansas kid, ocean deprived. Since moving to Scotland, he'd found the sea and its perpetual motion magical, its rhythms comforting. The men on the rig taught him how to identify the sea birds. He loved watching the wide white wingspreads of kittiwakes and gulls and the inky black cormorants flying overhead. He liked observing them as they gathered in conventions on the rocks of the tidal pools, calling to each other amiably.

Atop the cliffs the fields spread out away from the sea. The stubble from the harvest was so thick you couldn't see the dirt. The sprawling fields with their isolated farmsteads reminded him of Kansas, as did the Big Sky. He was glad he'd taken the risk and left home to relocate here, thousands of miles away. Way to go, D.J., he congratulated himself. Mom and Uncle John probably thought they were the only ones who wanted him to find his way, but he wanted to feel at home in a place and commit to some kind of work. Knowing you're disappointing folks sucks. One thing about being here...he was too far away to see Mom's "I need to encourage him" face or the anxious look in her eyes.

He felt the wetness penetrating his shoes, glanced down at his soggy feet, and wiggled his cold toes. He noticed a shining spider web stretched from the nearby gravestone to the grass. Perfect circles of shimmering light lay along each blade of grass, so bright that it took him some moments to realize what they were--the residue of raindrops, caught and held by the surface of each blade. The recent rain had deposited these water gems like rows of tiny diamonds glimmering in the afternoon sun. The grass bent with their weight. He watched them, transfixed.

Drew touched his shoulder. "Okay, man, time to find the antiques store before it closes," he said. D.J. picked up his backpack and slung it over his shoulder. Together they walked uphill to exit the cemetery where they had entered.

Unfortunately, when they got back to Seafield Street, most of the towns' stores were dark, locked up, shades drawn. Drew wanted to ask some of the locals about his grandfather's store in Portsoy and about the man who'd run it since his granddad's death, so they headed back down to the harbor to the old pub that the woman at the Coop Grocery said was the favorite of the locals.

At the pub an old timer told them that Cruickshank Antiques in Portsoy was only open by appointment now, but the Cruickshank Antiques Shop in Cullen was open till four most weekdays. The man Drew described could probably be found there. They thanked him, settled in for some fish and chips, and a pint, of course, and located a room at the Boyne Hotel for the night. The next morning, recovering from too many pints, they slept in, ate a full Scottish breakfast of ham, eggs, sausage, mushrooms, tomatoes, and toast, and then, feeling well stoked for the next leg of their adventure, hoofed it up to Seafield to get back on Bus 35 to Cullen.

They got into Cullen at noon, but the hand lettered sign taped to the door said the shop was closed until two. Drew suggested buying sausage rolls and wandering down to Cullen harbor where they could sit on the harbor wall and watch the boats. At Rockpool Café they bought sausage rolls and choco-late pastries. The woman who took their order chatted with them and, when she learned they were just passing through, suggested they might want to walk the old railway viaduct that ran parallel to the coast and eat their lunch sitting up there overlooking the city and the harbor. When they stepped out of the shop and looked north toward the sea, they could see the old bridge with its wide arches that formerly carried trains through Cullen. They fol-lowed her instructions to find the stairs leading up onto it.

It was a lovely early fall day, full of promise and sunshine. They enjoyed watching the sea and looking down on the steep roofs of the New Town where houses for the fishermen crowded close together just back from the harbor wall. Heading back toward Cruickshank's Antiques, they stopped off for a hearty bowl of Cullen Skink, the haddock soup the town was famous for, and some of the local dark, seed-dense bread. Drew joked that they were "growing lads." By then it was two-thirty and the sign on the door of the shop said OPEN, so they turned the knob and walked in to a cacophony of clocks announcing the half-hour.

The proprietor didn't look like a Good Samaritan, but Drew ploughed ahead with his prepared speech.

"I be looking for a man that helped me granddad run his antique stores for many a year. Granddad was George Cruickshank."

The stern faced disheveled man looked sharply at the lad, his closed face a cypher. Drew came up blank when he tried to read the man's expression. All he could make out was distrust.

"Why are you looking for this man?" The man's voice was gravelly and suspicious.

"This may sound daft to you, sir, but every Christmas my family lifts a glass to toast this man's kindness to Granddad. I've seen them do it many a year for as long as I have remembrance. But to my knowledge none of us has ever been in touch with the fellow since Granddad died to tell him how grateful we be. Me and my buddy here, we work the rigs and had two weeks' holiday, so we decided to come look him up and remedy years of the family's neglect." He was stretching it a bit to lay their entire holiday on coming to thank a stranger, but his smile and the way his eyebrows were drawn together, his blue eyes so earnest and childlike, well, it was sort of convincing. Drew Cruickshank could charm the ear off a pig, his mother always said. He waited for the man to respond.

The man was clearly considering his options. He took his time. Finally he shrugged and said, "I guess you found him." His accent was a queer mixture of American Midwest and Scots flavored with a bit of the King's English—hard to place. He seemed uncomfortable when Drew stuck out his hand and with a grin half shouted, "Well, I'll be damned! We did it. It warms my heart to meet you, sir. On behalf of me family, of all Cruickshanks, please accept our thank you for what you did for Granddad in his final years. I loved him greatly and am in your debt forever, Sir."

The man shook Drew's hand with some hesitance and they thought he muttered something like, "Your granddad was proud of you." Then he seemed to retreat behind the worktable piled with books and bric-a-brac.

D.J. picked up a porcelain dog that he thought his mother might like and took out his credit card to pay for it. The man grumbled under his breath about the charges he paid on credit card transactions, but he swiped the card and passed the receipt to D.J. to sign, saying nothing more.

The young men waited, hoping for more response from the man, but he seemed closed down, hiding behind his books and collectibles. A long, awkward moment passed, anti-climactic and disappointing. Drew said they'd been to the cemetery in Portsoy and visited Granddad's grave. He asked the man who had been taking care of it, to which the man replied, "That would be me." He appeared exhausted by their brief interaction.

Drew glanced at D.J. who shrugged his shoulders. They thanked him, said goodbye, and left the shop. Walking back to the bus stop, they agreed that this man was totally weird. "Have you ever met anyone more uncomfortable around other people? I thought Dick Anderson was strange, but this guy, well, he makes Dick look normal." D.J. was referring to a guy who worked the rigs with them who the rest of them thought strange and sometimes bullied.

The visit to Cruickshank's Antiques left them both feeling down. At Drew's suggestion they stopped by a pub for a Guinness before catching the bus to Buckie where they would spend the night.

"Fuck it, we never even got his name," Drew swore as they settled themselves on the bar stools and took their first sips.

"Well, I think going back there would be a waste of time, man. That dude must of drunk vinegar instead of his mother's milk, poor guy. You did what you came to do. We found him and you thanked him. Now we can find us some fun." D.J. noticed two attractive girls who looked to be their age enter the pub and glance at them. He was ready to shake off this strange day of cemeteries and families reuniting in the grave and an anti-social older man who didn't know how to function around other people. They picked up their drinks and moseyed over to the round table at which the girls had seated themselves, and he banished the miserable man from his thoughts.

Inside the shop Duncan Allan locked up and carried his cash box to his car, which was parked in the alley behind the shop. He would drive home and go over the day's receipts in the Wee Cottage in Portsoy. He was glad to meet Drew Cruickshank, glad to know he remembered his granddad enough to make this trip to his grave. He drove past the house where Mr. Cruickshank had been living when he first fell, when Duncan had found him and nursed him. He remembered how fortuitous the Old Man's fall had been for his relationship with Ineke. "Without his fall, would I ever have acted on the attraction I felt for her?" He heard his voice inside the car and smiled to himself.

It felt strange to smile. I don't do that often, he thought. Well, thank you, my friend, for bringing us together. I hope you know you made your mark on us all, including your young grandson.

He turned left to drive by the Cullen house the four of them had shared.

It showed no signs of life, garden untended and window shades drawn.

He pulled up in front of the house and turned off the engine, letting his thoughts come. The car windows were up and, anyway, who cared if anyone heard him talking to himself. "I could have offered this place to the grandson as lodging for a night or two. No one's using it. But I'm out of practice being hospitable. Like smiling, it doesn't come easily any more.... Come to think of it, being hospitable to Mr. Cruickshank opened up what was good in my life."

That was nineteen years ago!

"It also brought me the pain of losing them." For seven of those years he'd lived alone, except for Needja, without any of those people who had become his family, who he had loved, who anchored him to the sunny side. Needja had kept him going, but he was getting on, not nearly as spry as he'd been. They had their rituals that would keep them both going until.... He sighed, not wanting to think about losing Needja, too.

He was glad to meet the Cruickshank boy, who he vaguely remembered as one of the rambunctious grandkids from their trips to bring the Old Man to the Borders to visit his sons. He'd probably not see the boy again, which might be different if he'd had the sense to offer hospitality. Oh, well. Too late to look for more in this life.

He started the car and drove back to Portsoy, pulling into the driveway that led back behind his neighbor's house where Wee Cottage stuck out like a thumb, invisible from the street. It was only accessible if you knew which driveway to enter. A perfect place for a hermit. He put on the electric kettle and, when it was boiling, poured water into his tea pot and let it steep while he got out some shortbread. It had been a strange day, with Mr. Cruickshank's grandson coming by to thank him. If he'd had his wits about him he'd have told the boy that it was he who should be saying thank you, since his years with Mr. Cruickshank, Ineke, and Elleke were the happiest of his life. Too late now. He sat on the ladder back chair that wobbled uncertainly on the cobblestone floor of the cottage and went over the day's receipts while he had his tea.

He had folded the credit card receipt. Now he unfolded and smoothed it and recorded the amount paid. As he was setting it back in the box where he kept receipts, his eye noticed the almost illegible, American signature, vertical letters, large and almost printed but too close together to be easily read. He looked closer. There was no mistaking it. The signature read Duncan J. Allan.

He went to the table that served as his desk and powered up his laptop, waiting impatiently as it clicked and tinkled loading and cycling through its security checks. He googled "Duncan J. Allan" and then on impulse added, "Wichita, Kansas." When the screen opened to a dozen entries, he exhaled loudly, surprised to realize he'd been holding his breath. Several photos in small boxes lay across the screen like railroad cars carrying faces of men of various colors and ages all named Duncan Allan. One brought him up short. It was himself when he joined Ameriprise back in his twenties. He scrolled through the Google results. He found a resume that listed under experience an assortment of jobs in retail and service, including working at a nursing home, all of them briefly held. There was a Facebook account with no photo, only, "To see what Duncan shares with friends, send him a friend request."

He found a website for aspiring musicians to post their songs. A promo photo showed three guys in saggy jeans and T-shirts, arms tattooed with dragons more or less artfully burned into their skin with red and green and black dye, two of them with guitars and the third behind a set of drums. He thought the drummer might be the young man who'd been in his store.

He made a mental list of what he'd learned. There was a Duncan J. Allan in Wichita, a young man who held a variety of jobs and played in a band. That was it. Nothing announcing sports teams or awards or graduation from any school, no home address or parents named. Not much to go on, but enough to suggest he might have kin still in Wichita. This Duncan Allan could be the child Amy was carrying, could be John's child. He supposed it was even possible that the kid was his own.

The thought terrified him.

It had started to storm and the television weather report said they were in for a gusty one. He put on his boots and rain parka, pulled the hood up, and left the cottage with Needja to walk to the harbor. He could hear the sound of waves crashing noisily against the walls of the harbor and the after sound of frenzied foam arcing over the harbor wall and shattering on the cobblestones. He loved storms like this, loved how out of control the sea was, surging from several directions at once, waves running into each other and exploding as they made contact. Old timers, lifelong fishermen, talked about the sea as a living being who could not be pacified once riled. They talked of it "taking my brothers, my father." Standing on the cobblestones with only the low harbor wall between him and the waves, he understood. There was an anger in its churning and a dominance that would brook no dissent. Giant waves pummeled the walls and assailed everything within their reach.

He was standing three feet from the retaining wall watching their drama when a shaft of erupting water hit him from the side, buckling his left leg and knocking him off his feet. He gasped in surprise, sucking in some of the salty spray. He pulled himself to his feet, coughing and spitting, and looked around for Needja. The dog had retreated to the doorway of The Shore Inn, where he stood shivering, head and tail down, wet fur slicked to his body. Duncan backed away from the harbor wall and joined him, flattening himself against the roofed doorway to the pub for protection. He felt exhilarated and terrified. The storm before him matched the one in his gut, and he feared both had the power to destroy him.

Wichita, Kansas: October 2013

She'd gone to a concert at Century II with a woman friend. Afterward, because it was late by the time she got home and she'd not eaten supper, she heated a bowl of stew for herself and put together some greens for a salad. Before sitting at the kitchen counter to have her meal, she gathered the day's mail where it had spattered across the entryway from the mail slot in the front door. She was tired. It was one of those nights when she was glad to have her house to herself. Sometimes she missed D.J. and wished he wasn't so far away, but increasingly as the months passed she was enjoying the freedom of her solitude.

The letter lay amongst catalogs, fast food coupons, and appeals for donations, the detritus of what kept the US Postal Service in business in the twenty-first century. She leafed through the latest catalog from her favorite store for "mature" women, bending into careful triangles the corners of the pages featuring handsome women in swishy tunic tops that disguised their muffin-top midriffs. When she finished her stew and salad, she dished herself two generous scoops of ice cream, empowered by how well the clothes she liked on the catalog models hid their mushrooming waistlines.

She carried the mail and her recycling box into the living room and sat on her still-purple sofa to sort it, turning on the ten o'clock news for background noise. She rifled through all that paper, tossing 90% of it into the recycling bin, retaining only bills and an occasional ad or charity appeal that caught her eye. A hand-addressed letter barely missed being tossed. What saved it was the writing on the envelope, which was vaguely familiar, though the return address—Cullen, Scotland—meant nothing to her. She knew no one in Scotland other than D.J. She turned the letter over several times trying to place the handwriting before sliding her forefinger under the fold of the envelope and tearing it open. Ouch! The tiny slice of a paper cut on the inside of her index finger commanded her attention as it leaked a drop of blood onto the open flap and hurt like hell. She set the letter aside and returned to the kitchen for a Band-Aid. Finger wrapped and protected, she sat back down, heavily, wearily, to read whatever had come all the way from Scotland. Then she reread it. Several times.

Thirty minutes later, despite the lateness of the hour, she phoned John. He and Cliff were still together, but Cliff should be at his bar working at this time of the night.

"John, it's Amy. *He's still alive.* In *Scotland.* He met D.J. He wants to know who he is, if he is *your son."*

"Whoa! Slow down, girl. Who are we talking about?"

"Duncan."

"Wait a minute. *My* son? That's a hoot." She imagined John, too, sitting down with the impact of her news. "Does he say what he's been doing?"

"He's an antiques dealer."

"That's novel. Living in Grandmother's house of precious antiques we were forbidden to touch, the man becomes an antiques dealer. Sweet revenge!" She was no longer surprised by John's sarcasm. Their childhoods must have been rough, Amy thought. John continued. "Does he say how long he has lived in Scotland?"

"He doesn't say much of anything about his life. He hopes I've had a good life!!!!! That's pretty funny!" She read the letter aloud to John.

"Honey, you know he's crazy. But what an astounding coincidence that he would meet D.J. Read me that part again." She read Duncan's cryptic message that a Duncan J. Allan had entered his shop with a friend and made a purchase with a credit card, and that when he saw the name, he had to check if this young man could be related to him. Though he realized her address had probably changed long ago, he thought he'd try to contact her at their old address just in case.

"Has D.J. mentioned this?"

"No! I've not heard from for a couple of weeks. He did say he was going on a trip across Northeast Scotland for his two week break, so I suppose it's possible they met up."

Amy fidgeted with the tassels on the sofa pillow trying to calm the racing of her heart, wanting to restore some normalcy to her life which Duncan's letter had upended. "Do you think we should go and see him? We could see D.J. also, since they are both in the same part of Scotland."

"Amy, the man doesn't say he wants to see *any of us,* just that he wants clarity who Duncan J. Allan is."

"But he wrote, after all these years!"

"Let's sleep on this and if you get a call from D.J., see what he thinks. Don't get your hopes up, if you have any hope left for my brother. Honey, it's been almost twenty years since you've seen him."

She could tell by his voice that John was upset. She heard Cliff call to him and pictured him coming in the door from work. John would want to hang up and talk with his partner. She thanked him for his advice and signed off. Then, her mind careening, she tried with little success to sleep.

She got up several times during the night. The first time she went to her computer and did a search for Duncan Allan, Cullen, Scotland. Cruickshank's Antiques came up, three shops along the Northeast coast, wherever that was. Nothing else. No photos, no personal information, just a website that hadn't been updated in a long while.

The second time she awoke, she went to the hall closet and pulled a box of old photos from way in the back of the top shelf. She sat on the sofa looking through them. Some, the ones of D.J., were in small albums and labeled with dates and where they were taken. Underneath the albums were lose photos of her life before D.J., her life with Duncan. She was surprised how pretty she looked and thin. She'd always thought of herself as overweight and had been embarrassed by the image she carried in her head of what she must look like to others, but now she was pleased to see that the young woman in these photos was quite attractive, as was the young man. She looked at the photos of him closely, something she hadn't done in years, scrutinizing his expression, whether he was or was not touching her, looking for clues to explain his angry departure.

The photographs set off an avalanche of memories that made it even harder for her to quiet her thoughts. She finally slept but awoke again at five a.m., her mind throwing out options and questions with a rapidity that left her giddy. She got up and returned to her computer where she opened a new document and simply listed everything that coursed through her. After half an hour, depleted, her obsessing subsided and she fell into a deep, dreamless sleep. Finally.

She went in to work late. "Is everything all right?" her co-worker asked.

"Yes. I just couldn't sleep last night but I'll be fine. I have a number of houses to show today."

She didn't allow herself think more about Duncan's letter until that evening, after work. The advantage of being a workaholic, she told herself. After a second night of obsessing she was no closer to knowing how to respond.

The third day she received a call from D.J. He and his buddy Drew were about to board a ferry from the Orkney Islands to Aberdeen. They'd had a great holiday, he reported. He launched into an account of hitching a ride from Wick with a couple of young women and staying together in little house that they'd rented when the first big snow storm of the season hit Scotland. They'd gone snowshoeing and he'd tried to cross country ski! It had been a blast, he reported. He was more excited and chatty than she'd heard him in a long time.

He was about to hang up when she told him about the letter and read it to him. There was silence on his end of the phone. She hoped he was trying to reconstruct their time in Portsoy at the antiques store. She wondered how this news affected her son but knew she couldn't ask, not now. D.J. needed to process his feelings before he could talk about them.

D.J. told her about Drew trying to locate, "the dude who had helped his grandfather—apparently he cared for Drew's granddad after he hurt his hip, took him into his home for a while till he could manage on his own. We went into a bunch of antiques stores along the coast looking for the man so that my buddy could say thank you." D.J.'s voice went quiet and she thought they'd been disconnected. Then he spoke again like he'd suddenly thought of something important.

"Mom, there *was* this ratty looking old guy, shoulder length gray hair and eyes that darted around like a rodent's. I remember now. I bought something for you in his store. He might be the guy. This is really weirding me out, Mom. The guy we found was so strange that it was hard to believe he could have helped a disabled old man. He seemed more like the type to smother him with a pillow or chop him up and eat him for supper." D.J. chuckled at his own joke. "You really think that creep could be *my father?*"

The curious part of her wanted to learn more about Duncan's experiences in Scotland, but her son's description of this strange, anti-social man diverted her interest in his adventures. If Duncan met his father and his father was a disaster, how would that benefit any of them? She felt a heavy weight bearing down on her and didn't know what to say or do.

"My father can't be that weird, Mom, not with such a cool son like me!" She could picture the way D.J.'s nose crinkled when he found something funny, especially some witticism he'd come up with. Best to leave it there for now till she had more information.

"They've called us to board the ferry, Mom. I'll call you tomorrow before we go back on the rigs. You wouldn't believe how beautiful it is up here right now with the snow. You gotta come to Scotland some time, Mom. Stay cool. I love you." The call was over before she got in her formulaic "I love you very much, D.J." Obviously he was enjoying his new life there, making friends and having international adventures. That made her happy. Reassured that her son was thriving, she had no trouble falling asleep that night.

The following day when D.J. checked in by phone from Aberdeen, she picked up on his suggestion that she come to Scotland some time, throwing out an idea that had been germinating since Duncan's letter had arrived. "Maybe I could come to Scotland next month and we could go together to see this man? Maybe Uncle John would join us? What do you think?"

"I don't know, Mom." She could hear his resistance. "If this guy *is* my father, well, that will really rearrange my head. It would be great to see you, but you might want to wait till spring. Winter is sometimes mild up here but, like we found in the Orkneys, sometimes it can really kick ass."

The next morning she got up early and drove to Midtown, parking just north of North High. She removed her heels and put on her walking shoes. Then she left the car and walked onto the embankment on the east side of the Little Arkansas River, heading north. She did this fairly often when she needed to think. It also allowed her to stop at the Donut Hole on her way to work and not feel guilty about the two double chocolate donuts she consumed.

The east bank of the river rose upward in what Kansans would consider a hill, then sprawled a couple of house-lengths back from the water. The embankment on that side was mostly grassy with the occasional ancient oak or poplar or elm reaching its long arms toward the river and back toward the houses behind the embankment, as though trying to mediate between the two spaces. The trees were very old, at least by Kansas standards. Some dated back to when this area was an oak orchard a hundred years ago. Across the river the trees massed together at water's edge, their cargo of leaves obscuring the riverbank with a blur of gold and tan.

Normally she saw herons, mallard ducks and squadrons of Canadian geese. Today the embankment was hers alone, not even a dog walker to distract her. The grass of early fall rose up the embankment carpeting the east bank. In the early morning light of this autumn day, the grass was pink and salmon, tan and chartreuse, as though an artist had dotted a canvas with these colors and then applied translucent white paint on top to lighten and blur them. Fan shaped leaves that had prematurely given up their attachment to branches lay at the base of the grandfather trees.

The south wind pushed the river's skin into wrinkles and kept on pushing northward, defying the current that flowed south. Ah, Kansas! Land of the South Wind. The water was murky and dark. Soon the trees' branches would be leafless and the stark, monochromatic season of overcast skies and dead grass would be fully upon them.

She picked up her pace. She had decisions to make.

What would she write back to this man, still legally her husband despite all the years of no contact? Her therapist had trained her to pay attention to her feelings and to what she wanted. Okay. She felt anxious and apprehensive. If she made contact with him, if they went to see him, a lot of things could change. Maybe he's happily married and raising children. Maybe he's the crazy man D.J. met in the antiques store, strange or even mentally ill.

He is the only man I ever loved.

Maybe he would find her disgusting now, pushing fifty and overweight, her age disguised by expensive clothes, a wonderful stylist, trips to a spa every other week, and hair dye.

And what about D.J.? Would he be better off knowing his father, regardless of his father's state of mind? Or could meeting him raise questions about his own identity that would set him drinking more than he did already? She had been concerned about D.J.'s alcohol consumption and his inability to stick with jobs or relationships. With her alcoholic father and Duncan the runaway husband, could D.J.'s patterns be genetic? Would knowing make it easier or harder to redirect D.J.'s behaviors into more productive paths?

What if she never replied to Duncan's letter? How would that affect her? D.J.? John? She would never know why he left if she didn't reply to him. If she was honest with herself, that was the question that had flowed like an aquifer beneath her public life, preventing her from entering other intimate relationships, tying her to silence about her past, and causing her overwhelming sadness sometimes. To know the Truth... You will know the truth and the truth will set you free. Where had she heard that? But, couldn't the truth also make you miserable? She remembered someone—her therapist?—saying that the truth *will* set you free, but *first* it will make you miserable. Maybe miserable is worth it; anyway, miserable comes *without* knowing the truth.

By the time she checked her watch and made a fast tack, jogging back to the car so that she could arrive at work on time, she had made a decision.

That evening she called John again.

"I've decided to write him back and to ask to see him. If you and D.J. don't want to do that, I certainly understand. It's something that I need to do for myself. Of course, he may not be willing for us to meet. But I need to ask."

She could hear John's protracted sigh. "You know how I feel about conflict, Amy. I don't know if I have the emotional strength to hear from my long lost brother how much he hates me for reasons I've never understood. It might be different if he wanted to see me, or if D.J. felt he needed me there to support him.... I do think you are doing the right thing, by the way, and I am proud of your courage."

Amy reassured John that she was fine with his decision. After they hung up, she sat down at her computer to write. It took several drafts till she got it right. She saved a copy to her "Family" file, printed the letter, signed it, addressed the envelope, and at eleven p.m. drove to the post office to send it on its way before she could reconsider.

Portsoy, Scotland: late October 2013

Duncan opened the shop just before noon, barely managing the key in the lock. His hands shook and his head felt like it would split in two from too much Scotch the night before. The mail was already puddled on the floor just inside the door. On top, as though the postman had presorted the day's offerings and ordered them by what he thought most important, was a business size envelope postmarked Wichita, Kansas. He picked it up. It was from Amy. Something about the reality of that return address, that postmark, left his knees shaky. All these years of no contact with that place where he had experienced love and family, and then betrayal... He'd put it out of mind. The grief and loss of the last seven years replaced those earlier emotions connected to Wichita. Now here it was, slogging its way back into his consciousness, a real place with a postmark, a real person he had once been intimately connected to. He moved to his worktable and sat down, leaving the rest of the mail in disarray on the floor.

Could he handle this? He needed to know, so he split open the envelope using Mr. Cruickshank's fine brass letter opener with the carved elephant handle. Inside was one sheet of 8 x 11 paper and it was typed.

Dear Duncan:
Your letter arrived a week ago. It took me that long to decide what to write back to you.

First, the young man you met in your shop is your son, our son, who goes by D.J., though his name is Duncan John Allan. He works on the oil rigs off the coast of Aberdeen in the North Sea. He is a good young man, although he's probably drinking too much. He's unsure what to do with his life and I worry about him and delight in him at the same time.

Second, I still live in the house in Eastborough. I have my own real estate business, which has done well. Mother died a year ago. She became less judgmental in her old age, you will be glad to know.

Third, your brother John nursed his partner Phillip (do you remember him?) through a terrible death from AIDS. After Phillip died, John moved to Wichita, took a job at W.S.U., and lived with D.J. and me until he fell in love with another man. He was very involved with D.J.'s growing up, a surrogate father, I would say. He and his new partner, Cliff, are happy together, I think. I see John most weeks and we talk on the phone.

D.J. vaguely recalls meeting you in your shop. I am encouraging him to go to see you when he gets a break from work so that he can know you and you can know your son. I don't know what he will decide to do.

Your Wichita family are doing well. We have had mostly good lives, though not without pain, of course.

Duncan, I would like to come to meet you in Scotland. I never understood why you left. It is something that I want to understand in order to free me to move on with my life. I don't know if you will agree to this. I can take time off from work next month, my least busy time, and arrange to come, if you are willing to see me. I can come to Cullen, or is it Portsoy? Or we can meet somewhere else. I don't know if you are married or single or anything about what has happened in your life these almost twenty years. I just know that for me, seeing you and hearing from you the answers to the questions that have haunted me is important.

Please let me know as soon as possible if you are willing to see me and where you want me to come.

Sincerely,
Amy Allan

He sat in his chair unmoving for a long while. He read and reread her words. He had a son. His brother was not the father of Duncan J. Allan. His brother was gay! Amy wanted to come see him. She was still Amy Allan. Those were the basic facts, all of them very different from his assumptions.

"Your Wichita family"? He had discarded his Wichita family a lifetime ago. It was an odd, disquieting concept, that he had a Wichita family.

Gradually Duncan became aware of his surroundings. His shop was a disaster, dusty, dank, and cluttered with so many things that your eye could not settle on anyone of them. Mr. Cruickshank would be disappointed in him. So would Ineke. And Elleke.

He sat down again, feeling ashamed of himself, wanting to crawl back into his bed in the Wee Cottage and withdraw from the world.

He got up and walked slowly to the front door, locked it, and bent down to retrieve the rest of his mail. That was when he noticed the other hand-addressed envelope. From Elleke. There was also an embossed orange envelope from the University of Utrecht. He carried the mail back to his worktable and sat down to read Elleke's letter.

Dear Pappie Duncan--

I apologize for not replying to your last letter for so long. Vader has been very strict with me since Gaza. He was clear that he'd cut off my funding for university if I had any contact with you. But now I am graduating in December and he will have no power over me.

I've decided to attend graduate school at the University of Edinburgh! I want to be nearer to you as I miss you very much.

In a few months I will begin to be a serious archaeologist! I am especially interested in doing field work south of Elgin. Did you know that a Pict site was discovered north of Pluscarden Abbey? So many stones have been found there fairly recently! It amazes me how much our understanding of this ancient civilization has changed from what we are now learning. It is phenomenal what a difference uncovering a site like this can make to how we understand the past.

Pappie, I've sent you an invitation to my graduation ceremony in December. I would so like to have you there. I miss Mom every day and miss you almost as much. If you would come, it would seem like she was there, too. I hope you will come. My Vader, as he insists I call him, is a cold person, so wrapped up in his own world that he never thinks of how what he does or doesn't do hurts those around him. I need you, Pappie. Now that I'm finished with my undergraduate work and no longer needing his financial support, he cannot prevent me from seeing you. Please say yes!

Much, much love,

Elleke

Duncan sat down heavily on the beat up captain's chair behind his cluttered desk with its piles of unattended catalogues and reference books that nearly screened him from his shop and his occasional prospective customers. He occupied that chair each day he came to work, staking his right to hide out there. The chair was worn, its seat shaped to receive him. His body sagged, his joints seeming to come undone, lose and disconnected. With effort he raised his arms and leaned on the desk. He could not think. His feelings floated nebulous and inarticulate.

He heard the clocks break the silence with their interminable, chaotic clanging of the hour.

Gradually he seized hold of one of the fragments of thought circling his brain. Elleke had stayed away because her father forbade her from seeing him and would end her financial support if she did. In seven and a half years of crushing loneliness and no contact other than occasional letters, he had ached in his gut over his loss of her and believed she had simply moved on with her life, leaving him behind.

To lose Ineke and Elleke at the same time had been devastating. But losing Elleke was perhaps even worse than struggling through Ineke's dying. The dying they had done together, up to her final day. He had cared for her so tenderly, washed her body, held her through the pain, cooked the broth that was all she could keep down, gently massaged her wasted limbs, wept with her, and carried her to see the sea and back to their bed when she wore out. They had been so close in those last two months, so intimate.

Losing the child who had brought him back to life, losing her by what he thought was rejection….he had no words for this. He'd assumed that Elleke's connection to him was only because of her mother, that with Ineke gone, she felt they were no longer a family. After all, he had betrayed her by not stopping Jens from taking her away.

The afternoon light pushed through the dirty windows into Cruickshank's Antiques and fractured into small spots of brightness. It landed softly on the sundry objects cluttering the tables, leaving shimmering polkadots of hope. Did the sun do this other afternoons? He had not noticed.

Guilt warred with the joy of discovering that Elleke wanted to be near him. Why was he so quick to misread those who loved him?

He reread Amy's letter and then Elleke's. Elleke would be doing her research less than two hours away. In a month he would see her for the first time in nearly eight years. She wanted to move to Scotland for graduate school to be near him. The realization thrilled him.

But she would be dismayed at what he had become. What she wrote about her father was true of Duncan if you asked any of his "Wichita family"... *or* the people in Portsoy, for that matter. He lay his head down on the worktable and wept. When he had no tears left, he sat up and looked around the shop. He guessed he had better get to work cleaning things up.

When he left the shop at six that evening he carried with him the two letters, the orange graduation invitation, and two DVD envelopes he had found among the mail that had come in during the year after Ineke died. He'd been unable to deal with any of it that first year, piling up all of his mail in a box beside his worktable that spilled over and proliferated into wobbly towers of paper. He had not touched it until today. All these years later, as he started sorting, the manila DVD envelopes emerged from his stacks of unread mail from that terrible time. They were hand addressed but the handwriting was shaky and he didn't recognize it.

One DVD was addressed to Elleke and one to him. He didn't recognize the return address, some videographer in Elgin.

He decided to go to their home in Cullen rather than to the Wee Cottage. If Amy was coming, it would be a preferable place for her to stay. Also, the Cullen house had a DVD player in the living room.

He parked the car in the drive and walked up to the house. The remains of the first snow of the season lay in patches on the walk. He inserted his key in the lock, turned it, and opened the door.

The house smelled of dust and neglect. He had forgotten that he'd had the power turned off years ago. It was dark and he felt his way into the living room where he unplugged the TV and DVD player and loaded them into his car. He would need to get this house, Elleke's home, ready to receive her and to host Amy. He drove back to Portsoy, made two trips to the car to carry the heavy TV and then the DVD player into Wee Cottage, and connected them. He didn't take time to make supper. Instead he opened the DVD addressed to him and inserted it. Despite years of dusty hibernation, it worked.

Ineke appeared on his television looking as she had looked several weeks before her death. Pale and a bit jaundiced, her clothes hanging on her thin body, she sat on a bench up on the railway bridge, the wind ruffling her hair and the sea calm and gray behind her. It was an overcast day and the blue of her eyes looked especially bright. She looked straight at him with her familiar affectionate smile. She was addressing them both, Elleke and him, asking them to please take care of each other.

Duncan played and replayed the brief video, pausing it after she said she was most proud of how she had raised her daughter and of how she had helped him rise out of barely functioning despair. "Oh, Ineke, I've sunk back so often since you've gone." He startled, hearing his own voice say the words. He pushed Rewind, then Play again. He sat there in front of the television gazing at the woman he loved, still beautiful to him despite the ravages of cancer, the woman who should not be dead, who should be here beside him now, not a flickering image on his screen.

He awoke about four a.m., the cold of late October seeping into his bones as he sat in the chair before his TV. He turned the DVD player and the television off and lay down on his bed, pulling the duvet around him and slept more deeply than he had since Ineke became ill. When he awoke, a section of Elleke's letter held fast to his mind: "It is phenomenal what a difference uncovering a site like this can make to how we understand the past."

Over breakfast he tried to recall what Ineke had said, something like, hold onto caring and connecting....It will save you.

Before him on the table lay the letters—Elleke's and Amy's. Amy's letter uncovered truth about the past that he could hardly believe. What she said, about the young man being his son and about John being gay, stunned him. Could he have been wrong about her all these years? Her letter implied so. Was that who he was, a person who left his faultless wife to raise their child alone?

Ineke had experienced him as a caring person who took the risk to connect with her, her child, and Mr. Cruickshank. Elleke's letter affirmed him as a person who cared for her and was important to her. And Amy wanted to reconnect with him now in spite of everything.

Who was he, really?

He sat until his coffee was cold trying to sort out what to do. Then he located a pen and a piece of paper. He wrote first to Elleke, telling her he would be there in December and that he was thrilled that she was returning home to do her graduate work.

Then he wrote to Amy. "I am glad you want to come. Fly to Aberdeen and take the bus to Portsoy on the North Sea coast. I have a shop there and a short drive from there a house where you can stay while you are here. John and his partner are also welcome. I just need a month to get things in order here. Thank you for wanting to come."

He walked to the Coop Grocer that also served as the Post Office and mailed both letters. Then he stopped by the bakery for tea and shortbread. He'd forgotten how much he liked their shortbread—it was so much better than the Coop's cello wrapped kind. How good it made him feel, that buttery sweet softly dissolving in his mouth. Why had it been so long since he'd stopped at the bakery for shortbread?

He opened Cruickshank Antiques at the ungodly early hour —for him-- of ten a.m. and started going through years of accumulated clutter.

His feelings careened from exhilaration to trepidation and anxiety, from regret and shame to giddy glee. He could hardly take in how much his mistaken assumption about Amy had cost him, how much it changed his life. But the change had not been all bad, at least not for him. He had met Ineke and Elleke and George Cruickshank, had found a career that he enjoyed, he had experienced ten years of happiness with his Scotland family. He felt the cauldron inside that held his emptiness beginning to fill, as though he'd been living on thin porridge and was finally tasting the thick warmth of a nourishing stew.

A voice inside cautioned him. Apparently Amy had not found someone else. She was the victim, *his* victim. His stomach churned and nausea crept up and nested in his throat. He felt ripples of heaving moving up from his stomach and ran for the toilet, where he retched the nourishment that had so recently begun to reach him. He flushed the toilet and rinsed his sour mouth. He caught sight of his face in the mirror and stood for a long time staring at this man he barely recognized. His haunted face peered from behind furry eyebrows and an overgrowth of beard. There were white hairs among his brows, his beard, and his hair, but most alarming was the expression in his eyes that jumped out from under the alarming V of his ferocious brows. The eyes bored into him from the mirror. I look like I could be a serial killer, he thought, shocked.

That thought carried him back to the first time he entered this store, seeking work. An elderly gentleman sat at this desk working on a clock whose innards lay in neat piles before him. The man looked up at him over his magnifying half-glasses, gave him an appraising look that later he would recognize as the look the man gave to prospective purchases. He beckoned him forward. Walking toward the desk he'd caught sight of himself in a mirror framed in elaborately carved wood. The appearance of the young man in the mirror had jolted him then: Alarmingly disheveled, long straggly hair and unshaven face, haunted, wary eyes, bone-showing body. He remembered hesitating, shocked by the hopelessness of his situation. Who would take a chance on the Duncan he saw in the mirror? But the man spoke to him and invited him in. It had been the beginning of his new life.

The man in the mirror on October 31st, 2013 was probably thirty pounds heavier and going gray, but, other than that, he looked much the same. It struck him that in these years since Ineke's death—especially in the past three years when the absence of contact with Elleke had worn down his hope—he had practiced depression and despair as his vocation, the way a doctor practices oncology or pediatrics. He wasn't sure he knew any other way to live. It was familiar and seductive, even more addictive than the Scotch that had allowed him to survive the darkness.

Gradually a new insight surfaced in his consciousness. Without his first descent into despair in Wichita in 1994 and his desperate flight to Scotland he would never have known Ineke or Elleke or Mr. Cruickshank. He felt his mind grab ahold of this realization with the strength of a hand tightening around a tool. He wasn't sure how long he could keep holding on. He feared his grip would weaken, but for now he held on.

He turned away from the mirror and went back to the worktable where George Cruickshank had sat in the spring of 1995. He resumed the work of preparing for the visits that he hoped would turn his life right side up, cleaning and sorting and disposing of things.

That night he shaved his beard.

Wichita, Kansas: early November 2013

Duncan's letter relieved and pleased Amy. She passed on to John his brother's invitation for both John and Cliff to come to the North Sea coast. She booked her ticket to fly to Edinburgh November the 21st, take the train to Aberdeen, and then a bus to Portsoy. She allowed herself ten days to meet Duncan and, hopefully, see D.J., although D.J. had not called. She emailed D.J. telling him what his father had written and her travel plans. If he couldn't get off work, or if the reunion went badly, she would use the rest of her vacation days to sightsee in Scotland. The Highlands should be beautiful despite the cold.

As she prepared to leave for ten days, she saw her house from a new vantage point. Why did she need all this space? Perhaps when she returned she would look for something smaller.

A few days before she left for Scotland, Amy attended a meeting of her women's book group. They were meeting at Linda's elegant home on the east side of the city. It was Amy's turn to lead the discussion.

They sat on the leather covered sofas and chairs that made a rectangle in front of the fireplace in Linda's den, nursing glasses of red wine that glimmered in the firelight. It was a week before Thanksgiving. Linda's house was decorated with pumpkins and gourds and potpourri simmered under a candle on the coffee table, giving off a pleasant spicy perfume. They'd sat like this in one or the other's home to discuss serious books and catch up on each other's lives for several years. These were the women she knew best in Wichita, the women she liked most. Tonight they were discussing Rachel Maddow's latest book, and, though Amy had prepared to lead the discussion, she changed her plan in the minutes before they started. When the group quieted and their faces turned to her expectantly, she announced the change.

"There's something I need to share with you," she began, launching herself on what she realized with dismay was her first self-revelatory conversation with anyone other than her therapist and John. "I leave Thursday for ten days in Scotland." The room buzzed with ooo's and ahh's and someone said, "Lucky you!"

She took a deep breath and continued. She needed them to know the significance of her revelation, so she pushed on. "I've never told anyone other than my brother-in-law and my therapist what I am about to tell you." She was looking into the fire, avoiding their inquiring eyes. "I am going to see my husband who disappeared more than nineteen years ago, leaving me pregnant." She heard their sudden intake of air, like the synchronized breathing of a chorus. She could feel a heaviness descend on the room. She knew that each woman present was focusing intently on her. Their faces displayed their shock and concern. Sharon's eyes were brimming with tears. Cornelia was looking at her lap, her head moving slightly from one side to another in silent protest, "No." Linda's forehead was wrinkled and her mouth drawn in so that her lips didn't show at all, just a straight, forbidding line. Lakshmi's brown eyes were round and deep and her right hand covered her mouth. Vicky, sitting beside Amy, reached over and laid her warm hand on Amy's arm.

Then Amy told them the story of Duncan's disappearance, of raising her son alone, of her shame and secrecy about this central fact of her adult life. She didn't cry, not until Cornelia spoke.

"Honey, I want to knock his lights out." Her voice was fierce and the solidarity that Amy felt in those words overwhelmed her. When she recovered her composure, others of them spoke.

Sharon said she'd been abandoned when her daughter was a baby, so could well imagine, "how much courage it took for you to wade through all that pain and make a new life for yourself."

Linda got up to pour more wine. "You are so brave to go see him," she said. "Are you afraid of what you may learn?"

Yes," it was the first time she'd named it to herself. Stating it publicly felt good. "I'm afraid I may still be in love with him. I'm afraid he's happily re-married with children and that I will look like a plump, middle aged woman who's desperate for love. I'm afraid he may be crazy from D.J.'s description of him, mentally ill, I mean. I'm afraid of what this visit might do to my son, who's still working out his own identity. *Yes, I'm afraid.*"

"But going and seeing *for yourself* will be freeing." Lakshmi spoke quietly and they all looked at her. "Everyone has secrets, Amy, places in our lives we don't share, pain that overwhelms us at times, guilt we can't bear to speak. It can be paralyzing. You have this opportunity to face your fears and get answers that you need. And you're giving Duncan that chance. All will be well."

They asked clarifying questions, nodding and making supportive sounds as she replied. Then Vicky, still with her hand on Amy's arm, rose. "I think we need a group hug and a prayer," she said.

They'd never done this before. They prided themselves on being an intellectual group, not some churchy women's group. Still, no one dissented when Vicky suggested it. They stood around the coffee table with its fragrant potpourri, aware of the firelight's crackling noises and its soft glow that lit their faces from below. Arms around each other they each blessed Amy with a sentence. Vicky went last. "We will think of you every day you are gone and send you energy and light. Thank you for deepening the relationships around our circle by trusting us."

Vicky offered to drive her to the airport and Lakshmi suggested they burn candles each night while Amy was away as a reminder to think of her. Amy left the meeting feeling fortified.

When she got home, she called John to say goodbye, even though it was late. Cliff answered the phone. "John can't come to the phone, Amy. He's quite distraught about whether or not to see his brother. I'm trying to convince him to go. I've suggested we go together and, if meeting his brother is a downer, turn it into a ski trip in the Highlands. He seems quite paralyzed by indecision, so I have no idea whether we will see you in Scotland! But we'll keep in touch. I hope it goes well." She was surprised by the warmth in his words and by his encouragement.

She was sorry not to talk with John, but she was doing what she needed to do, whether or not she did it alone. She folded the clothes she was taking and packed them in her roller bag. This would be her first trip outside the U.S. other than a week in Cancun to celebrate D.J.'s sixteenth birthday. In all of her forty-five years she had never made a major trip alone. Why hadn't she traveled more? It wasn't for lack of money. Her business was quite successful. Maybe this would be the start of her new life as an international traveler.

She emailed Duncan her cell number, told him she'd be coming alone, gave him her itinerary and when she'd be catching the bus in Aberdeen.

As she stepped onto the plane in Wichita for Chicago, the first leg of her journey, she felt some trepidation, but when the plane lifted off the Chicago runway, next stop, Edinburgh, a kind of euphoria settled over her, banishing her anxiety, at least for the next eight hours.

Changing from plane to train in Scotland went surprisingly smoothly, thanks to the friendliness of the Scots. Young and old people would notice her hesitancy and ask if they could help. That was lovely because she was quite tired.

In Aberdeen she tried phoning D.J. again. After several tries, she tracked him down. He was on the rig and would not have a day off for about five days.

"I don't really want to see him, Mom," he told her. "I am proud of you, though, coming all this way by yourself to find him. My buddy Drew says a woman your age who's never traveled alone outside their country coming to Scotland to see the man who left her twenty years before shows remarkable 'thrawn.' That means strength. I agree."

She imagined that this was a side of his mother that D.J. hadn't seen before. She wasn't sure how she felt about being identified as the woman who crosses an ocean to see a man who left her twenty years before. Did that make her pathetic? Or romantic? In fact, she felt neither. She just wanted answers. The Truth.

She joined the queue to board the mid-afternoon Stagecoach 35 bus shivering from the damp cold and took a seat a third of the way back next to a window on the right side so she could look out at the countryside and the sea. She asked the driver to let her know when they arrived in Portsoy.

Her seatmate was an elderly woman with white hair that stood out from her head from the static electricity. The woman smiled and assured her that she would let Amy know when they reached Portsoy. Her faded blue eyes peaked out from folds of eyelid and her round, doughy face was worn with wrinkles. She looked kind. She told Amy that the trip took an hour and a half, so there'd be time for her to rest. "You're not from here, are you?" she asked. When Amy said she'd come from Kansas, in the middle of the United States, the woman's face lit up. "Home of Dorothy and Toto and tornadoes!"

Amy could tell she was proud that she could make this connection. She wished there were other things Kansas was known for, but she imagined for the next ten days she'd be hearing that same refrain.

The bus was quiet, and Amy was too tired to talk. She barely noticed the sea coast that came suddenly into view as the bus turned west onto the highway that paralleled the coast. She dozed most of the way. Her seatmate kindly shifted position so that Amy's nodding head could rest on her shoulder.

Duncan had called when she was in the bus station to tell her to get off at the second Portsoy stop and walk just a few yards to the right where she would see Cruickshank's Antiques. He would be watching for her.

Hearing his voice on the phone threw her. Her mother had always said Duncan had a voice for radio. She had loved that voice. Hearing it now was confusing and oddly exciting. It was the same yet different, still deep, but quieter, even gravelly, like someone who hadn't spoken much. His betrayal had hurt her so deeply that she had expected her challenge during this trip would be controlling her anger at him, remaining calm and detached. To her surprise, his voice set off a rush of sensate memories of the years when she had adored him and he her. That felt uncomfortable and disturbing and gnawed at her self-confidence.

Portsoy & Cullen, November 22, 2013

Her seatmate nudged her gently and whispered that the next stop was Portsoy Village. Disoriented, Amy gathered her purse, zipped up her turquoise down jacket, wrapped her colorful turquoise and purple scarf around her neck, and pulled on her matching gloves and ski cap. The woman arose to let her step into the aisle. Nodding thanks Amy positioned herself behind the yellow line beside the driver, waiting for the bus to stop. The occasion merited a drum roll, she thought. Apparently her pounding heart agreed.

A man entered her peripheral vision, emerging from a store on her right. He looked dreary—pants, coat, shoes, and hair all shades of brown, though his hair was salted with gray. She wondered if living this far north produced dun and drab attire in most of the residents. Dismal thought. Grateful for color and her turquoise jacket, she climbed down the steps of the bus and waited for the driver to open the luggage hold beneath the chassis. When he did, she pulled out her purple roller bag and turned right to scout out the antiques store Duncan had said was a few yards away.

The brown man approached the bus stop. His gait, loose and loping, was vaguely familiar.

"Duncan?"

"Amy.... You must be very tired. Come on in the shop and have a cup of tea before I take you to the house."

Duncan was struggling to get out sentences. Amy looked quite different to him, like someone he would not recognize were he to pass her on the street. She was plump, but pleasantly so, and attractive. Her purple and turquoise attire engaged his eyes. She looked middle aged, and carried herself with an air of competence. She was no longer the young woman whose small, curvy body he had known so well and cherished. The gap between then and now felt infinite and confusing. He reached for her bag and led the way to his shop. A bell tingled as he opened the door.

The shop was noticeably different from even a week before, though of course Amy could not know that. Duncan had worked cleaning and tidying it, throwing out boxes of old mail and disposing of items that he had never taken time to sort, repair or catalog. You could actually walk between the tables of knick-knacks without setting off an avalanche of precariously wobbling china.

He pulled her bag to the back of the shop. There two chairs faced each other at a small table on which an electric kettle, a tea pot, a pitcher of milk, and upside down cups on their saucers sat awaiting them. He had planned ahead. He plugged in the kettle and, when it was briskly boiling, poured water into the teapot, dangling a tea ball from the lip of the pot and covering the whole with a colorful knitted tea cozy.

"You're probably very tired," he said again. She nodded, unable to respond further.

She was mesmerized by the changes in his appearance and behavior—he was now a drab shades-of-brown older man, no longer the handsome dark haired husband who had left her, and his behavior was unfamiliar. When last she'd seen him he disliked tea, didn't know how to boil water, and was unacquainted with anything remotely related to food preparation.

"I'll drive you to the house shortly," he said. "I thought you might benefit from a cup of tea first. I have some shortbread, too, if you're hungry."

He passed her a plate and she helped herself to two pieces of shortbread shaped like wedges of pie. She hadn't eaten since the plane, and that was many hours ago. They both sipped tea and munched shortbread in silence. Then he collected their dishes, washing them in the utilitarian sink attached to the interior wall of this all-purpose rear room.

"My house is here in Portsoy, but it's too small for company. I still own a house in Cullen where I thought you could stay. I can take you there now and you can catch up on sleep. You have my cell number and can call me whenever you're ready tomorrow. Do you want to have a meal before you crash?"

She was hungry and knew she would not sleep well without something in her stomach besides shortbread. But she was too exhausted to talk now.

Duncan read her uncertainty and suggested that the groceries he had purchased for her use that were at the house in Cullen might provide enough for tonight. She agreed and they left the shop by the rear door and loaded her things and themselves into his green Scion. It was already getting dark.

Twenty minutes later he pulled up at a gray stone house in Cullen with a small front garden on a hill overlooking the harbor. He brought in her things, placed them in a bedroom on the ground floor next to the bathroom, and showed her the kitchen and how to work the heating. Then he made a hasty exit, reminding her to phone him when she felt rested and ready to talk.

Like a robot she scrambled some eggs with onions and peppers and made toast. Comfort food. Then she crashed.

When she awoke, unclear where she was, the clock in the kitchen told her it was after noon. It had snowed during the night, muffling the sounds of the road and wrapping the house in glistening white. She looked out, curious about this place that she had not been able to see in the gathering dark when they arrived. Snow continued to amble lazily down from the sky, obscuring the harbor and neighboring houses. Duncan had left oatmeal and milk for her, so she cooked herself a bowl of porridge. She dressed in the most flattering of the six outfits she had packed, made up her face, and phoned him. He said he would be by in about thirty minutes.

She sat down in the living room wondering what they would say to each other. A DVD lay beside the television marked with thick black letters, "FOR ELLEKE." She wondered who Elleke was—his new wife, perhaps?

Duncan drove slowly as the roads were icy. He pulled up in front, set the emergency brake, and walked a path to the front door, entering the house covered in snow and stamping his booted feet. He removed the boots and put on thick wool socks that he pulled from his pocket.

"Are you warm enough?" he asked her. "Many of these old cottages don't have central heating, but we renovated this one and put in the radiators. Did I show you how to use them?"

He'd said "we." She didn't acknowledge that he'd showed her the night before how to work the heat as she had found the unfamiliar technology a bit daunting and welcomed another lesson.

He walked to the radiators and demonstrated how to raise and lower the room temperature.

She wondered who "we" referred to but didn't ask. "Thank you for the groceries," she said. "I made some coffee if you'd like some. Or do you prefer tea?"

They moved to the kitchen and sat at the table while Amy got their drinks. "Do you take milk in your coffee now?" she asked.

"Yes, and in my tea. I guess I've become a true Scot."

They sat silent in the cozy kitchen facing the window watching languidly falling snow obscure everything except the brilliant sunshine. Amy could hear the drip, drip of snow melting off his gloves and dropping to the floor from where he'd draped them on the edge of the sink. They were both waiting, neither of them clear for what.

"Is John coming?" Duncan asked her.

"I don't think so. Although Cliff, his partner, said it's still possible he could change his mind and come. I don't know if D.J. will come either. Lots of ambivalence, I think."

More silence.

"Tell me about your life, Duncan?" She asked hesitantly, afraid of intruding, afraid of what she might hear. She did not want him to walk out again.

He sighed audibly, then launched into the explanation he'd prepared. "I fled Wichita and drove until I had to stop. Ended up in North Dakota quite by accident. I couldn't think straight. Just had to get away."

"*Why?*" Okay, here it comes. He saw her face muscles tighten.

He resettled himself on the chair and crossed and uncrossed his legs before answering. "I'd been told that John and you were having an affair and when you said that you were pregnant, I thought it was John's child. I wasn't able to live with that knowledge."

Dead silence.

"So you never checked it out with me or with John but took someone else's suggestion as fact?" Her voice was intense and angry. His answer seemed to take her by surprise, as though she wasn't prepared for it. She stared at him unblinking, then began blinking rapidly.

"I felt so betrayed. You and John were all that I had and...I loved you both so much." He was looking at his hands which were artificially arranged in his lap, fingers interlaced.

Whoever holds their hands like that unless they're having a portrait painted? Amy wondered, surprised by how strongly disapproving she felt of his folded hands. His reason for deserting her was preposterous.

She wanted to slap him hard across his face, to erase that hurt little boy look. How dare he pull that on her? Instead, she stood, excused herself, and headed for the bathroom, locking the door and sitting on the toilet trying to process what he had just said. After a time she returned to the kitchen. He was still seated in the same chair, elbows on the table, head in his hands. She stood in the doorway, arms folded protectively across her chest.

"I don't understand why you never checked out whether what this person told you was true. If you loved me and John, didn't that require you to talk to us about what you had heard before vanishing from our lives?"

He said nothing. Then he mumbled, "I tried calling you for a couple of weeks but no one answered the phone. I assumed you were with him and gave up."

She moved from the doorway to the table and sat down. "That's when I was living in the apartment while they repaired the damage to the house from the fire."

His head jerked up and he stared at her. "What fire?"

Amy chose her words carefully. "When you pulled me into the bedroom, a pot holder or towel or something landed too close to the burner and caught fire. I blacked out when I fell." She didn't mention his hitting her. She had never told anyone about that, other than her therapist. "When I came to, the house was filled with smoke. I called 911 and got out onto the deck. There was a lot of damage and I had to move into an apartment while they refurbished the house." Her voice was emotionless, recounting the facts like she was reading items on a menu. She was processing the new information that he had tried to call her, repeatedly.

"You tried to call me." She felt regret pour over her like a fast flowing stream that threatened to carry her under, and she struggled to reach the surface. *He had tried to call.* How differently their lives would have turned out if they had been able to talk on the phone! The years of not knowing why he'd left, of feeling discarded, thrown away like something putrid and disgusting, the dissembling she had done with D.J. and her mother, finding excuses for why he left, the fury she had felt gnawing at her gut....Had his phone calls reached her she could have told him why she was in John's bedroom patting his hair and holding his hand. Now she summoned the words she would have said twenty years before.

"John and I were friends," she told him. "Nothing more. His partner was dying of AIDS, and he needed to talk with me about what they were going through. He couldn't talk to you. You didn't hide your disapproval of men who love men. Duncan, *I never slept with anyone other than you,* not until years after you left.... No, let me be absolutely truthful: I have *never* slept with anyone other than you. *Ever.*" She was trembling with anger at her lost years, the chances for love she had been unable to let herself take.

He could not raise his head to meet her eyes so they sat across from each other, Amy watching him, and Duncan shrinking into himself before her, looking mortified and ashamed. He raised his head and looked at her, his eyes penetrating. "It was all my fault," he said. "All my fault. I'm very sorry, Amy, for all of it." He pulled himself up to standing, grabbed his coat and boots, and was at the front door in a minute. Amy got there first.

"Don't you *dare* leave again, Duncan Allan, not until I get the answers I have traveled all this way to get." She physically blocked him from leaving, standing like a bouncer, arms akimbo and legs spread. The look on her face was so fierce that he looked away.

They faced off for some moments. Then Duncan set his boots down, laid his coat on a chair, and returned to the kitchen.

"I guess I owe you that," he said.

"I guess you do." She followed him back to the kitchen and sat down, watching him warily.

For several hours they talked, haltingly and with silence spacing their sentences. Amy suggested they each ask the other questions and give whatever time was needed for the answers. She asked him to speak first. Duncan told her about his lost months in North Dakota and the winter months he hibernated in The Wee Cottage in Portsoy. He told her about Mr. Cruickshank befriending him and giving him work. He did not tell her about Ineke and Elleke or about his caring for Mr. Cruickshank the last years of his life. That felt too intimate, too invasive. It did not affect her, he rationalized. Anyway, maybe it would anger her.

When Duncan stopped talking, Amy thanked him. "I guess it's my turn," she said. "Are you hungry? I am. Such intense conversation calls for sustenance." She moved to the frig and set out bread and cheese and fruit while she told him about the house fire, D.J.'s birth, confronting her mother, and about Phillip's excruciating death. She told him about John moving in to help her with D.J. and then moving out after he and Cliff became a couple.

She didn't tell him how jealous of Cliff she had felt. She told him she was a real estate agent with her own company, doing well financially, and ended with her concerns that D.J. seemed unfocused and unable to stick with anything, school or career. She even told him about D.J.'s friend Adam who the police shot.

When she finished, she stated that they had actually done fairly well surviving as a family despite their unconventional configuration. "I don't mean that we didn't need you, no, not at all. I just mean that it all seemed to work out in the end."

Duncan said he was glad of that, but the anguished look on his face told her there was something he was leaving out. She wondered if her face showed the same strain, the same mix of exhaustion and confusion.

"Has your life in Scotland worked out?" she asked, not wanting this time of openness to be over.

His voice was bitter. "You've been better off without me. I'm a drunk and a recluse who perpetually walks a tight rope debating whether I and the world would be better off if I simply gave up trying to remain upright and let myself fall into oblivion."

She gasped, overwhelmed by the misery in his words. He wasn't looking at her so she doubted he could see the tears making tracks down her cheeks or the caring that softened her face and replaced the anger.

Outside the window darkness had returned though it was only four thirty. They could see the snowscape eerily lit by a bleached blur of moon. It felt foreign and unfamiliar. For a moment Amy wished she was back home. She wanted Duncan to turn on the lights, the radio, the TV, anything to penetrate the heaviness that filled this space. Finally, she got up and turned on the kitchen and hallway lights. When she returned to the kitchen, they sat in silence for a long time.

She didn't know what to say. She wanted to help him. That yearning felt familiar. Wanting to help him had been a dynamic of her attraction to Duncan since she'd first talked with him after Miss Davis' algebra class in middle school. A voice inside cautioned her to stay back. Focus on what you are feeling, her therapist taught her. I'm feeling sorry for him and wanting to help. And I'm feeling wary, because that wasn't enough before, not enough for him to trust me with his pain back then, not enough to keep him from leaving me with no explanation. That thought brought the anger back. Best to back off, at least for now. Let the oppressive air around them laden with pain and regret dissipate.

She stood and walked over to the kitchen window, her eye drawn by a porcelain figurine on the window sill. The figurine depicted a young red-headed girl lying on her back in a grassy area, hair blown by the wind, a smile lighting her face. When Amy looked more closely, she noticed tiny fracture lines and one small spot where the glaze had chipped off the red hair. Some-one must have meticulously glued the pieces back together! The Duncan she had known would have tossed out a broken figurine and bought a new one. Could he have spent the time repairing this one? She looked back at him where he was seated at the kitchen table, face frozen, eyes unfocused, the antithesis of the reconstructed figurine. There was so much she didn't under-stand about him. Or about myself, she acknowledged. Well, she did know that they needed a break from all this heaviness and that she, anyway, needed something to eat.

"Why don't we go get some dinner? I'm hungry and we could do with a break from this conversation, don't you think?" She recognized the voice she used selling houses, her take-charge positive voice. No harm in that. Some-one had to take charge here. "Can you take us to dinner since you have the wheels? My treat. Okay?"

Duncan raised his head but didn't look at her. His voice was low, and she strained to hear what he was saying. "There really are no places to eat open this late, other than carry outs or pubs. I don't want to be in a public place just now. Not sure I'd be able to contain my feelings sitting in a public place talking with you tonight. I guess I could purchase fish and chips from the carry out and bring it back here. How would that sound?"

Why didn't he want to be seen in public with her? Was there a woman in his life now? If so, it must not be a happy relationship, as down as he sound-ed. Well, she could use the time alone to think about what she'd learned from him while he went for fish and chips.

"That would be great." She walked into the living room, found her purse, and carried it back to the kitchen. Holding out a pile of pound notes she said, smiling, "You'll have to tell me which notes will cover the fish and chips. I don't understand your currency."

He waved away her money. "This is on me. I owe you…" His eyes glazed and his voice cracked. She felt sorry for him.

He gathered his outer wear, put on his boots, coat, muffler, and mittens, and went out into the cold, mumbling something she didn't quite hear but assumed was "Be back soon." She was surprised that he didn't look at her when he left.

She made herself some tea and munched on the left over shortbread as she sorted what she had learned from their conversation. She could almost hear John's voice in her head cautioning her to slow down and step back, to comprehend what a strange man her husband had become. She thought about her friends back in Wichita lighting their candles for her and Lakshmi saying that she was giving herself *and Duncan* the opportunity to face their fears and get answers. What did he fear? She wondered.

The cold and the dark felt oppressive, like a gigantic malevolent creature crawling over the town, over the house, over her. She got up and walked through the downstairs rooms turning on more lights, needing their reassurance, needing to see the shadows retreat as light flooded each room.

She was hungry and weary and alone in this strange, frozen place. Frustrated as she was with him, she wanted Duncan to return.

Portsoy

Duncan drove from the house in Cullen back to Portsoy. The roads were slick and he drove slowly. The only restaurants open in Portsoy were the Boyne Hotel and The Shore Inn, where he often hung out. He intended to go to the Fish and Chips Carry-Out on Seafields down from the Coop, but first he needed some Scotch. He made it to his Wee Cottage, poured himself a drink and wolfed it down. Its warm downward slide through his body felt momentarily reassuring. He sank onto a kitchen chair and Needja lay on his feet and nosed his calves until he reached down and ruffled the fur on his neck.

Then he felt himself begin to shake. He had made such a mess of it all. Even Ineke and Elleke. If he'd married Ineke, if he'd submitted the adoption paperwork for Elleke in time... Maybe Ineke's death was payback for what he'd done to Amy? As distorted as his mental processes were, he knew that kind of thinking would anger Ineke. His mind deleted that thought, striking it out letter by letter. Plenty of other reasons to castigate himself were piling up. His gut spasmed and he thought he might be sick. He forgot that Amy was waiting for him, forgot about his promise to get fish and chips, forgot everything except what a miserable fuck-up he was.

His gut cramped again and he grabbed a bottle of Xanax, taking it with him to car and driving downhill to the harbor and The Shore Inn. He wasn't sure what he intended. The sea was churning and growling, throwing waves

above the harbor wall. Arcs of salty, foaming water splashed on the snow
covered cobblestones, their sound strangely muted. He parked his car in the
shoveled space farthest from the lighted doorway and went in.

Not many folks were out on this snowy night, mostly the regulars for
whom every night ended here in slurred conversation and too much alcohol.
He ordered a double Scotch, and then another, and a third, drinking them
down rapidly. He was overcome with guilt and inadequacy. Depression had
him in a headlock. He couldn't see beyond the pain that his behavior had
caused others. In his misery he forgot that Amy was waiting for him back at
the house. He just wanted the pain to go away. He asked the bartender for a
tall glass of water and began swallowing the Xanax, several at a time, until he
had consumed the whole bottle. He chased the pills with a double Scotch,
paid his tab, and went out to his car.

He sat shivering in the driver's seat, his back to the harbor and the roiling,
freezing darkness.

Cullen, Scotland

At the house in Cullen, Amy responded to the knock on the door eagerly, throwing it open and exclaiming how happy she was that he had finally come back with food!

But it wasn't Duncan.

Standing before her was an attractive young woman with long red, curly hair. She appeared to be close to D.J.'s age. The look on her face told Amy that she was not expecting to find a strange woman answering the door.

"Where's Duncan?" the young woman asked.

"He went out to get fish and chips a couple of hours ago, but he hasn't returned," Amy told her. "Come on in out of the cold. I don't mean to be rude, but who are you?" Amy looked intently at the young woman.

"I'm Elleke." She extended a mittened hand. "Who are you?" She took off her heavy coat and hung it in the closet as though this place was familiar to her.

"I'm Amy Allan. I was married to Duncan back in the States twenty years ago. I came to learn why he left us." [There, she had said it, those words that had caused her to feel shame for so long.] "He ran away from us, and we never knew why or where he was, not until about six weeks ago when my— our--son happened into the antiques store and bought something, and Duncan saw that his name was also Duncan Allan. Are you Duncan's girlfriend?"

The young woman laughed. "Oh, no! He has been like a father to me, at least until my mom died and my dad took me back to Holland. I think of him as my other dad, my Pappie."

Okay. He hadn't been fully honest with her. He had another family. She walked over to the television and handed the young woman the DVD addressed FOR ELLEKE. "I found this here this morning. It seems to be for you."

Elleke's eyes widened and she opened the envelope very carefully, pulling out the DVD and placing it in the slot in the DVD player beneath the television. "Do you mind if I see what this is?" she asked.

"Of course not."

The video was slightly shaky, probably taken with a hand held camera. A thin young woman sat on a bench with the Sea behind her. From the emotion on Elleke's face, Amy guessed she must be someone very close to Elleke, maybe her mother. The woman on the DVD spoke briefly and movingly about her coming death. She asked Duncan and Elleke to take care of each other. Elleke began to cry, and Amy sat beside her on the sofa, her arm around the young woman.

This was a major part of his story and Duncan had not told her. He had found another woman and moved on with his life, while she had remained faithful to her phantom husband.

"Duncan loved your mom." Amy stated it matter of factly, and Elleke nodded.

"He loved us both and lost us both seven and a half years ago. I haven't seen him since, although we usually write at Christmas and birthdays. I wrote him a couple of weeks ago that I was moving back to Scotland now that I am graduating university. I'm going to grad school here in Scotland so we'll be able to see each other several times a year. He wrote back that he would come for my graduation next month and that he longed to see me, but that he didn't deserve my love. After I got that letter, I decided to come see him now rather than wait to see him next month at my graduation. Something in it sounded so sad."

"I wonder where he is," Amy said. "It seems he would have been able to get fish and chips and return by now." Her face went suddenly pale as she thought back on what he had said before leaving the house.

"He was very upset before he left to get us some supper. I guess I wasn't paying attention, trying to absorb all I learned from him today. Now that I think about it, he seemed very depressed, said he was a drunk and a recluse... never sure if he should remain alive." Remembering these words startled her.

"Do you have any idea where he might go feeling so low?"

"The Wee Cottage. In Portsoy. It's where he lived when he first came to Scotland."

"He said that's where he lives now," Amy told her.

Elleke looked scared. "We've got to find him."

"I'm here without a car. Can you get us there?" Amy had grabbed her cell phone and was dialing Duncan's number as she spoke. No answer. Then she texted him. "Elleke is here! We need you."

The two women shrugged into their coats and pulled on their boots as they hurried to Elleke's rental car. Driving as fast as she could in the snow and ice, Elleke made it to Portsoy in twenty-five minutes. Amy noticed a message on her phone, but it wasn't from Duncan. It was D.J., calling to say he'd persuaded his boss to let him off for the weekend; he would be arriving the following morning despite the forecast of more snow. For the moment she set aside her worry about his traveling in a snow storm. It was his father she was more worried about.

The Cottage was unlocked and Elleke opened the door for Amy and followed her in. No Duncan. The place was empty except for a grizzled black dog whose tail wagged non-stop at the sight of Elleke. The girl had come from Holland to Scotland in late November because she loved this man who was like a father to her! Amy wanted to know more. She wondered if the girl had had anyone taking care of her during the—was it eight?—years she'd lived away from Duncan.

The dog licked Elleke up one side and down the other. "He still remembers me!" She looked at Amy with an expression of such sheer delight that Amy suggested they bring the dog along with them.

Amy felt drawn to the young woman and most grateful for her presence on this impossible night when Duncan seemed to have disappeared. Where was he? One thing was becoming clear to her: They must find Duncan and be sure he was all right.

Elleke thought Duncan might have gone for a drink at the tavern by the old harbor. With the dog in the back seat and the window wipers working overtime, they inched their way along the street. The snow was piling up. They could feel the rental car shaking from the wind off the sea. Elleke was afraid to drive down the steep hill to the harbor. Ice leveled the cobblestones, making them treacherous. She parked in the town square, and the two of them carefully made their way downhill, holding on to each other for support. The dog followed, darting from doorway to doorway as he descended.

Amy recognized Duncan's car in front of The Shore Inn. The dog ran to the driver's side where they could see someone slumped over the wheel. Amy yanked open the car door and an empty bottle of Xanax rolled off Duncan's lap and out onto the cobblestones, skidding dizzily on the ice.

Amy froze. She'd been around this man, for barely twenty-four hours. Why was he sitting in his car? Why was he curled into the steering wheel like someone who had had a heart attack? Nothing made sense. She felt the dog push in front of her and heard him licking Duncan's face.

She heard Elleke shouting, *"Pappie! Pappie!"* Both women were screaming now. *"Help us! Help us!* Someone please *HELP us!"*

At their screams, half a dozen men poured out of the tavern and made their way to the car. The tavern owner pulled Duncan from the car and asked for help turning him upside down to try to empty the contents of his stomach. "I was afraid of this the way he was putting away Scotch and those damned pills," he muttered. Someone called 999, but in these weather conditions there was no chance any help would arrive in time. They carried Duncan out of the cold into the tavern's toilet, bending him over the bowl while the owner called Doc Elliott who had retired to Portsoy and might know what to do. The tavern owner brought charcoal from the fire in his hearth and mixed it with water as Doc instructed. They tried to force it down Duncan, but he gagged repeatedly on the charcoal solution. "Duncan, lad, Duncan!" The tavern owner kept talking to him loudly while he slapped his face. *"Ye must drink this,"* he commanded.

Briefly Duncan opened his eyes and took in the group of people surrounding him in the small bathroom. His eyes locked on Amy and Elleke who stood together, holding each other, willing him to stay alive.

After he finally vomited the men carried him into the main room and laid him on a leather sofa at the east end of the tavern. Amy and Elleke sat beside him. Both appeared dazed, unsure what to do, other than to sit near him. Someone had to remind them to take off their coats.

"You can *not* die on us, Duncan," Amy said to him. "You cannot leave us again. Your son is coming tomorrow to see you." She heard the anger sharpening her voice. Yes, she was angry! Furious, for that matter. She felt Elleke's eyes on her.

Elleke whispered into his ear, "Please don't die, Pappie. I could not bear to lose you, too. Mama told us to take care of each other. Please, Pappie."

Amy thought they must look like representations of Ying and Yang, "wife"-"daughter," older-younger, furious-nurturing. That was all right. They each had their separate roles as they shared the space beside him. Together they might keep him alive.

Doc Elliott had said to keep Duncan awake, to get him up and moving every half hour and to continue force feeding him charcoal in water. The tavern owner organized the men into teams that would lift him and walk him around the tavern.

Amy was amazed at how they rallied to help. Elleke said it was common in these small fishing villages where most folks know each other.

Doc Elliott was too elderly to risk coming down the steep hill to the tavern in the storm, but he stayed by the phone. When Amy asked to speak with him, he answered her urgent question: They would not know if Duncan was going to survive until morning. If he hung on through the night, the chances were in his favor.

About four in the morning, Amy noticed Duncan's cell phone lying on the floor under the sofa. It must have fallen out of his pocket while the men were getting him up. She looked to see if he had received her call and found an outgoing call he had made about fifteen minutes before they found him: 999. She nudged Elleke, who was half asleep with her feet up on a second chair. "Elleke, look! He changed his mind and called 999. Maybe he decided he wanted to live!"

Amy's cell rang in the next half hour. It was John calling from the States to let her know that he had booked a ticket and would be there in two days. She caught him up on her conversation with Duncan and his regret and despair that had led to this crisis. She could tell John was shaken. "Tell him I'm on my way," he told her. "He is still my brother."

She spoke to the comatose Duncan using her most authoritative voice and declaring herself as she had to her Mother all those years ago. "You cannot die. Your son, your brother, your....daughter Elleke, and I are all going to be here to get you well because we want you in our lives. We need you, Duncan. Hang in. That's an order!"

Duncan floated in a gravity-less space, drifting, lazily out of his body above the sofa and the people gathered in the tavern. He wanted them all to go away. He just wanted to hibernate, to sleep so deeply that all thoughts would vanish, all feelings disappear. Let me alone, he tried to tell them, but the words were trapped inside his skull, bouncing from one bony side to the other.

He saw himself sick with chickenpox curled up in his mother's lap. He felt her cool, soft hands stroking his forehead. He tried to touch her hands but the effort was too much for him.

Now he lay with his head in the lap of another woman, a small and lithe young woman who he adored. She smiled down on him and told him she loved him and would love him forever. He wanted to tell her that he loved her, too, but he could not find the words.

A small child held a dandelion up to his lips, her face glowing with delight as she urged him to blow it and watch the magic fly. She so wanted him to blow this one, to share her delight with her. He couldn't find the energy to blow that dandelion.

Ineke sat beside him. She was smiling, too, her face full of love. He reached for her, marshalling all his strength to close the space between them, to hold her body next to his. He felt her words enter him. "You can't hold me, not now, my love. They need you, all of them—Elleke, D.J., Amy, and John—and you need them. I am here. I will always be here. Receive my love and let me go."

With all of his heart he yearned to float in that space asleep in her arms, breathing her breath, just the two of them together.

Amy and Elleke dozed intermittently during the night, awakened every thirty minutes by the men returning Duncan to the sofa from his forced stumbling around the tavern and by changes in his breathing or a twitch of his arm. They awoke simultaneously at the sound of a car, its tires encased in chains clicking against the cobblestones, chewing the ice. It was still dark but from the east side of the harbor a faint, frail light stretched over the rooftops and onto the snow covered cobblestones, so fragile it barely whispered that morning was arriving. The tavern door opened and an icy wind blew elderly Dr. Elliott into the room. The tavern keeper had gone to fetch him. Above his giant muffler Dr. Elliott's face was red and his bushy eyebrows were covered with snow. He unwound his muffler, then removed and shook his heavy woolen coat, spattering the two women and the unconscious man sprawled on the sofa with icy droplets. The unconscious man did not react and the doctor's face showed his concern as he moved to the sofa with his stethoscope in hand. The women stood to make room for Dr. Elliott who sat down and began checking Duncan's vitals. Duncan emitted a deep sigh. Dawn was breaking the darkness. He had made it through the night.

Doc Elliott suggested the two women get some rest. He would remain with Duncan. In these blizzard conditions, the tavern was unlikely to receive many patrons, certainly not for a few hours, anyway. The tavern owner invited the women to use his flat upstairs over the tavern. His wife was in Buckie, caring for their grandchildren. They could eat, rest, and be nearby if Duncan's condition changed.

Amy noticed that her phone was dead. She worried about how D.J. would find them but, as there was nothing she could do to reach him, she let that worry go.

She felt her way up the narrow stairway that led to the tavern keeper's apartment. Exhaustion and the too narrow, steep steps forced her to palm the walls on either side to keep her balance. How many hands had palmed the walls of this passageway since 1723? How many fingerprints, invisible but leaving traces of DNA, remained on these walls? It seemed an important question, though she knew there was no answer. She pulled herself up the stairs, holding onto these walls, praying they would not let her down. If her tired body could not reach the top, she would plummet backward. This thought brought to mind an image of herself after a fall, broken into pieces, right arm here, left foot there, punishingly smashed and unrecognizable. Three more steps. She could do this. She shook off the image and pulled herself forward.

The apartment was spare but surprisingly modern in its appliances. To her right was a pedestal table and two captain chairs topped with one of those Danish red enamel electric kettles, two cups, a sugar bowl, and a porcelain dish with an assortment of tea bags someone had carefully fanned into a circle. Beside the table was a fridge, a stove and a dishwasher, also red enamel. The Ships Inn must provide a generous living, she thought. The shiny reds, modern and startling, reminded her of Cliff. Don't go there, she told herself.

To the left was the sitting room, open and contiguous with the kitchen but decorated more subtly in blues, a plump navy sofa flanked by two overstuffed chairs in a nautical plaid, navy, red, and white. Elleke had conked out on the sofa without removing her shoes. She lay curled on her left side facing the room, her red curls covering much of her face. Amy carried the white chenille throw from the chair on the right, unfolded it, and covered her. She's had a rough day, poor girl, learning about Duncan's deserting us, meeting me, viewing her mother's DVD, seeing him in such a state of despair, and now keeping vigil over him, trying to pull him back to life with her love. Was it weird that she liked the girl?

She got no further than that question before crumpling onto the chair nearest the electric heater where she hoped to be warm despite the blizzard raging outside. She had brought her coat with her and pulled it over her before crashing into sleep.

They were awakened by a knock on the door. It was the tavern owner with news. A young man who appeared to be family to Duncan Allan had arrived by bus and called from the Coop looking for Duncan and/or his mother. Someone directed him to the tavern. In a town this small everyone was informed of the dramatic goings on at The Shore Inn. The lad should be arriving on foot any moment. Exhausted, she fell back asleep until she felt the tavern keeper gently shaking her shoulder.

"Mu'm, there's a young man just arrived below quite concerned about ye. Maybe yer son? Do ye want I should send 'im up?"

She shook her head. She would go down to see him. "How is Duncan?" Her anxiety was showing. She didn't want D.J.'s first real contact with his father to be with a corpse. Was it wrong of her to be more concerned about D.J. than Duncan?

"E's made it through the night and to late morning, so that's a good sign. Still unconscious, but Doc Elliott is hopeful."

Amy washed her face, momentarily dismayed by her appearance when she looked in the mirror, and headed downstairs. Elleke, now also awake, said she'd remain upstairs until Duncan's son had time with his father. Amy thought she detected some sadness in Elleke's face.

Duncan hovered near the ceiling looking down on himself lying on the sofa. Sofa must be six feet long, he thought, seeing that all of him fit easily between its curved arms. Old Doc Elliott's eighty years were showing on him this morning, he noticed. Martin the tavern keeper appeared weary, too. Poor man, spending most his days and nights on his feet day after day. He'd never thought about that before. A couple of men sprawled on wooden arm chairs, their feet resting on one chair, their torso on another. One was snoring loudly. The other looked like he was dreaming. His face twitched and his mouth opened and closed. Now and again he emitted wordless noises. The fire in the massive fireplace crackled and sighed as the tavern keeper used the poker to raise one partially consumed log and insert another under it. Traces of smoke escaped into the room. Chimney needs cleaning. He could read Martin's mind.

It was pleasant in this very masculine room. Especially now with only a few people there, without the usual noisy banter of regulars who had consumed too many pints of ale. He took in the gleaming wood of the bar, the large containers of draft beer with their porcelain handles and brass nameplates, the three shelves filled with bottles of whiskeys, vodkas, rums, brandies, cordials--every imaginable brand of liquor stacked like books in a library. Ineke used to talk about drinking from literature. Did literature and drink serve the same purpose?

While he watched he heard Doc Elliott say to the tavern keeper something about Old Man Cruikshank. He couldn't make it out. That triggered a conversation he had had with Mr. Cruikshank after he'd moved to their house in Cullen. He'd not recalled that conversation for at least a decade. Cruikshank had been in a talkative mood. Duncan remembered him leaning back in his chair and pushing his glasses up so they half-framed his face. He had not looked at Duncan, his eyes seeing something distant. He could hear the old man now.

When my Molly died, I wanted no more of this life. She reflected the world back to me so that I saw it differently, and I did not want my own way of seeing to return. I knew it would pull me under.

One afternoon I drove to Sandsend and walked down the beach to where no one was within a kilometer. I took off my clothes and piled them with my shoes and watch on the rocks. Then I walked into the sea. The sky was very blue and the air crisp. The sea was so cold I thought the shock would kill me, but it didn't. I kept walking till the water was up to my arm pits. I wanted to keep going. Fish were darting between my legs. I could feel them nibbling. I heard someone saying, 'You've got to fan those coals, my love, and keep on fanning.' At first I had no idea what was meant by fanning coals far out in the North Sea. I stood there puzzling it. I hadn't recognized the voice, but the lilt of the words was familiar. I still don't know who spoke or precisely what they meant, but it was enough to turn me around and get me out of that freezing water.

When I arrived at me clothes, my peter was shriveled to half size and my balls had gone into hiding. I thought to me'self, whoever pulled me body from the water might think I was without the proper equipment. That thought kept me out of the sea till now."

When he stopped laughing, Duncan had asked if he'd figured out what the voice meant by fanning the coals?

"Maybe the coals of me heart? Don't know."

Why had Mr. Cruikshank's story come to him now?

Some moments later Duncan moved back into his body.

D.J. heard from the clerk at the Coop Grocery a version of what had occurred the previous night. The girl had wildly dyed blue and orange hair that was shaved on one side of her head and stood up punk style on the other. Noticing his American accent, she told him, "Most people come here from the States to see castles and dragons. When they meet my mother—or your Dad—they get a new appreciation of what dragons we have here!" She grinned at him to be certain he knew she was joking.

The woman at the next check out station interjected that Duncan had changed recently, not such a grumpy codger when he last came in to pick up food. "Don't give the lad a wrong impression of his da'! Your mum, yes, but that man.... He ain' so bad. Just carryin' a load o' pain, me thinks."

D.J.'s anxiety grew as he made his way down South High Street, across the square, and down the steep hill that was North High Street. He could see the sea breaching the harbor walls with great displays of froth and power. He turned right at the harbor, saw the tavern just yards ahead, and had a déjà vu moment of being there with Drew. He stood still in front of the pub taking deep gulps of air to fortify himself, feeling it cold and expanding in his chest. Then he opened the door of The Shore's Inn and stepped inside.

The young man stomped the snow from his boots and entered the tavern. His raw red face came into view as he unwound his muffler. Snow slid off his woolen cap onto the shoulders of his pea jacket and from there dropped to the floor, melting rapidly. Before he noticed the sofa, he saw the fireplace with its orange glow and shuffled awkwardly to the hearth. He extended both arms toward the flames and rubbed his hands vigorously. Only after his body thawed enough to enable him to move without shuffling did he glance around the pub. His eyes came to rest on the sofa and its inhabitant, and a troubled look took over his face.

That's when Amy saw him as she opened the door at the bottom of those treacherous stairs.

"D.J.!" She was hurrying toward him, crying, all of her resilience spent. She could feel his resistance as she hugged him. They had had this conversation about public displays of affection, his tight muscles reminded her, after Uncle John moved out with Cliff. She let go and stepped back. She knew he was afraid of her dependence. If she didn't pay attention to that, she might lose him, too. She wiped her eyes, brushed the tears from her face, took his hand, and led him to the sofa.

"D.J., meet your father." Someone brought up another chair so D.J. could sit next to Duncan. Amy watched her son studying the pale, long haired man who barely moved despite the fluster around him. She hoped he seemed very different from the unpleasant man D.J. had met in the antiques shop.

As they sat together she told D.J. what she had learned about why his father left and what his life had been since moving to Scotland. She could read in D.J.'s eyes the anger that vied with curiosity as he listened. They must find some private time to talk, away from this man who did not need their anger right now. There would be a time, after...*if...* he recovered, when they would have to speak it, and he would have to listen.

She hadn't heard the door to the stairway open or the soft sound of shoes meeting floor. She felt someone touch her shoulder and looked up to find Elleke standing there, sleep deprived eyes inquisitive and focused on her Pappie Duncan. She obviously did not notice D.J. For a moment that annoyed Amy. Then she realized that Duncan was Elleke's only living, caring parent. The emotional stakes if he died for Elleke were far higher than for either D.J. or Amy. She reached out to hug the girl and introduced her to D.J., choosing her words carefully. She had seen D.J.'s admiring look as he took in the tall red head. She did not want romance further complicating this strange joint vigil.

"Elleke, meet D.J., my son and your brother. D.J. meet your sister Elleke." Each of them sent her a look of confusion. She guessed they thought she was crazy. She plunged ahead with what she needed to say.

"D.J. never knew his father and you, Elleke, became the child Duncan never had, or so he thought. So I figure you are each his children, strangely enough." Amy felt Elleke's arm encircle her waist and was relieved that her words had pleased rather than offended the young woman. They sat in silence watching Duncan sleep until growling stomachs reminded them that they had not eaten in a long while. Leaving Duncan with Doc Elliott, the three of them ascended the stairs to prepare something to eat.

She and Elleke fixed eggs, tea and toast. All three of them were exhausted but needing to talk. Amy asked Elleke to tell them about her childhood memories of Duncan. Elleke shared her memory of the first time she saw "The Scruffy Man." More memories spilled out of her, vivid descriptions of the lost, morose man who the child Elleke had determined to bring out of his cocoon and into a relationship with her.

Having finished his food and unable to listen any longer, D.J. excused himself and went downstairs.

Amy paid close attention as Elleke provided details of the transformation of the man Amy had loved and lost. She found herself caught up in Elleke's stories, glad for Duncan's being found and saved by Elleke and her mother, glad the three of them could recover and shape their identity as a family. When Elleke told Amy about sitting with her mom and Duncan on the bench on the brae overlooking the sea and her mom saying with conviction that such a beautiful moments are delicate gifts to be handled carefully and preserved in memory, Amy found herself weeping.

"I'm so sorry! I didn't mean to make you sad. It must be hard to hear of us being so happy when you were missing Duncan."

"No, Elleke, that's not why I'm crying. All these years I haven't allowed myself to remember those moments in *my* life with Duncan, those lovely, gentle moments of joy. Your mom was a wise woman. I'm glad she and Duncan and you found each other." She wasn't pretending. Odd how her feelings kept jackknifing.

Downstairs people were gathered around the brown leather sofa on which Duncan lay, covered with a tartan plaid wool blanket. His skin was pasty looking and drab, his eyes closed. Amy sat by his feet, Elleke beside her, and D.J. near his father's head. Duncan groaned, opened his eyes, and studied D.J. with an unfocused, puzzled expression. Doc Elliott addressed the invalid, his voice overly loud as if talking to someone hard of hearing.

"Yer family is here, Duncan, all o' them. So what's it gonna be, laddie? The choice is yours."

Duncan mumbled a reply, his voice faint. Later they disputed what he had said, some hearing one thing, some another. D.J., who was nearest, was certain his father had said,

"Life."

The snow subsided by mid-morning Sunday, and someone shoveled the harbor in the hour that followed. By two most of the ice on the cobblestones was sanded, and Doc Elliott gave permission for Duncan to go home to the house in Cullen where he would be looked after by Amy, Elleke, and D.J.

At four that afternoon Amy stood in the kitchen fixing tea for Duncan, who was settled in the front bedroom, resting. She could hear the two young people in the living room getting acquainted. Elleke asked D.J. if he'd been in Scotland long, and he told her about working on the rigs the past few months and making a trip along the Northeast coast with his friend Drew.

Then he asked her how she knew Duncan. Elleke explained that she'd moved here with her mom when she was three and met Duncan and Mr. Cruickshank and eventually they all moved in to live together.

"Mr. Cruickshank?" D.J. sounded confused.

"Yes, George Cruickshank, the antiques dealer who Duncan worked for. Duncan bought his shops after Granddad died."

Amy carried a tray with biscuits, the tea pot in its colorful cozy, and two cups into the front bedroom for Duncan. The cups sat uncertainly in their saucers, rattling and causing him to open his eyes. He sat up, smiling sheepishly. "Thank you," he said. "I'm really sorry for the muddle I've made of everything."

"Your apology is accepted. But I don't want to hear anything more about muddles you've made," she said. "What's past is past. It's what's ahead that's the puzzle now." Even as she said the words, she knew they weren't true. She was not finished with the past. There was much more she needed to say to him out of the depth of her anger. But he needed to recover first.

She looked through the doorway toward the hall that led to the front room. "I thought we might want to listen in to the kids' conversation. They're getting to know each other, and we might learn a lot." She sat in the chair next to the bed and propped her feet in their warm wool socks on the edge of his mattress. He reached out to massage them, like he'd done hundreds of times before when they were married. It felt natural but also weird, and she was relieved when almost immediately he took his hands away and busied them smoothing the quilt. She'd been in Scotland only three days and she was exhausted. Still, the opportunity to fill in more of the blanks in what she knew about this man, his "daughter," and her son kept her awake and attentive.

D.J. was telling Elleke about going to the cemetery in Portsoy and his amazement at how whole families are buried in the same plot on top of each other, all of them listed on one stone.

Elleke said she'd been there and loved that place.

"There was another stone, a small one, next to the Cruickshank grave marker." D.J. was talking. "It said 'In-NEE-Kee.' Is that person a Cruickshank, too?"

Elleke laughed. "It's 'EE-ne-kah.' That's my mom. Duncan put it there for her. He said we were all part of Granddad's family, all honorary Cruickshanks."

D.J. was quiet, then he said, "Being an honorary Cruickshank sounds really cool."

"Granddad was a lovely man." Elleke continued. "So is your dad. I guess from what your mom told me that you don't know him."

"It's not exactly the best way to meet your father, when he tries to kill himself." D.J.'s voice was subdued.

In the bedroom Amy and Duncan were listening intently.

"When I first met Duncan, Mom and I called him The Scruffy Man." She laughed again. "His hair and beard were kind of wild and he wouldn't look people in the eyes. But he had a nice face, though he never smiled. I was pretty little, but I remember deciding I was going to make The Scruffy Man my friend. And I did."

There was no response from D.J.

"I remember Mom said something terrible must have happened to him. I guess from what your mom told me, that was losing her and you."

Elleke's interpretation startled Amy. She wanted to protest that it was his own damn fault; he hadn't needed to experience that loss. She decided just to keep listening. Apparently Duncan's reality had been very different from hers. From the information he *thought* was true, he would have seen *her* as having left *him*. So losing her—and their unborn baby—could have been his 'terrible loss.'

They heard D.J. asking Elleke something, but neither of them was certain what he'd said.

Elleke responded slowly, as though she was thinking hard before forming each sentence. "Well…he was a good person. He took care of me. He loved me. He read Harry Potter with me after Granddad died. He tried to adopt me, but Mom died before the paperwork was completed. After Mom died, when my father came to bring me back to Holland, I wanted to stay with him, and he wanted me to." Her voice trailed off as though her words couldn't keep up with her memories of her life in this house. It was quiet for what seemed a long time. Then she spoke again.

"Three and a half years ago when I decided to go to Gaza with the flotilla…"

Amy looked at Duncan gesturing that she didn't understand. He nodded but put his forefinger to his lips, signaling her to wait for the explanation and simply listen now.

"…my father was furious with me for tarnishing his reputation as a strong supporter of Israel. I had hurt his career as a rising Member of Parliament. He'd never forgive me. It didn't matter to him that Israel had killed nine of our group and put his daughter and six hundred non-violent peace activists in prison."

Amy could imagine her son's shocked expression as he listened. What was this all about?

"…but Pappie Duncan called the U.S. and Dutch governments, my stepmother, and whoever he could think of to make sure I was safe. He wrote me that he was proud of me. Can you imagine what that meant to me? ….You are very lucky to be his son."

Duncan's heart blossomed at her words. He felt giddy with gratitude for the constancy of Elleke's love for him. He felt Amy's hand slip into his momentarily, the pressure of her fingers squeezing his, and looked over at her. Her face looked tired and gentle. "It sounds like you've been one amazing pappie," she whispered. Then she looked away as her eyes began to overflow.

From the living room they heard D.J.'s voice. He sounded very impressed. "So you really were in *prison?* I wanna hear more about that. Hey, wanna get something to eat while we talk?"

Their voices grew faint as they headed for the kitchen, making noises that obscured their words—the refrigerator door opening, closing, opening, closing; the electric tea kettle starting to boil; plates clattering from cupboard to counter to table; the fizzy opening of two bottles of beer, knives on cutting board, the sounds of food preparation.

The regular, ordinary sounds of home.

In the bedroom Amy's anger caught up with her. So Duncan had been a good father to Elleke, *another woman's child,* while *she* struggled to raise DJ *alone.* She stood up and her heels sounded fierce against the hardwood floor as she strode to the door and closed it with a force that set the air in the room vibrating. She walked back to the bed on which her former husband lay. Her voice was intense and gritty. She no longer cared if this was the right time. It was the right time *for her.*

"I made sacrifices for the past twenty years to have our son grow up with a responsible man in his life. I brought John into our home. I brought John's boyfriend into our home. Even when he took charge of my home, removed things I treasured, and showed no respect for me, I let him stay *so that DJ would have a father figure.*" Her voice was no longer quiet and she shrilled the next words, leaning over the bed and almost spitting in his face. **"Meanwhile, you didn't give a damn. You were shacked up here raising someone else's kid. Did you even think once about your responsibility for your own child, your son?"** She was on a roll. Beads of sweat stood out on her forehead and upper lip. She was a force standing before him shaking with rage. **"How could you?"**

She turned and left the room, slamming the door behind her.

She put on her down jacket and gloves, pulled her ski cap low and wrapped her muffler around her neck over her hair. DAMN him! Then she left the house. The icy air tightened her face and made her teeth sore when she opened her mouth to scream. It did not deter her. She walked away from the house uphill. She didn't care if anyone heard her saying every cuss word she'd ever heard and railing at the "fragile," self-absorbed man lying in the downstairs bedroom.

When dark began to obscure her way, she turned back toward the house. She opened the door quietly, not wanting to run into any of them. Elleke stood in the kitchen, making supper. DJ was nowhere to be seen.

"He's with Duncan in the bedroom," Elleke called to her. That was the last thing she expected. Curious, she moved a chair into the hall outside the bedroom and sat down without removing her jacket. She didn't want to miss what this strange, irresponsible man would say to her son, and she didn't want either of them to know she was listening.

"This must seem crazy to you, the whole situation." Duncan was speaking.

"Yeah. It's scrambling my head."

"I am sorry that I wasn't there to watch you grow up, to help your mom. I've made so many mistakes."

"Are you really sorry you weren't with us? Seems like you made yourself a new life pretty fast."

In the hall Amy pumped her right arm and whispered "YES!"

"I didn't want to live after I thought your mom was through with me."

"So this trying to kill yourself isn't anything new?"

Her son was holding his own and she was proud of him.

"I've struggled with depression all of my life, and with alcohol when I get really down. I hope you can learn from my mistakes there. I began to recover when I met an old man, your friend Drew's grandfather. He gave me a chance and I took it and it changed my life. I found work I loved and friendships—Mr. Cruickshank, Elleke, and her mom. Gradually we all became close, family. I was happy again…. Then Elleke's mom got cancer and died a little more than two months after she was diagnosed. A few weeks after that, Elleke's father took her away from me to Holland. And my world crashed again. Needja, here, and my promise to take care of the antique stores kept me alive, but when I had no contact with Elleke the past three years, I just let myself go, gave up."

"When Mom told me that the weird man I met in the antiques shop was my father…well, I wanted no part of him. Are you going to be that man now? Do you have any choice?"

D.J.'s honest and insightful zingers left his mother marveling. Where did her son come by that wisdom? She strained to hear Duncan's answer.

"I've had three chances at happiness: with your mom, with Ineke and Elleke and Mr. Cruickshank, and now. It's time for me to get it right. I do have a choice…."

They were both quiet for a time and then Duncan spoke again. "Do you have any questions for me?"

"Yeah. Did you ever think about me, wonder how I was?"

"I thought you were Uncle John's son."

"No way!"

"Yes. I was convinced that Uncle John had replaced me with your mom and that you three were a family. When I learned you were my son, I began researching online to find out whatever I could about you. I learned about your rock band and the jobs you've had."

"I can't believe you didn't know Uncle John was gay."

"Any other questions for me?"

Silence.

"If not, would you tell me about your life? I really want to know whatever you're willing to share."

Amy leaned forward in her chair and took off her jacket. She continued listening while D.J. recounted his adventures on the rigs, telling story after story in his own inimitable way. The boy had a gift. He could find the funny in any situation and bring others into his stories. It was lovely to hear him chuckling as he told his tales.

She heard something else now, a voice that joined D.J.'s. It was Duncan. Laughing.

Afterward

A Happiness

Each second is birds singing in every tree.
Not real birds. Not real trees.

And my room is mornings stretching on forever.
Not real mornings nor that real forever.

A plough went into the ground. Corn rose from it.
I saw that plough. I saw that corn.

They were real. But for this fragile moment
The plough turns over the soil into the future

Where the corn sways
That was cut down long ago.

"A Happiness" from The Collected Poems of Norman MacCaig, courtesy of Birlinn Ltd.

Acknowledgements

Thank you to Michael Poage, Hildred Cassel, Sirana AbiMikhael, and Laura Tillem for critiquing and strengthening this story, to Kendra Eick for help with the ending, and to Khloe Skye Jackson and Kiah Revoal, my Ellekes. I am grateful to the people and places that inspired this story--the Northeast coast of Scotland and Wichita, Kansas.

About the Author

Gretchen Eick has worked as a foreign policy lobbyist and a professor of history. She lives in Wichita, Kansas and has lived in or visited more than forty countries. She is the author of three books of fiction and *Dissent in Wichita: The Civil Rights Movement in the Midwest.*